In the United States...

Mariana Mitogo is struggling to make ends meet. Then, out of the blue, she learns she's to receive a huge inheritance that would erase all her debt. The problem: she has to be married for six months to receive it, and her dating life is nonexistent.

In Spain...

Santiago de los Reyes, Mariana's Internet friend, has drained his bank account to support his family. Desperate to get his mom the heart surgery she needs, he interviews for a better-paying job that would take him from Madrid to Virginia. When he's offered the position but can't get a work visa, Mariana offers a solution that benefits both of them—a fiancé visa and a quick wedding.

If anyone finds out it's a green-card marriage, Santiago will be deported. Mariana would face a colossal fine and jail time. Good thing they're committed actors.

But as Santiago and Mariana pretend to build a life together, the lines blur between charade and reality. Will they dare to choose the love that feels more honest every day?

Border Ctrl+Esc is a lighthearted friends-to-lovers marriage of convenience between LGBTQ+ Internet friends (a demisexual woman and a bisexual man).

BORDER
CTRL+ESC

Ivy L. James

A NineStar Press Publication

www.ninestarpress.com

Border CTRL+ ESC

© 2021 Ivy L. James

Cover © 2021 Natasha Snow

Cover graphics: Neimy Kao

Edited by Elizabetta McKay

Printed in the USA

ISBN: 978-1-64890-356-4

First Edition, August, 2021

Also available in eBook, ISBN: 978-1-64890-355-7

WARNING:
This book contains sexually explicit content, which may only be suitable for mature readers, adult language, and depictions of religious shaming (brief), health problems, medical procedures (mention of), anxiety, and money problems.

For Liz

Chapter One

In Which Internet Friends Become In-Person Friends

APRIL

> THEHISTORICMARIANA: *This is going to be AWESOME. Less than a day!!* 🎉🎊

> SANTI17: *I'm looking at the plane ticket now and still can't believe it!*

> SANTI17: *[sent an attachment]*

> THEHISTORICMARIANA: *What's with the Post-it?*

> SANTI17: *So I don't lose it lol. You would do the same thing. Don't judge me.*

> THEHISTORICMARIANA: *Nah, I'd attach them to a cool keychain or something. Like an adult.*

SANTI17: *I need to finish packing.*

THEHISTORICMARIANA: *Wait, what time is it there?*

SANTI17: *Past midnight.*

THEHISTORICMARIANA: *Try to get a little sleep before your flight, okay?*

THEHISTORICMARIANA: *Sweet dreams, Santi.*

SANTI17: *Dulces sueños.*

Mariana Mitogo scanned the faces filtering through both the escalator and the stairs into the Arrivals area of the airport, hoping Santiago de los Reyes Martínez hadn't changed his appearance since his last selfie. She had assumed he wore his glasses all the time like she did, but did he? Maybe they were only for the aesthetic. What if he didn't have them on, or he cut his hair, and she didn't recognize him? What if his plane had come in somewhere else and this wasn't even the right flight?

Announcements squawked over the speakers; conversations murmured around her as a fresh wave of people came from the gates. The crowds swirled, heading to the luggage conveyors and the restaurants and the exit. She sidestepped travelers on their phones. She almost passed over the man who stepped off the escalator next—and then she couldn't look away.

Thick, mussed black hair curled over the edges of his ears and down the nape of his neck, too long to look professional. His naturally tawny complexion had darkened with exposure to the sun, and she could see those big, dark eyes from here, even with his oversized hipster glasses. The edges of him were soft, not harsh with muscle, but something about the angle of his shoulders and the way he filled out his simple T-shirt and jeans scrambled her insides.

Please don't be him, she prayed, ready to barter her health and wealth against her need to not have to deal with a cute guy friend. She hadn't been interested in anyone since she was sixteen—she didn't want to start now. Life was simpler that way.

As she stood there, appalled at her potential bad luck, he turned to meet her gaze, and he pulled back. No wave, not even a smile. He just pushed his glasses up the bridge of his nose, shoulders tense, lips pressed together.

Her throat prickled. *Of course I look different.* Cheeks hot, she smoothed her palms over the front of her yellow dress. *I guess I didn't expect to...to disappoint him.*

He hadn't even waved yet. She swallowed her embarrassment and, with a smile, did jazz hands.

A grin split his face, and it clicked.

She'd seen that grin in enough goofy selfies.

Damn it.

Santiago raced to her, dropped his suitcase, and swept her into a bear hug. For a split second she froze, not having expected outright affection—but then she relaxed and hugged him back, and her concern about attraction faded.

This is him, her heart and mind seemed to sigh, this time in relief. *This is Santi.* They already knew each other inside and out. Having him here in person, at long last, fit a piece into place she hadn't realized was missing.

When he finally let go, she tapped him on the chest. "I'm not sure I know how to talk to you face-to-face. Let's go sit somewhere so we can text."

He snorted with laughter, as she'd hoped. "Maybe we can turn around and pretend to talk to our phones." The lilt of his native language softened his English, prettier than her own slight Virginian drawl. Poor guy, having to practice his second language with a Southerner. He was going to end up with two different accents blended into one. Not to mention a propensity for the word *y'all*.

"How was your flight?" It seemed like the appropriate first question to ask.

He shrugged and rubbed his butt. "It was fine. Long."

She grinned.

This response, though, made his forehead crinkle. "I said that right, didn't I? Sorry about my accent."

"Yeah, you said it fine." She bounced on the balls of her feet. "Do you want any coffee or anything before we start the drive home? It's gonna be another two hours until we get there."

Santi glanced around the waiting area, probably looking for a coffee shop.

"Not here. There's a Starbucks a couple miles down the highway."

He half grimaced at the word *miles*. "And that's...?"

"Oh." She struggled to remember the correct ratio of miles to kilometers. Two to one? One to two? *Ugh, math.* She gave up. "About five minutes."

They both stared at each other, looking a little blank, until they shared a self-deprecating laugh, and he picked up his suitcase. "Yes, let's get some coffee. I'll still be able to sleep when we get home."

*

All the signs were in English units, not metric, as they blew down the highway in the evening sunset. This threw him off more than the Spanish-to-English switch itself. *What's a half mile? This is supposed to mean something to me? Americans always have to be special. The rest of the world uses the metric system, like sensible people.*

No, Santiago liked America, at least so far. It had its cultural quirks and problems, but it wasn't all bad. And everyone was so friendly. *Anytime you look at someone, they smile and nod at you.* Even strangers. It was weird. Nice, but *weird.*

They stopped at the Starbucks. Energy. Caffeine and sugar. He ordered a coffee and a brownie, but before he could fish his wallet out of his backpack, Mariana handed the cashier her credit card. "I'll have a triple-shot medium mocha, and that'll be it for us, thanks."

After the cashier left to make the drinks, Santiago nudged Mariana. "I can pay you back for that."

She shook her head. "I got you. You're fine."

Neither of them was fine with money, but he was here and they were together for the first time and he was interviewing for a job that might keep his mom alive. He thanked her and dropped it.

He picked up their order from the counter, and she pulled out her phone, a frown tugging at her full lips. He glanced at the screen as he passed her cup to her.

A banking app. Two credit cards maxed out. Three big loans. His own cup of coffee burned his hand before he could set it down.

"Anyway—" Mariana slid her phone into her purse and gestured toward the door. "We should head out. But tell me about the flight! Were there any screaming babies?"

They chatted with enthusiasm for the first half of the drive, but after that, jet lag hit him hard, and he drifted off almost midsentence. He woke when she parked outside her apartment complex, and he stayed sentient long enough to drag himself and his suitcase inside and collapse on the blankets she'd spread over the couch. He wasn't sure if he'd closed the door behind him.

She must have closed the curtains for him while he slept; the sun never broke through his dreams. Stirring naturally, he tried to register the foreign surroundings. His hostess's one-bedroom apartment framed an eclectic mishmash of the old and the new—an armchair topped with a lace doily, a framed print of the American Declaration of Independence hanging beside a floor-to-ceiling mirror. He wasn't much for interior decorating, but it captivated him. It fit her. So many years into their friendship, and he finally had a chance to learn details like this.

He liked it.

Shrugging off the giant quilt she'd draped over him, he pushed himself to his feet, slipped on his glasses, and dragged himself into the bathroom. His entire body creaked from the long flight followed by the long nap. *What time is it?* The analog clock on the wall read 7:45, but the hour and minute hands weren't moving. The second hand twitched occasionally, like a death rattle. Broken, then. Not helpful. Unable to summon the energy to care, he turned on the sink water, then puddled some in his hands and splashed it onto his face. The shock of cold startled him into full consciousness.

Wiping away the wet with a yellow hand towel, he smacked his lips and grimaced at the sour taste of morning breath in his mouth. *Where did I stick my toothbrush?* He wandered back into the living room to rummage through his suitcase and found it in a weird bottom pocket. *Why did I put it there?* He went back to the bathroom and had just started scrubbing with foamy toothpaste when the other door to the bathroom opened. In the mirror, Mariana's sleep-glazed eyes widened.

"I'm sho—" He almost sprayed foam on the sink.

She held up her hands as he quickly finished and spat. "No, it's fine! You're the guest."

He swiped a hand over his mouth. "No, it's your home."

"I can wait."

"I'm already done anyways." To prove the point, he set his toothbrush on the counter. Then he picked it back up, in case leaving it was presumptuous. "I can do my hair in the living room."

She let out a long breath and relented. "Okay. If you need anything, come on in. I shouldn't be long."

He had no intention of initiating another awkward you-first-no-you-first bathroom encounter. He'd stay on the couch until she was done. "Okay, thank you." Taking his toothbrush with him, he retreated to his suitcase to attempt to tame his tangled mess of hair. To pass the time before food, he pulled out his phone and checked the Internet for nearby barbers.

Yikes. The closest one was half an hour away. His city life had had its advantages.

Mariana emerged from the bedroom in a pastel-blue off-the-shoulder blouse and white short-shorts that showed off her dark skin and thick thighs. Her close-cropped curls gleamed, and a touch of pink glossed her full lips. Her soft, round cheeks had been cute for as long as he'd known her, but in person, she was all curves, full and rounded and way too tempting.

More than cute. Sexy as hell. That hadn't come through on social media, and Santiago hadn't been prepared for it. That first look in the airport had almost killed him.

He forced himself to look away. "I need a haircut before my interview."

Her gaze darted to his unkempt hair long enough for him to feel a flicker of the embarrassment that thirteen hours with the lip-curling white guy in 12C had failed to elicit.

Averting his gaze from her casual perfection, he held up his phone. "Is there really nothing around here?"

She shrugged. "Nah. I warned you that I'm out'n'mil'nowhere."

He leaned in and squinted, as if that would help him hear better. "You're what?"

It registered in her face how quickly she'd run through the phrase. "Sorry. Out in the middle of nowhere." This time, she slowed down and enunciated more clearly, and he was able to pick out the individual words. He knew the phrase itself; he'd just never heard it so blurred before. "We can take a trip up into town before your interview. You wanna go today or tomorrow?"

He scratched his ear where a tuft of hair tickled sensitive skin. "Today, if we can do that."

She cracked that familiar grin. "Yeah, I think we can manage that. I can't believe you let your hair get that long to begin with." Ruffling his hair, she sat beside him on the couch.

He snuggled up against her, but she stiffened. *Oh, right. Americans. So weird about touch.* He straightened up and tilted his phone toward her again. "Do you know any of these places? Where should we go?"

She took it and scrolled through the options. "Ummm...This one."

"Okay. I trust your judgment."

"Well, you shouldn't. This is the place that helped me dye my hair pink in college."

"I thought the pink was cute!"

"It was adorable, but that's not the point. I could totally be tricking you into messing up your hair right before your interview."

"You wouldn't do that to me."

"Oh, wouldn't I?" Mariana winked and stood. "When can they take you today? I can make some eggies for breakfast if you want."

"That sounds good, thanks. Scrambled?"

"Can do." She draped an apron over her head and tied the red ribbons behind her back. The pattern looked like...

a bunch of old white men striking silly poses in historical costume.

He followed her into the kitchen and tugged at the fabric. "What's on that?"

"This thing?" She laughed. "It's some of the presidents. Washington, Jefferson, Lincoln...uh, Madison..." She pointed to each one as she named them. "I got it for my birthday a few years back from my mom. I think she hoped that appealing to my actual interests would make cooking more fun. It did, but not enough for me to become a cook." She pulled a dozen eggs out of the fridge, cracked them into a cup, and added salt and pepper to the mix.

Basically twiddling his thumbs, Santiago sank into a seat at the small, round kitchen table. It was weird to let someone else do the cooking, even if he was only visiting. "Is there anything I can do to help?"

He didn't expect her to say yes, but she jerked her thumb toward the refrigerator. "If you want, you can peek through there and see what fruit you like. I have a few different kinds of berries, and bananas and apples are on the counter by the pantry."

"Berries are always good." He especially liked them with oatmeal, although he wouldn't say so at the risk of making it sound like he was ungrateful for the scrambled eggs, which he also liked. He opened the fridge and pulled out a container of strawberries, which he rinsed off in the sink. "Is it okay if I cut them up?"

"Go for it." She pulled a knife out of the block and passed it to him handle-first. "The cutting board's right there on the counter."

He set about slicing the berries into quarters, happy to have something to do with his hands to help.

Mariana drizzled some oil in the skillet as it heated on the stove. "What are you most excited to do while you're here? Besides getting hired for a job that would make bank, of course."

"Don't jinx it! I haven't even interviewed yet."

"Yeah, but you're the best. You deserve the position."

"Thanks—*ai!*" He nicked his fingertip on the knife blade when his hand slipped. The cut stung. Blood welled up, and he stuck the wound in his mouth.

She froze. "Oh, shit! Are you okay?"

He shrugged, not pulling his finger away.

"Let me grab you a bandage." She set aside the egg mixture and rummaged through a drawer on her other side. Triumphantly, she pulled out a white box with a red cross on the front. "I knew I had it in here."

He lowered his hand and showed her the cut. Not deep, but it stung in the air conditioning.

Mariana pulled a Band-Aid out of the first aid kit, peeled away the backing, then wrapped the bandage gently around his fingertip. It was nice to feel taken care of, he had to admit. Her hands were warm and soft as she fixed him up, her touch gentle. It was almost worth cutting himself like an idiot.

"*Sana, sana, culito de rana,*" he said under his breath without thinking. *Heal, heal, little frog bum.* Some habits died hard; he'd lost track of how many scraped knees he'd cleaned up as a kids' soccer coach.

She processed the translation and came up with "What?"

"*Si no sanas hoy, sanarás mañana.*" He finished the rhyme as if that would answer the question. *If you don't heal today, you'll heal tomorrow.*

She stared at him. Shook her head.

Right. If she didn't know the shorthand, the long version wouldn't make any sense either. "Uh...I don't know. It's what we say to kids when they hurt themselves."

"Aw, you're saying you've got a boo-boo," she teased. "*Pobrecito.*"

He nudged her playfully. "You called the toilet 'a potty' last week. Don't talk to me about baby talk."

"I was being ironic!"

"You were not. You said potty because it's fun to say. Don't lie to yourself."

She huffed. "Rude. I don't think I like you in person after all." A smile tugged at her lips though.

"Aww, that hurts my feelings." He wrapped one arm around her shoulders. To his surprise, she was almost as tall as he was, not as short as she looked in pictures. "Come on. You love me."

Her arm went around his waist in return, a display of affection he hadn't expected but was delighted by. "Yeah, okay. Maybe so." She stretched her free hand toward the stove to pour the eggs into the skillet. "Are you okay to finish cutting up the strawberries, Mr. Frog Butt?"

He stuck out his tongue and released her so she could finish cooking. "I'm injured, and you're bullying me."

As the eggs firmed up in the heat, she layered a handful of shredded cheddar cheese on top and stirred. "So is that a no?"

"It's a 'yes but just so you know, I'm wounded.'" He sliced the last of the strawberries, with more caution than before his slipup.

She stirred, stirred, stirred. "You're pitiful. Do I need to scoop you up some ice cream to soothe you?"

Santiago brightened. "Ice cream would definitely help me feel better."

Mariana patted him on the cheek. "You're precious. Never change." Once the cheesy scrambled eggs were done cooking, she spooned them onto two plates and passed him the one with a bigger portion. "Here. They're eggs-cellent."

He laughed despite himself. "No. That's horrible."

She grinned, and he loved it. "I've done better, but it wasn't half bad. Don't eggs-aggerate."

"Stoooppp." He added some strawberries to his plate as well and then dug in. He didn't really mind the puns, but she got a bigger kick out of them when someone hated them. He was happy to oblige because her smile was the sun. He'd thought he knew that when they were only internet friends, but now that he'd seen it in person, he was worried about what he'd do to bring that smile out.

Meeting Mariana had messed with his head. At least he'd only be here for a few days. Once he got back to Spain, the distance would sort him out again.

At least he'd have to hope so.

Chapter Two

In Which the Interview Goes Well but the Visa Situation Does Not

APRIL

The hair stylist offered to pull up a spare chair for Mariana to sit in, but she leaned against the wall and occasionally interjected into the small talk about Santiago's visit, his interview, and his pending work visa. He chatted easily with the stylist, a natural conversationalist even in his second language. It warmed her heart to see him in day-to-day activities, and even more to see him so sweet to a stranger. If she weren't determined to wait on a relationship until she got her life together, she might be tempted to want him to charm *her*.

Ragged tufts of hair dusted the black cloak over his torso and drifted to the ground. Finally, the stylist blow-dried the last of the spritzed water and combed his hair along its natural wave. She turned his chair toward the mirror: "What do you think?"

"Ooh" burst from Mariana's lips before she could think to formulate a more coherent response. Santiago had looked good before, but *now*, trimmed neat and classy... Mariana nudged his shin with the toe of her shoe. "Now you don't look like a hobo."

The stylist laughed. "Definitely not a hobo, I should hope."

He pretended to fluff his hair. "This was my real reason for visiting America. In my country, we have only hobo salons. Now I can go back and show them all the light—"

The theme song of their favorite show interrupted him. Mariana looked down at her phone, grimaced, and flashed the screen in his direction: an unknown number, no ID. She flicked Decline. "Stupid telemarketers."

He put on a robotic tone. "He-LLO. This is your. Bank. We need your. Credit card information. Because this is really your bank. And not. A scam."

Mariana feigned robot moves. "Your mortgage is. In danger. We need your. Social security number. Because you definitely have. A mortgage." She laughed. "That's pretty much the only type of debt I *don't* have. Makes it easy to tell that they're fake."

Her phone beeped. She groaned at the new voicemail notification. "I haaaate when I have to listen to them even though I ignored the call." She dismissed the icon and slipped her phone into her back pocket. "Anyway."

The next morning, Santiago looked even less like a hobo when he emerged from the bathroom, ready for his interview. She knew he preferred a more casual style—in his clothes, in his mannerisms—and she had assumed that would carry into his work life. *But I was wrong.* The crisp plum button-down shirt, the pressed slacks, the gleaming shoes. The sleeves rolled up to his elbows. The perfectly combed swoop in the waves of his hair.

"Wow," said Mariana.

Grinning and then turning it into an over-the-top model pout, Santiago placed his hands on his hips and strutted over to her. He pivoted for a half-turn to the left, then to the right.

She laughed. "If teaching doesn't work out, you could model for a living."

He returned to his normal posture and flashed his dimples in a smile. "Thanks. It's natural."

"You look awesome," she told him sincerely. "Very professional, all spruced up like that."

His smile turned confused at the last bit. "Isn't a spruce a tree? I look like a tree?"

She shook her head. "No. I mean, a spruce is a tree. But 'spruce up' means more...getting all fancy so you look nice. Which you do."

"Oh. Thank you." His brow creased. "That's a weird idiom. What does a tree have to do with looking nice?"

She snorted and held out her hands, palms up, in a helpless shrug. "English is weird."

As they drove to the school, she asked him standard interview questions, and he perfected his responses until his shoulders lowered from his ears. After she parked, she gave him a hug from the driver's seat. "You're gonna be great. Go impress them."

"Thanks." He let out a long breath and shook himself out. "Do I need to send you a message when I'm done?"

She shook her head. "I'm gonna get coffee and park here in the visitor's section. You can come right out."

In the back of the school lot, she sipped her triple-shot mocha and called her coworker Omar Khan at the Historical Society of Northern Virginia. "Morning, Omar. Have a minute?"

Paper shuffled on his end. "Sure, what's up?"

"I wanted to talk to you real quick about a project idea of mine. How much do you know about James Farmer?" Wind whistled around her car, and she sent up a silent prayer that he couldn't hear it.

"Uh...not much."

She wiggled in her seat. "Here's the thing—he was a huge influence in the Civil Rights Movement. He co-founded the Congress of Racial Equality, which was all about nonviolence. Think sit-ins and Freedom Riders. He worked with Martin Luther King, Jr."

"Okay, cool. What about him?"

"He lived in Fredericksburg." The city was a mere forty minutes from the Historical Society, practically next-door neighbors in rural Virginia. "That makes him a local! So I was thinking, why don't we do an exhibit about him? Everybody's heard of George Washington and the other local Founding Fathers. This would change things up."

"James Farmer, you said?" Omar's keyboard clacked. A pause, then: "I could get behind that. Have you talked to anyone else about it yet?"

A number she didn't recognize popped up on her screen as an incoming call. *Wait, is that the same one from the other day? Lay off.* Again, she flicked Decline.

"No, not yet. I wanted to run it by you first, see what you thought."

"Yeah, I think it's a great idea."

Her phone vibrated. Another voicemail. *Ugh.*

Upon draining the mocha, she chewed on a pen while she brainstormed with him—until a knock at her window startled her into dropping it. Santi leaned down to wave at her through the glass. Quickly, she told Omar she'd catch up with him later and rolled the window down. "Hey, stranger. How do you think it went?"

He shrugged, but his eyes shone with hope. "I think well. They said I'll hear back from them in the next few days."

"That's awesome!" Beaming, she patted the passenger-side seat. He rounded the front of the car, opened the side door, and slid inside. She yanked her hand away to keep him from sitting on it.

As soon as they got home, they changed into comfortable clothes and flopped onto the couch for Netflix. She propped her feet up on the long coffee table, and he followed her lead, although his longer legs meant his heels came dangerously close to hanging off the edge. Resting his arm behind her over the back of the couch, he shifted close so that their sides pressed together. She hesitated, nervous about the unfamiliar close contact, but he only relaxed against her. Reassured, she pulled a blanket over both of them and leaned back.

They watched twenty-minute sitcom episodes until the sky darkened to the point that Mariana had to turn on a light to go to the bathroom. When she reemerged, she headed for the fridge.

"Food?" She looked in the pantry and the fridge, and her motivation wilted. "Eh. I don't feel like making anything—do you?"

He waved a hand lazily from where he'd slid down in his seat. "No, I'm tired."

"Me too. I'm thinking leftovers. Wanna do that?"

"Sure." He leaned his head back and closed his eyes, and Mariana sent up a silent prayer of thanks for friends who didn't have high expectations for every day of her adult life. Some days it was all she could do to put on real clothes before she left the house to buy groceries. With her friends and coworkers already years into full adulthood, Mariana worked hard to convince them she was in tip-top shape at all times. Santiago, from across the Atlantic, had been her sole confidant about how false it felt.

Somewhere inside her, she felt like a teenager playing dress-up, playing a game she was still learning the rules for. Maybe other adults felt this way, but she couldn't bring herself to ask. Couldn't bring herself to admit that, as successful as she worked to be, she had no idea what she was doing 90 percent of the time.

But Santi understood, and that was enough.

*

The email verdict on his job arrived earlier than expected—barely a full day after the interview. They perched on the edge of the couch, the afternoon sun warming her living room. He gripped her hand for support as he read the decision. She read over his shoulder...and gasped.

He beamed. "They want me to do it!"

She threw her arms around him. "Of course they do. They know you're an amazing teacher."

But when they read over the email again, she noticed a condition that might cause him some trouble. The school wanted him stateside by June for training and summer school, rather than at the beginning of the school year in September. And it didn't look optional. "Are you going to be able to get your visa that soon?"

He sucked in his cheeks. "I think so. I hope so."

"Didn't they bring that up during the interview?" That kind of deadline was critical, too critical not to have been stated up front.

"They said they wanted me early." He grimaced. "I told them I didn't think it would be an issue—I didn't think it would be. I thought they meant August, maybe July."

Mariana took his phone, frowning at the screen as if that might change the school's mind. "You should call them and ask for an extension."

So he did...and he ended the conversation with concern creasing his brow. "They gave me until the end of June, but they need me in the summer."

She chewed her knuckle, pensive.

"So I'll just get the visa fast." Santiago forced confidence. "I needed it fast anyway. It's not that big of a timeline difference. I'll explain, and my lawyer can...extricate it."

It took her a moment to unravel the sounds. "Expedite?"

He shrugged. Word choices were the least of his problems.

*

Santiago flew back to Madrid as planned, and Mariana didn't hear from him other than the requisite "landed safe" and "got home okay" messages. He was recovering from jet lag, she figured.

And after that, she had other things on her mind.

She'd let the little voicemail icon sit all day...and the next day too. Halfway through day three of pretending it didn't exist, she got a lunchtime call from her mother. "Hi, Mom. What's—?"

"Why haven't you called the lawyer?"

Mariana rocked back on her heels. No pleasantries today. "What lawyer?"

"He called you twice!"

Oh. *Heh. Whoops.* "Uhhh...I must've missed it." She straightened her shirt. "What's it about?"

Her mother told her.

Mariana hung up and called the lawyer.

That evening, she walked into a cluttered office and sank into a hardbacked chair. The citrusy scent of the wood floor and furniture tickled her nose, the fake lemon of cleaning products. A tight-lipped man sat across from her, framed by the folders scattered in stacks across his desk. Leaning toward her, he shook her hand and introduced himself as Fredrick Cho.

Given the situation, small talk escaped her. "I have... how much?"

He straightened one folder and pulled out another. "Your great-aunt left you $200,000."

Her breath caught. So many zeros. She could pay off her student loans, her car loan, and both her credit cards. And buy a new vacuum. A *nice* vacuum. "Are you sure? I didn't even know her that well."

Mr. Cho nodded. "But to clarify, you don't *have* the money."

Mariana's stomach fell through the floor. "I don't understand. I thought you said she..."

"It's in her will, yes. But on one condition."

Of course there's a condition. Why would it be easy? Still, she wasn't about to walk out without hearing the requirement first. "Okay, so hit me with it. Do I have to kill someone? Steal the Declaration of Independence?" *I'd consider it, for the chance to be debt-free like a real adult.*

He looked at her askance. "Nothing so dramatic, Ms. Mitogo. But your great-aunt did stipulate that it was for you to, er, establish a family."

Complete silence.

He shifted in his seat awkwardly. "Not that you have to have a child to inherit the funds. You'll receive them when you've married. Well, six months after you've married."

Mariana stared at him. She considered her options for a mature, adult response. She went with "Are you *kidding me*?"

He fidgeted with the legal papers. "Er, no. I'm not."

"How is that her business?!"

Mr. Cho looked like he would've preferred to be somewhere else. Anywhere else. "She wrote that she hoped you would settle down. That she wanted to provide for your family."

She dug her nails into the chair arms. She didn't even know where to start with that nonsense. The assumption that she *needed* to settle down? The idea that her great-aunt would provide for her *theoretical* spouse and offspring but not for her alone? *Mind your own, Auntie!*

"Whether or not you're presently in a relationship is irrelevant."

Like that made it better.

He talked some more about legal things, but it barely registered. At the end of the meeting, she stumbled to her feet and lied that it was nice to meet him. As soon as she was out of the building, she sent Santi a Snapchat video about how ridiculous this whole thing was.

He watched the video. He didn't respond.

Unsettled, she sent a follow-up message the next day.

THEHISTORICMARIANA: *Hey, you doing okay?*

It was unlike him to have nothing to say. He would have told her if he had something going on...wouldn't he?

His brief response only worried her more.

SANTI17: *Having trouble with the visa.*

With a period at the end, not even a frowny face. Whatever the holdup was, it was serious.

At work, she got wrapped up in promoting her new project on James Farmer, researching and emailing and calling until the days blurred together. Local restaurants saw an uptick in delivery orders to the Historical Society at all hours of the day. Tuesday became Thursday became Saturday at the office, and she was eating takeout at her desk when she realized a full week had passed since she'd heard from Santi.

Her Skype complained that she had an incoming video call. Frowning in confusion, she accepted the call. "Hey, did we have a Skype session today? I don't remember scheduling one."

"No, we didn't." Santiago sounded drained—and despite the blur of a bad laptop camera, she could make out the shadows under his eyes, the wan dullness of his skin. He scrubbed at his face, but that only made it look worse. "I need to talk to you."

"Yeah, of course. Go for it." She shifted into a more comfortable position, ready for whatever story he would relate about the visa issues.

But the story, as it turned out, was only a single-sentence summary. "I won't get the visa."

Her eyes widened, and she struggled to understand exactly what he meant by that. "As in, you changed your mind, or the school, or the government...?"

Upset and drained, he strained for his English. "The government—they have no more work visas."

"*What?* How can they *run out of visas?*"

"There's only a few." He scrubbed his eyes. "They don't accept *applicac*—applications after that."

Oh no. "How long until they accept them again?"

"Not for another year."

Her breath caught in her throat. *No.* He might not get an opportunity next year. Worse, his mother might not make it through the year without the surgery that job would allow her to get.

"Okay," she forced herself to say. "Okay, we'll find a way around it. There has to be something. I'll look around." She was no lawyer, but she would dig through horrible documents for a friend, especially one for whom English was a second language.

She could see in his eyes he didn't expect this to end well, but he mustered up a smile. "Thank you."

They talked for another half an hour, and then Mariana let him go so she could research visa types and regulations.

She would be damned if she let Santi's opportunity slip through his fingers.

Chapter Three

In Which They Pull a Hail Mary

APRIL

In the Madrid family apartment, Santiago and his older sister, Maca, bent over their mother's bank statements, bill receipts, and budget that had several months ago become insufficient for her needs. Their father had been absent almost all their lives, though he'd at least sent money regularly. But he'd died at the beginning of the year. Since then, Lola Martínez Rubio had struggled to make ends meet. When her employer cut her salary, it had gone from difficult to almost impossible. And then the coronary disease diagnosis.

"I'm already transferring my extra money into her account." Maca's voice thickened with tears. Every leftover cent from almost sixty hours per week between three part-time jobs, all at a meager pay. She threw her hands in the air before shoving the offending papers away from her. "I don't know how we're going to pay for a caretaker." The bypass surgery itself was free, but neither of them could leave work to take care of their mother afterward. They'd have to hire someone full-time...which they couldn't afford. And without a caretaker waiting for her afterward, she couldn't have the surgery.

He couldn't keep his mom safe. He might lose her.

Teeth clenched against the overwhelming worry, Santiago raked a hand through his hair. "I don't make enough here." They both knew this already—as well as the fact that he was sending their mom money out of his personal savings *and* what remained of his monthly salary stipend after paying his own bills. He was in danger of bleeding himself dry, and it still wouldn't be enough.

And now this American teaching job, which would pay almost twice as much as his current salary, was about to blow away in the wind because of *bureaucracy*.

Maca pressed the heels of her hands into her eyes and choked back a sob with an ugly noise. "What are we going to do?"

Nothing. They could do nothing. Without the job, there was nothing more *to* do.

Eyes burning, he shoved his chair away from the table. "I need to go for a walk. Do you want to come?"

Maca nodded, hands over her face, but she didn't move. With a deep breath to steady himself, Santiago stepped over to her and pulled her against him. Her shoulders shook as she dug her fingers into his shirt, ugly tears dampening the fabric. Pressing his face into her hair, he hugged her until she softened into hiccups, and then they took that walk around a few city blocks.

Though the exercise helped disperse the most acute pain, the problem still darkened the backs of their minds: *how were they going to keep their mother alive?*

*

The cap was on *work* visas. Not visas in general. There had to be another visa type he'd be eligible for.

Mariana worked through her lunch break, but once she was home, she reheated some leftovers and lay on her stomach on the couch to research all the visa types on her phone. They all fell into either nonimmigrant or immigrant status—either for a temporary event, such as tourism, school, work, or business, or for actual immigration to become a permanent resident.

He obviously wouldn't qualify for an A visa—nonimmigrant for representatives of foreign governments. Santiago wasn't an ambassador by any stretch of the imagination. The B-1 visa—temporary visit for business—was too short for his needs. He wasn't a NATO member or international athlete or some kind of extraordinary talent or criminal informant...but oh.

The K-1 visa. The fiancé visa.

They could meet the requirements if he agreed to it.

And she'd get her money too.

That would be a big jump. Huge. She wouldn't bring it up except as a last resort. With a sigh, she rolled over onto her back to stare up at the ceiling and think. Was it too much? Was she overstepping her bounds as his friend?

Don't do it. It's ridiculous. No.

Her phone buzzed with a message from him:

SANTI17: *Do you have time for a call?*

Rather than respond with a redundant yes, she pressed the little video-camera icon. Santiago picked up after only two rings. "How are you?" she asked before he could say anything.

His connection stuttered, but she caught his last few words. "...what to do." He heaved a weary breath. "I don't qualify for other visas."

No. Don't do it. "Not even the short-term ones?"

He shook his head. "I wouldn't be able to work." His hands twisted at the bottom of the screen, almost out of view, as he plucked and rubbed the St. James cross on his bracelet.

Mariana stared at the repetitive nervous movement. "Is everything okay? How are you feeling?"

He froze, then dropped his hands. He looked down. "It's my *mamá*," he said to his knees, so quietly she almost didn't hear him. "Maca and I are running out of money to help her pay her bills. *Really* running out now. And her heart disease..." His voice cracked. "She needs the surgery, so I'm going to have to find another job fast. Somehow. I'm just worn thin. We all are."

Mariana pressed her lips together, dug her nails into her thighs, sucked in a deep breath to steel herself, and prayed she wasn't about to take a sledgehammer to their friendship. And to both their lives. "I have an idea. But it's a little...drastic."

He looked up at her then, hope and confusion warring in his expression. "What is it?"

Grimacing, she bit at her knuckle. "Don't get mad, but...how would you feel about marrying me?"

Santiago's eyes blew wide open. "Sorry, what?"

Embarrassment warmed her cheeks, but she didn't back down. "I'm a US citizen. You could get a green card as my fiancé and then as my husband, and you could take your job here. We act like we're madly in love for a few years until they're convinced and stop checking up on us. Then we get a quick divorce and go back to being friends."

He seemed stunned. "I... Is that legal?"

No. No, it wasn't. But she shrugged. "I don't see why it's their business. You have to get your mom that surgery—and this is the only way I can think of for you to do that."

He scrubbed his face with one hand. He didn't agree. But he didn't shoot the idea down either. "Why would you do that for me?"

She tried to sound light. "Tax benefits. Shared rent. Twice the movie collection. Someone else to cook. Plus, it's basically a three-year sleepover with my best friend. Seems reasonable to me."

He snorted—even managed a small smile—but his dark eyes remained cautious. "Really. This could ruin your life."

"You'd better be a good actor, then." She managed a sympathetic, almost sad smile and reminded him about her great-aunt's stupid condition. "I want to help you. And if I'm being honest, I want to help me too. That $200,000 would pay off the loans looming over my head. And some of the money can go to you, to help your mom." She sighed. "If you have a better option, take it, but I'm offering, Santi."

Silent, he looked around himself as if the right answer might be written on the walls. "I don't know. I know you aren't Catholic, but marriage is a sacrament, you know? It's... I don't know." It wasn't a no, but he sounded broken. What other option did he have?

"Think about it," Mariana said gently. "It's late for you anyway. Go to bed."

He took the out, and she plotted a plan of action in case he was indeed desperate enough to take her up on the offer.

Desperation drove people to difficult solutions. Santi would have to decide for himself how far he could go.

*

Santiago lay in bed, staring up at the ceiling and rubbing the cross on his bracelet. It was one thing to move to the US for a job to pay for his mom's surgery. It was something else entirely to marry a friend so he could move to the US for that job. Mariana was beautiful and a joy to be around, but he didn't think of her romantically. He would have to play a part, to lie, long term. And to marry under false pretenses...wouldn't that be a sin? Or at least strongly frowned upon? A *sacrament*.

He wouldn't have chosen this for himself. Not at all. But he was running out of options. And who could he ask for advice? The mother and sister he would have to lie to in order to make it work? The friend willing to put her reputation—her way of life—on the line for him?

He drifted off out of sheer exhaustion. His alarm rang early, a too-happy song cutting through the silent darkness. Eyes squeezed shut, he reached out with one hand and groped around for his phone. He flicked at the screen in the way he'd perfected so that he could snooze the alarm without looking *and* without accidentally turning it off.

But the noise didn't stop, and it wasn't his alarm.

He slitted his eyes open to take the call before it went to voicemail. Why was Maca calling him?

He threw an arm over his eyes. "Nnggaatt?"

An ugly, ragged sob cut through the line like a serrated knife.

Santiago bolted upright. Adrenaline, fear, pounded in his neck. "What happened?" Was she hurt? Or their mother?

"Mamá—Mamá had a heart attack. She died."

Santiago woke for real this time. His pulse pounded; sweat clumped his hair and stuck it to his forehead. His trembling hands were twisted up in the sheets.

A nightmare.

Breathing hard, he forced himself to lie back down. *I'll get a glass of water when I stop shaking so much.*

So, the next day, on top of his usual my-family-is-unraveling exhaustion, he was frazzled and jumpy from the too-real dream when he found an envelope from the school board in his work mailbox. Once he'd torn open the top and unfolded the letter inside, it took him a few tries to understand what exactly those printed words meant— and then the floor dropped out from under him.

"It's just budget cuts," the principal explained to him in a private meeting that afternoon after the students had gone home. "The school board reduced the languages budget, and the other teachers are on a continuing contract." She touched an age-lined hand to his arm. "We're truly sorry to see you go, Santiago. You're a great teacher. If you need a letter of recommendation, anything, let me know."

He nodded. Mind blank, he somehow made it through the meeting with his dignity intact. He drove home in silence, staring flatly into the road in front of him. Pulled into the parking lot. Shut the door. Let himself in the tiny apartment.

Only after the latch clicked into place did he let himself think—let himself sink back against the wall as frustrated tears burned his eyes.

They weren't going to renew his contract.

He had assumed that even if the American job fell through, he would have this private school position to fall back on. But no. It was almost summertime and he had nothing waiting for the autumn. Maca couldn't handle that kind of burden financially, not to mention emotionally. There were so few openings available to him. Maybe he could juggle a few customer-service jobs, but that would barely cover his own bills, let alone pay for a caretaker for his mother's surgery.

He needed a miracle. Something, *anything*, to shove him in the right direction. He needed—

His phone beeped. Vision blurry, he dug it out and saw the yellow blinking notification light. On-screen: *TheHistoricMariana te envió un Snap!*

Santiago sucked in a breath.

She was the only one who could save him, save his family, and she'd contacted him in his darkest hour. Maybe it was nothing more than coincidence, but

Santiago's chest clenched, then steadied with resolve. Staring down at her nickname on his phone, he realized what he had to do.

(First, he opened her photo. It was a picture of a dead raccoon with the caption "relatable." He snorted.)

He sent her The Message—on Snapchat of all platforms.

SANTI17: *I think you would make a great wife.*

Her response was immediate, the words bold against the blurred, out-of-focus image of her carpet:

THEHISTORICMARIANA: *Are you sure?*

Despite everything, he was.

Later, he knelt in his church and, rosary in hand, prayed along every bead. *Forgive me for what I'm about to do. I can't lose my mamá to what would happen if I didn't.*

The guilt probably should have lingered after that... but it dissolved.

Hail Mary.

Chapter Four

In Which They Declare Their Love

APRIL

During her lunch hour the next day, Mariana split her screen between Skype and her visa research notes. "So we need to have met at least once in person within two years of applying for the visa. No problem. We just did that."

"Nailed it." He flashed a dimpled grin.

Though she rolled her eyes, she smiled. "Yeah, we're practically psychic. We'll also need evidence of a relationship."

"I have all our messages from back in, what, 2013? I can print them off." He looked down toward his phone. "Ooh, *2012*. We're relics."

She laughed, pleasure warming her cheeks and chest. "We are. I can't believe you kept those."

Head jerking up to look at her again, he placed a hand over his heart, the picture of wounded love. "Are you saying you *didn't* keep them?"

"No, yeah, I kept them too."

He pretended to wipe sweat from his forehead. "Okay, good. If you hadn't, I would have divorced you."

"We aren't even married yet, Santi!"

"A preemptive divorce, then."

"You're ridiculous."

"Well, you're the one who wants to marry me, so..."

She snorted. "Point taken. Anyway, my distractible future husband, we need proof of a romantic relationship. Messages from years ago yelling at each other about our interpretations of two characters sharing the screen for ten seconds probably don't count."

He sucked in an argumentative breath. "Seraphina and Ainsley were in *love*."

"They were *not*. They were part of that coup in season four."

"In love *and* part of the coup," he insisted.

She threw her hands in the air. "We don't even watch *The Frat House Gang* anymore! It doesn't matter!"

"It matters," he muttered.

They had definitely not been in love, but she forced herself to get back on task. "The point is, we need sappy, I-love-you-more-no-I-love-you-more messages and photos and physical proof like that. I have some saved selfies of yours, but that's it." She stopped to consider this. Typed love notes over the web were doable, but they'd only spent a few days together in person, and they hadn't taken a whole lot of photographic evidence since the primary focus had been overcoming jet lag and nailing a job interview. "How good are you with Photoshop?"

He made a face. "Not good—and that wouldn't help us anyway. As soon as they figured out we faked photos, our case goes out the window. We need real pictures."

How do we get those? They both fell silent, searching for feasible options.

"Do you have any vacation time?"

She clicked her tongue as she mentally reviewed her employee handbook and time card. "Yeah, I have something like a week of PTO—paid time off. Why?"

"How would you feel about coming to Spain?"

Surprised, she leaned back. "I might be able to swing that. Don't you have to work?"

He shrugged, a shadow passing over his face. "What are they going to do, not renew my contract?" Then he shook off the bitter tone. "I have some vacation available, and we have a five-day weekend next month. I can make that a week, and we can go out on dates. Maybe a road trip or something. Lots of photo taking."

"Oh. That's a great idea, actually." She sucked in her lower lip and held it in her teeth. "That would work. I can't think of any reason it wouldn't. Would your family be okay with me visiting?" The shared apartment would be close quarters.

"I'll check, but I think they'll be glad to meet you. We won't go out to eat or anything expensive."

Okay, good. She didn't want to stress them out even more. "So I come out there, we cheese it up for a week, and then we announce what? That we're dating, or engaged?"

He thought. "How about we start dating now, and then before you leave my country, I'll propose?"

Slowly, she nodded. That seemed like a reasonable timeline, given the circumstances of their pretend romance. "For the fiancé visa, we have to get married within ninety days of you getting here."

Uncertainty shifted his expression. "How? Do we sign a paper?"

Mentally reviewing what she knew of marriage legalities, she guessed, "We should be able to do a civil wedding fast. It would be a judge, witnesses, and paperwork. We could do a church wedding, too, but that needs more planning and is ungodly expensive."

He winced. "No church wedding. It seems... sacrilegious."

"Oh." She bit her knuckle. *Does it speak badly of me that I didn't think of that?* "Okay, that's fine. Of course. No worries. We'll do the civil wedding thing ASAP, and you'll move in with me, and it'll be fine."

"You only have one bedroom."

She squinted. Had the logistics of this not been obvious? "Where did you think you were going to sleep, in a cardboard box on the street?"

He looked straight into the camera to glare at her.

"We're about to spend three years acting like we're a madly-in-love married couple. We're going to live together, and until my lease is up, that means sharing a bed. Or you can sleep on the couch if you're that freaked out about it." More for her own benefit than his, she clarified, "We'll have to touch in public, some kissing, too, probably. It won't mean anything. As soon as we're home alone, we can go back to normal." She wasn't looking forward to all the public displays of affection.

A suspicious cough sounded like he was covering a laugh. "America must be so sad if you can't hug and kiss your friends when you see them."

"You know what I mean!"

He made an I-don't-believe-you expression.

With a scowl, she leaned back in her chair. "Anyway. So we're officially dating now. We should—"

"No, we're not."

She furrowed her brow, cocked her head in confusion. "Yes, we are. We said so two seconds ago."

He shook his head, adamant. "If we're doing all this, we have to actually do it. Actual asking out, actual proposing."

"Oh, okay." She shrugged. "Probably a good plan. After lunch, I'll send you a message telling you I love you. Would that work?"

He had the nerve to laugh. "That's the dramatic, romantic confession of love you want to go with? Really?"

Mariana huffed. "That's how I'd do it if I were serious, so yeah. Why not?"

"When was the last time you went on a date, Mari?"

Her lips pressed together, and she looked away. She didn't answer. She didn't have to.

He softened. "I'm not judging you. Just let me handle this part, okay?"

Gaze skirting back to him, she nodded once.

He smiled gently. "Don't worry. It will be great."

*

SANTI17: *I've been thinking, Mari, and I have something important to tell you, or to ask you, I guess. Can we Skype again during your lunch break? I need to talk to you.*

The message came the next morning, and Mariana sent back a quick *of course, I hope everything is okay*. But when the video call connected, she all but spit fire. "How is that any different from what I was going to do?"

Santiago held up his hands. "I set the tone. Awkward, embarrassed, but resolved to let my passion be known. And now we need to run Skype for an hour minimum for the grand confession, and the excited gushing to each other afterward about how happy we are." He cracked a tiny, hopeful smile. "Isn't that more convincing than one message that says 'I realized when you visited that I like you, let's date'?"

It *was* better. Although it shouldn't have mattered, it clawed a hole in her gut. She wanted to be competent— any adult knew how to ask someone out, didn't they? She couldn't even manage basic romantic gestures.

How had she thought this was a good idea?

"Hey, what's with the face?" He deflated. "I was playing, Mari. Are you okay?"

She forced a smile. "Yeah, I'm fine."

Clearly unconvinced, he watched her for a minute. "Okay, forget the declaration of love thing. Did you watch that new Spanish movie I told you about?"

It wasn't the smoothest subject change ever, but she appreciated the distraction from her own thoughts. They went back and forth until she was relaxed and laughing.

*

Santiago relaxed, too, when the last of the defensiveness smoothed from Mariana's expression. She'd taken his teasing about her lack of experience (and, to be honest, lack of general romanticism) badly, and although he wasn't sure why she had, he had enough common sense to know he'd better leave it alone.

They did need to act out their cover story though. "Hey, what do you think is the absolutely most ridiculous declaration of love we could get away with?" He posed it gently, as a laughable extension of the conversation rather than a segue into the more serious real issue, and she didn't tense.

She tilted her head toward the ceiling, a smile tugging at her lips. "You rent a cruise ship and reenact that scene from *Titanic*."

That mental image made him grin. "As long as I get to be Rose."

Mariana gasped through her laugh. "Rose is the one who survives, you jerk! You're gonna leave me to freeze to death in the water?"

"At least you get to be the selfless one." He laughed. "What about if I bought a roomful of roses and did my confession there?"

"That would be absurd. If you buy the room now, it's too late. We're already Skyping. The timeline wouldn't match up."

"A) that would apply to a cruise ship too. B) I could chicken out during this call and have to try again in a few days."

"Is someone donating the flowers? They're pricey. I don't think it would make sense given your financial situation."

"And a cruise ship *would*?"

She dissolved into giggles but found the composure to muster, "Maybe you snuck onto the cruise ship?"

"How—in what world—does that make more sense than me sneaking into a flower shop?" His rising voice cracked from suppressed laughter, and they snickered.

"Okay," she managed. "Okay, what about a PowerPoint montage of our selfies and one of those composite things of what our children would look like?"

He choked. "If they're based on our selfies, we would have unusually ugly children."

"It would just prove how much you love me that you want to reproduce." She grinned. "Are you sure we can't say you did one of those ideas?"

She was only half joking, and he sobered. "We can, but if people press, we need a serious answer. Mind if I…?" He gestured toward her.

Though concern flickered in her eyes, she settled back and nodded. "Sure, go ahead. Make sure it's good, or I'll break up with you."

He flashed the playful grin he knew she liked. "We aren't even fake-dating yet, Mari."

She pursed her lips against an amused smile. "I'm waiting for you to convince me of your undying, passionate love. There's thirty-five minutes left on my lunch break. Hurry up."

"Ooh. Pressure." He straightened up in his seat, shook out his arms. He was joking, but at the same time, he wasn't. Sure, he'd planned out a romantic speech this morning, but if he tried to act sappy in a fully serious way for after-the-fact credibility, she would be uncomfortable. At the same time, if he gave her some silly spiel that was obviously a joke...sure, she'd laugh, but they would have to bullshit a story whenever anyone asked how he'd confessed his love.

They were already faking their love. They might as well make things easier for themselves and make some of the details true.

"Listen, I really enjoyed coming to visit you." He let his voice drop to a huskier tone while keeping the mischievous teasing in his eyes. (He hoped this translated well over Skype.)

"I liked having you here," she replied diplomatically.

"But when I stepped on the plane to fly home again, I realized something." He paused for dramatic effect.

Her eyebrows rose. "What was that?"

Placing a hand over his heart, he looked right into the camera. "I realized that it wouldn't be home if you weren't there."

She stilled, clearly unsure how to play it now, so he barreled onward.

"We've been friends for years. I'm so glad that show brought us together. Even if you ignorantly insist they weren't in love," he added in his normal voice, and she laughed. Back to the I'm-sultry-and-in-love-with-you voice: "I spent so long thinking of you as my best friend that it didn't occur to me you could be anything else. But then I saw you at the airport and, well, it occurred to me." That, he didn't have to BS. She was gorgeous in a nontraditional way, and he couldn't deny his body had reacted. It hadn't truly changed his feelings for her, but still. There it was.

Mariana ducked her head. "It occurred to me too," she said, so quietly he almost didn't hear her.

He nodded at her surprisingly believable contribution. "I know we didn't do a lot while I was there, and I wasn't there long, but when I left, I felt...alone. I think I left part of me with you." He winked. "It was my PowerPoint montage of our ugly children."

Her laugh surprised her into looking toward him again. "I looked at it. They're horrendous little goblins."

He held up his hands. "Whoa, now. That's half your genetics."

"The recessive half, clearly." She tried to stop laughing and only ended up snorting. "Anyway, you were saying."

"Right, right." He screwed up a rueful smile. "I was saying it doesn't feel right, being here without you. I can't focus. I can't sleep. All I can think about is how much I need you."

Her smile faded, and worry clouded her face, her posture. Her shoulders tensed and drew upward; she wrapped her arms around herself—she didn't even seem to realize she was doing it.

"And how much I need—what is it? Life Alert," he added in the same earnest tone, "because I've fallen for you, and I can't get up."

The terrible pickup line drew out a relieved smile, though she didn't relax completely. "That's because you're getting old, Grandpa. You're gonna break a hip if you ever get down on one knee."

He could think of a different kind of rigorous physical activity that might actually mess up his back for a while. But he opted to pass that particular joke by, given he was currently straddling the line between funny and uncomfortable for her, and she was ambivalent toward sex anyway.

Back on track, Santiago.

"All that to say"—he rushed for the sake of time and their attention spans—"I want to be with you as more than a friend." A quick switch to Spanish, since people seemed to think oops-I-forgot-which-language-I-was-speaking was romantic: *"¿Quisiera ser mi novia?"* He gestured grandly to her to indicate the fake-relationship ball was in her court, and he did his best to look romantically conflicted about her potential answer.

Mariana touched her palm to her cheek in an overdone Southern-belle expression of flattered surprise. "You want *me*, the unassuming Mariana Mitogo, historian and former shotput-thrower, to be *your girlfriend*?"

"If you'll have me!"

She flung the back of her hand to her forehead. "Oh, my stars and body! I do declare I never thought this day would come! Yes, yes, a thousand times yes, Santi!"

At least, he was pretty sure that was what she said. She had turned on a thick, twangy accent that made her harder to understand. But hey, they now had an official Declaration of Affection to report to friends, family, and Facebook, and that was what they had needed.

"Nice." He air-high-fived her. "I vote we tell our families first, and change the Facebook status tomorrow. Good?"

"Great. Sounds like a plan."

They signed off at the end of her lunch break, but Santiago fended off a fresh worry: as they were right now, no one would ever believe they were dating.

How would they pull off realistic romance when they only thought of each other as friends?

Chapter Five

In Which Internet Friends Are All Serial Killers

APRIL

During the school year, Mariana's Wednesdays were taken up by volunteering as a mentor at the local high school. After the last teenager had left, she and one of the other mentors, her friend, Embry, loitered beside Embry's SUV in the school parking lot. The spring air smelled of daffodils and coming rain as Mariana took a deep breath to prepare herself. "So, you know Santiago, my friend from Spain?"

Embry leaned back against the hood of her car and tilted her face up to the gray sky. Her long natural curls shivered in the breeze. "Yeah, the one who just visited you. Why?"

Mariana shoved her fists into her jacket pockets. "Well, we're kinda...dating now."

"Heyyy, congrats!" Straightening, Embry hugged her and grinned. "Must've been some visit, huh?"

Mariana laughed. "Yeah, you could say that."

"All right, so show me a picture of him."

Embry planted her hands on her hips when Mariana didn't immediately whip out her phone. "Come on. I need all the information. Tick tock." She tapped the hood impatiently.

Pulling a face, Mariana scrolled through her saved Santi selfies until she found one that was true to reality. "Here."

Embry took the phone. "Aww, he's cute, in a nerdy way." Liking girls didn't mean she couldn't appreciate a guy's aesthetic. She leaned back against the SUV. "So who asked who out?"

Mariana was now glad they'd actually done it so she didn't have to lie. "He called me over Skype and asked me. He said something about feeling alone when he left me behind."

Embry clapped a hand over her grin. "That's so freakin' cute. And unfair. When will I find a beautiful lady to sweep me off *my* feet?"

"I don't know, but until then, she's missing out."

Embry chewed the inside of her cheek. "Not to be a downer, but how are you going to manage the whole long-distance thing? I mean, being friends internationally is one thing, but dating is another. It's hard." Her last girlfriend had broken up with her because the distance was too much, and that was only from Virginia to Ohio.

"I'm gonna try to visit him soon." Mariana hesitated. What could she say? *Don't worry, we won't be dating for long?* "We video-call all the time, but yeah, it still sucks to be so far away from him." Was that good enough?

It must have been. Embry nodded. "At least there's technology. Imagine if we were stuck with just snail mail."

Mariana laughed. "Oh, now *that* would suck. Waiting for my letters to get there, and then waiting to hear back—plus, global stamps are not cheap."

"Postage is a bitch for sure." Embry shook her head. "Anyway, all that to say, congratulations on your new partner in crime. I hope you're able to go see him."

Since Embry had taken the news of the new long-distance boyfriend so well, Mariana hoped her parents would take it, if not as well, at least with the same level of grace. She had, unfortunately, forgotten one important difference.

Embry understood the concept of Internet friends.

"Where is this coming from?" Eyes wide, Carmen Mitogo looked one step away from getting off the couch to shake some sense into her daughter. "You only met this boy, what, a week ago?"

Mariana sighed. "He visited two weeks ago. But we've been friends for almost a decade."

Her father, Rafael, gripped the armrest until his knuckles paled. "You don't know anything about him. You hadn't seen each other before that."

"No, we did." She summoned all her patience. "We talk all the time. We do video calls, Snapchat, emails, Facebook...pretty much every way you can be in contact with someone who lives in a different country. Since 2012."

Carmen adjusted her headwrap. "That's not the same, Mari. You can't know someone until you spend time with them."

Deep breaths. She gave up on them understanding Skype calls as quality time. "Then you don't have to worry. I'm gonna go visit him."

This did not, in fact, reassure them. "You can't go overseas by yourself! What if he's a serial killer?"

"He's not a serial killer," she gritted out. "You remember all those times I've talked about Santiago, my friend from Spain? That's this guy."

Both her mother and father leaned back, trying to process this revelation.

"I thought that was someone from school, or history camp, or something." Rafael scratched his head.

"Nope. Internet."

Carmen looked away and blew out a breath. "I don't know, Mari. You never mentioned that you liked him."

This, Mariana knew her answer for. "I didn't really, not until I met him in person. But I do now." She let herself go girlish, coy. "I'm so excited to see him again. We've been Skyping every day." That was true, although not for the reason she implied.

They eyed her skeptically.

"We can video-call you when I go over there," she promised. "Y'all can talk to him. I think you'll like him—I hope you will." She smiled. "He means a lot to me."

At that, they softened, as she'd hoped they would. Carmen spoke first. "You really like this boy?"

Mariana nodded.

Her parents exchanged a silent look until Rafael said, "We'll talk to him, if that's what you want."

She beamed. "Thank you!"

They didn't smile back.

She understood that her parents were looking out for her. She did. But not accepting her relationship was too much. It crossed the line from looking out for her to distrusting her judgment.

I am an adult. She flexed her hands. *I make decisions. I pay bills. I feed myself—some days better than others.* It didn't seem like much to ask—for them to treat her like an adult who could make her own choices.

But her indignation faltered in one aspect: she didn't feel as grownup as she looked. *Tried* to look. Mariana wanted to set a good, responsible example for her mentees. And on the flip side, it was all she could do to look competent around her older friends, like Omar and Embry, who knew what they were doing.

She had a job in her field, sure, but three massive loans and two maxed-out credit cards shadowed her entire life. She had one meal she made well, so she cooked it family-size and ate the same thing for days on end with minimal effort. She vacuumed when she had company. She watched Netflix at night instead of doing any of the 500 tasks on her to-do list. God help her if someone was rude at work.

She had her life "together," but not...*together*.

If her parents didn't believe in her, who would?

*

Maca sat in the tiny kitchen with Santiago, staring at him, lips pursed. The silence concerned Santiago more than an outright rejection.

"I mean, you don't have to talk to her if you don't want to." He wasn't going to drag them together. "But she'll be here, and she's important to me."

More silence. Finally, Maca sighed. "No, I want to get to know her. I only... Is this the best time? Partners are expensive, especially long-distance, and it's not like you have a lot of spare time either."

Jaw clenched, he looked away. His last partner, a local man named Paolo, had often complained that he wanted more gifts and more dates, but Santiago hadn't been able to meet the ever-increasing demands. He would care for Mariana. He had to. He couldn't lose her too.

"Have you told Mamá yet? Or do I get to watch that horror show tonight?"

He snorted. "No, I wouldn't do that to you. I told her already."

"Boo. I wanted to see her face." She cracked a grin. "At least now I know I'm the new favorite child."

"It would take more than that."

"Oh, not even. I know how she feels about Internet friends."

Apparently that much was universal. Santiago's talk with his mother had gone the same way as Mariana's with her parents, right down to the serial killer theory. The older generation clung to that stereotype as if they'd never heard of pen pals. And the fact that they'd already spent almost a week together—with no murders to speak of— meant nothing.

His sister smacked him lightly on the arm. "When's this girl coming to visit, anyway?"

"Next month, when I have that long weekend." It was actually only a few weeks away, but it made him less anxious to think of it as a month, like it was way off in the distance.

"Aha. Excellent." She rubbed her hands together.

He shot her a suspicious look. "What?"

"That gives me time to plan how to show her what a terrible person you are."

"Well, if my horrible sister doesn't scare her off, I'll know she's a keeper."

"Hate you."

"Hate you too."

She blew him a kiss, and he pretended to slap it out of the air. An easy light shone in her eyes, and he hoped that—if nothing else came of this visit—it would give his sister a fun distraction from everything else going on. She needed it. She'd earned it.

And if this worked and he got the teaching job in America, he could take the burden from her altogether. Then she wouldn't need a distraction at all, and he could sleep easier at night.

It was a big *if* though.

Mariana's visit would make or break their plans.

Chapter Six

In Which They Get an Unexpected Tutor

MAY

Mariana had expected the jet lag to be worse. After all, Santi had crashed on her couch right after his flight. But the exhaustion came in waves, and she was in an energy upswing when she stepped off the plane in Madrid.

She looked around the airport and sucked in a deep breath against rising worry. What if she couldn't find him? What if she was a stereotypical American and everyone hated her? Was she going to embarrass herself?

"Mari!"

She recognized the voice even in a single word. Santiago stood waiting for her, waving his hand high over his head so she would see him through the crowd milling about. She waved back, and when he grinned, she saw the dimples all the way down the hall. As she approached, she saw someone else with him—a young woman who looked so like him there was no mistaking they were related. His sister.

He pulled Mariana in for a big hug as soon as she drew close enough, and spun her in a circle. Surprised but delighted, she laughed and held on tightly. When he set her down, he kissed her cheeks. Flushing, she tried to act like she was used to outright affection.

He introduced them in Spanish. "This is my sister, Maca. Maca, this is my girlfriend, Mariana."

Then Maca hugged her, too, which somehow surprised Mariana more. "I'm sorry you met my brother first. He doesn't represent the family very well." The same playful sense of humor as her brother.

Mariana laughed. "I'm here, so he did something right." She added, "Sorry about my accent." She'd learned Spanish all through high school and college, and between that and Santiago's tutelage, she could hold her own in conversation. However, no teacher had ever been able to get rid of her southern drawl.

Maca waved this off. "It's fine. I think it's cool that you can speak it while you're here. My English is terrible."

"That's true." Santiago elbowed his sister in the side. "I teach English as a *job*, and I can't help her."

"You see how mean he is?" Maca planted her hands on her hips. "You see what I have to put up with?"

Mariana fought to keep a straight face and lost the battle. "He's a jerk. Let's leave him here."

He spun on her, affronted. "Betraying me already? Does my love mean nothing to you?"

"Nothing at all."

Maca draped both arms around Mariana. "She understands me."

"I'm going to leave you both here." He rolled his eyes. "Now give me back my girlfriend so she can pretend to think I'm cool."

Mariana grinned. "That *is* why he invited me here."

Maca laughed and released her. Santiago immediately took Mariana by the hand and tugged her to his side. His arm draped around her to keep her snuggly-tight against him. "Ready to go?"

In the family's apartment, Santi set a neat stack of sheets and blankets on the twin-size air mattress in the living room, and Mariana tucked her backpack and suitcase behind the corner of the couch. With a goodbye hug, Maca went to pick up their mom from the doctor's office, leaving Mariana alone with Santiago in the apartment. Biting the inside of her cheek, she perched uncomfortably on the edge of the couch. *Our relationship is different now. What does he expect?* When he brought out a DVD of *El Ministerio del Tiempo*, she hedged. "I'm pretty tired. Is it okay if I shower and take a nap?"

The nap lasted too long. When she woke the next morning, jet lag dragged down every inch of her body as if someone had attached weights while she slept. With a groan, she pulled the blanket over her head, but someone who smelled like coffee tugged it back down. The sunlight burned. "Nuuu."

Gentle fingers slid between her shoulder and the couch and pushed her upward. "Come on, *querida*. Up. I made coffee."

Eyes squeezed shut, she poked one hand out from under the covers for the mug, but he didn't pass it to her.

"You have to sit up first."

She scowled but forced herself to sit all the way up. As soon as he handed over the coffee, it went to her mouth.

He had the good sense not to start a conversation until she'd downed it and started in on the refill he brought her—long enough for the caffeine to kick in. Only when she looked him in the eye did he move on. "Do you want to get started on our romantic field trips? We can do all the touristy things around Madrid, and take selfies and stuff."

She was now awake enough for that to sound appealing. "Like where? Museo Reina Sofía?"

"Yeah, that's one. I think you'll like it. And there's lots more."

So, after a shower and a short metro ride, she found herself outside this building she'd only ever seen in pictures—a huge tan exterior with windows in rows for miles. The entrance was framed by two soaring glass columns that read REINA and SOFIA.

Entranced, she waved her phone at Santi. "Photo time."

"Already?" Surprised, he fished his phone out of his pocket. "It's not even noon yet. You look like a zombie. A *cute* zombie, but still."

"It won't be getting any better." She stuck out her tongue. "You did this to yourself. Come take a picture with your zombie girlfriend."

"Is that necrophilia?" He slung an arm around her and pivoted them so that the art museum towered behind them, a gorgeous backdrop.

His half embrace felt conspicuous, even though she knew people here on the whole were touchy-feely and probably thought nothing of this. His acting wasn't going to be the problem—hers was. She had so little to go on. Did she even know what romantic and sexual attraction felt like? How was she supposed to mimic something when she didn't know what it was?

"Hey, your Thinking Face looks a lot like your Angry Face. Stop frowning, or people will think you don't like me." A light, nonaccusatory half joke.

Worry (exacerbated by jet lag) clogged up her sense of humor. Switching back to English, she turned to press her forehead into his shoulder. "I don't know what I'm doing."

"You're taking a selfie." When she didn't respond to the teasing, he ducked his head to get a look at her face. "You don't know what you're doing with what?"

"All of...this." She squeezed her eyes shut. *You're a failure.* She'd been the one to suggest a fake relationship, and now she was going to be the one to ruin it. "I don't know how to be all romantic and touchy. I just know how to be friends."

"Hey. Hey." He wrapped his other arm around her. "It's okay. We can figure it out. Do you want to sit down?"

She nodded against him.

He led them to a bench off the beaten path, out of sight of the other visitors wandering around. She sat down, leaned her head back to try to get her emotions under control. Once she was no longer in danger of crying, he pressed, "Can you explain for me?"

She ran her hand over her close-cropped curls. "I don't...I *can* feel attraction, I have before, but it's been a long time. I was a kid. I don't know what it's supposed to look like now. I'm afraid I'm going to do it wrong."

He pushed up his glasses, serious for once. "You're really worried about it?"

She shot him a dirty look.

He held up his hands. "All right, all right." He clicked his tongue as he thought. "Okay, how about this—let's not think of this as romantic. We're two friends going sightseeing, right? We'll be hugging as friends. Holding hands as friends. It doesn't mean anything, so you don't have to worry about whether or not you're doing it right."

Pretending they weren't pretend-dating. Hugging herself, she sighed. "I guess that makes sense." Getting rid of the "romance" mental gymnastics might help her chill out and actually make a convincing fake girlfriend.

He gave her a reassuring smile, and when he touched her arm, she didn't stiffen.

"All right, loser, let's go take a bunch of cheesy selfies."

In front of the façade, she lined up the shot for the best angle, framing them with the glass columns. Once again, Santiago slung his arm around her shoulders and tugged her flush against him. She took a deep breath...and, letting it out, relaxed against him. *Friends hugging.* She flashed a huge smile and took the picture.

"Another!" He held up their clasped hands with a grin.

Mariana cocked her head, kept the smile, and saved a second selfie.

*

At dinner, Mariana gushed to Santiago's mother and sister about her favorite aspects of the Temple of Debod and Palacio Real, her eyes sparkling. "So we're in the Royal Library and, Lola, you would not believe what he—"

Lola. Hearing Mariana address his mom by the nickname...Santiago didn't expect the warm satisfaction that bloomed in his chest. He laced his fingers with Mariana's atop the table.

"I—um." She stared at their intertwined hands before remembering this was supposed to be normal. She flashed a grin and relaxed, but she didn't lean into the touch, didn't initiate anything further. "What was I...?"

Maca grinned. "It sounded like an embarrassing story about Santi?"

He scowled.

"Oh, right!" Mariana brightened. "Listen. Santi was looking at one of the globes, and he went to look at the placard, but he moved too fast and—" She made a *shoooom* motion, complete with sound effect. "—his legs went out from under him. It was *suuuper* dignified."

Later that night, he pulled Maca into her and Lola's bedroom. "I need to ask you something," he whispered, closing the door behind them.

"You're being weird," she told him, "but fine. What?"

"Do you...?" He scrubbed a hand over his face. *It's not a hard question. Get it out.* "I wanted to ask if you like Mariana." It might be too soon for deep bonding, but he'd take any positive impressions.

Leaning against the wall, Maca ran her fingers through her thick hair. "She told us about how you tripped over nothing and fell on your face in that library, so yeah, she's cool with me. Why, are you—?"

"I'm going to ask her to marry me," he blurted. *Maybe it'll sound more rational if I say it quickly.*

Maca reeled. "I'm sorry, you're *what*?"

"*Shh!*" He pushed her head down as if that would lower her volume. "*Don't yell.* I want to marry her. And you said you liked her."

"No, I... It's a little *fast!*" She flung her hands in the air. "Romance makes people idiots. Maybe try dating for longer than a *month* before you get engaged?"

"We've been friends for years. We know we want to be together...and I want to propose while she's here."

Closing her eyes, she pinched the bridge of her nose. "And, what, she's going to move here just like that?"

"No." He stuffed his hands in his pockets. "I would move there."

She sucked in a breath and looked him in the eye. "You're really moving away?" Her gaze was sad, injured.

Tenderly he ruffled her hair. "She has a job there, and so will I. I can take care of everything once I start working in the States. I'll have money for a caretaker after Mamá gets her surgery."

She snorted, ducked her head. "I know you wanted that job, but this seems like extreme measures to get a green card," she joked despite the sadness in her voice.

It shouldn't have surprised him she'd jumped to that conclusion—she wasn't *wrong*. "Of course it's not for a green card." He thought that was a reasonable tone.

Too late: *I should have run with the joke*.

Oh no.

Maca stiffened, and slowly, she raised her head to squint at him. "Tell me you didn't."

"Of course not."

Her eyes widened and she gasped. "*Santiago Mateo de los Reyes Martínez!*"

From the kitchen, Mariana laughed. "Someone got full-named."

Lola snorted. "Leave each other alone, you two!"

Meanwhile, Maca hit him on the arm with every syllable: "San-ti-a-go!"

"*Huy!* Don't *do* that!"

"How can you use her like this? This is a terrible idea!"

If he couldn't convince her otherwise, she could and *would* derail the whole thing. "No, listen, it was Mariana's idea. She needs to get married to get some big inheritance. And you know Mamá needs the money. We'll just be married for a few years, pretend we're madly in love, and then divorce as friends."

She gaped at him in horror. "You really think it's going to work? You could go to *jail!* Both of you!"

As if he hadn't had this argument with himself a thousand times. "Do you have a better idea?"

With a huff she crossed her arms. "Literally anything else. Play the lottery?"

He bopped her on the head. "This is my absolute last resort. But Mariana and I are best friends, and we think it'll work."

"I figured it out in, like, thirty seconds."

"Well, you're basically me, so it doesn't count. Anyway, we need you to help sell it, all right? No one else can know."

"Unless they figure it out too."

"*No one else is allowed to figure it out*," he grumbled. "Come on. Mariana's having a hard time with the acting. We could use a wingwoman."

Maca rolled her eyes and gritted her teeth. "You two are incompetent." Finally, she threw her hands in the air, playful interest gleaming in her eyes. "It's time for the professional to step in."

*

"And tomorrow we're going sightseeing again," Mariana told Lola, who was leaning against the kitchen counter. "Is there any place in particular we should fit into our itinerary?"

"The Museo del Prado, for sure. I used to take the kids there all the time when they were younger." Lola beamed. "Did Santi ever tell you about the time he got lost there?"

Mariana clasped a hand to her chest. "Awww, no. Poor thing. How old was he?"

"Eight. And when we finally found him, he said it was on purpose so he could spend the night there. Can you believe that?"

"You know what? I absolutely can."

The second bedroom door creaked open. Santiago emerged and came to stand beside Mariana, looping his arm around her waist. On his heels, Maca took Mariana by the hand, pulling her away from the conversation and into the bedroom.

Mariana sat on the quilted bedspread. "Is this the family meeting room? If so, I'm honored to be included."

"Santi told me what's going on. Well, I made him tell me," Maca corrected herself. "So he's going to propose before you leave?"

Mariana shifted her weight. Had they been that obvious? "Um, yes. I don't know exactly when."

"Okay, great. Keep the surprise real." Maca tilted her head and tapped her cheek, looking Mariana up and down. "You aren't very affectionate. Is that an American thing or a you thing?"

"A me thing? I don't know. Maybe both."

Maca combed her fingers through her elegant ebony waves and gathered all her hair over one shoulder. "All right. You're just going to have to do your best while you're here. You aren't actually kissing?"

Mariana quickly shook her head no.

Maca muttered something that sounded like *I have to do all the work.* "You have to make all the smaller touches count. Hand on his lower back. Trail your thumb over his knuckles. Play with his hair. I don't know, you should be draped over each other."

Shouldn't he have been able to detail what he wanted? "Why isn't Santiago the one telling me this?"

"Boys are useless." Maca rolled her eyes. "If I thought he could do this talk justice, he'd be here instead of me."

Mariana squinched up her brow. "I thought Santi told me once you didn't like romance."

Waving this off, Maca inspected her nails. "I don't like to *participate*. In dating, sex, any of it. Zero percent. But I like games, and I like to watch other people's romances unfold. So here I am, coaching my brother's fake girlfriend." She raised her eyes to the ceiling. "What did I do to deserve this?"

By the time Mariana was finally allowed out of the bedroom-turned-conference-room, she still wasn't sure exactly what romance was, but she at least had specific instructions for ways to imitate it. Santi's advice had helped her lower her inhibitions about touch; Maca's advice had helped her know what kinds of touch to aim for.

She rejoined her fake boyfriend in the kitchen, running her fingertips along his back as she leaned against the counter. He leaned into the contact with a smile that, for all the world, looked like a man satisfied by being stroked by the woman he loved. She returned a lazy, crooked smile she hoped accomplished the same effect.

"There are other people in the room," Maca complained. When Mariana glanced her way, though, her smile shone with approval.

This was good, then. *Maybe I'm not a lost cause after all.*

After darkness fell outside, she and Santi crawled onto the couch to watch TV, but she drifted off before the first commercial break.

She stirred later, bleary and barely awake, a late-night show playing onscreen. Santiago napped, too, his head resting on hers where she'd fallen asleep on his shoulder. Nothing romantic, just two friends who cared about each other.

I should get my headwrap and move to the air mattress. Instead, she closed her eyes and slipped back into sleep with a small smile.

She liked this.

Whatever this was, she liked it.

Chapter Seven

In Which the Question Pops

MAY

The Museo del Prado bustled with visitors. Santiago had been here plenty of times, so he was more excited to see Mariana's reactions to the beautiful architecture and fine art. But first, it seemed nature called.

"I have to use the restroom. Give me five minutes." Mariana disappeared into the ladies' room.

Santiago leaned against the wall by the auditorium and pulled out his phone, but a touch at his shoulder stole his attention. A tall, broad-shouldered man with freckles and a trimmed brown beard smiled at him. "Hey. Do you speak English?"

Santiago nodded. "Can I help you?" Surely this guy didn't think he worked here?

The bearded man stretched, flexing his impressive biceps. "Where's the best place to get a drink around here?"

Santi struggled not to stare. *Keep it together.* "Depends on what you want to drink. Are you looking for a coffee shop, or a bar, or what?"

That muscled arm rested against the wall. "What do you like best?"

"I'm a coffee guy."

The guy flashed a grin, not taking his eyes off Santiago. "Coffee, then."

Santiago smiled in response and raked his fingers through his hair. "Toma Café is great."

The bearded man leaned in. "Can I tell you something?"

"Sure."

"I hate drinking alone. Would you want to go grab a coffee with me later? I mean, I saw you with a woman—" He inclined his head toward the bathroom. "—but I figured, no harm in asking if you're single, right?"

Warmth bloomed in Santiago's cheeks. "Thank you. I—" *I'd love to get to know you* almost slipped out.

No, wait. I'm not single. Not anymore.

"I appreciate the offer," Santiago backtracked, frowning slightly, "but I'm actually in a relationship."

"No worries. Have a good one." The guy disappeared into the crowds, and Santiago sank back against the wall.

He was off the market. Officially. For the next several *years.*

A selfish thought. Not worth lingering on, and certainly not worth reconsidering the arrangement. Still, a thread of disappointment wound around his stomach. As beautiful as Mariana was, as much as he cared about her as a friend...she was only a friend. And with their situation so precarious, he couldn't risk a date with anyone else, much less anything intimate.

He loved her, in a way, but he would miss that.

Dwelling wouldn't help though. *Enjoy what you have. Don't linger on what you don't.* When Mariana emerged from the bathroom and dragged him off down the hall, he jogged to keep pace, and smiled at her when he caught up.

On their way to the Flemish collection, heat rushed to Santiago's face when he caught a glimpse of the bearded man again. Quickly he looked away. "Mari, does it ever bother you...?"

She cocked her head. "Does what bother me?"

He swallowed the regret. "That you can't see anyone while we're together?"

A shrug. "Not really. I don't really think of people like that, at least not right away." She hesitated. "Does it bother *you*?"

He grimaced. "I wouldn't say it bothers me, but I...I'll miss it." He gave her a quick rundown of the cute stranger who'd asked him out. "He was handsome, and there's still part of me looking for the right person, you know? Now, I'll never know if it was him."

Mariana touched his arm sympathetically. "I'm sorry. I didn't think about that. If you want to back out—"

"No, this is too important. I'll survive." It would be difficult some days, but he would make it through. His mom's health took precedence over his dating life.

Taking his hand in hers, Mariana led him into the next room, where she recognized an artist. "Hey, it's

Bosch!" She indicated a triptych without looking at the info beside it.

He checked the artist's name, and she was right. "Look at these tiny weirdos. Tag yourself, I'm the pig nun." Grinning, he pointed at the small figure in the corner.

She evaluated all three panels before something lit up her smile. "Ooh, I'm the naked people getting smushed by a giant strawberry."

A laugh burst from him, too loud for the museum atmosphere. "I don't think the artist meant this to be funny...but our way is more fun." Both for appearance's sake and to cement his mindset, he raised their joined hands and pressed a kiss to her knuckles.

She kissed his in return, her gaze serious. Too serious. He fluttered his eyelashes to make her laugh—and she did, relaxing again. And she still didn't let go of his hand.

Santiago pivoted on his heel so that the painting was to his back. "Let's take a selfie here."

Without hesitation, she leaned into him with a smile. "Your phone or mine?"

She's already doing so much better. The two of them genuinely looked like a couple. "I'll take it." He tugged her closer. In return she slinked her hand over his hip, let her fingers dangle intimately low. He pressed a kiss to her cheek, and she playfully scrunched up her face and shoulders.

Phone up. Quick click.

"No photo! No video!" A museum employee glowered at them.

"Oops." Santiago pretended to delete the photo before he tucked his phone back into his pocket. Mariana covered her mouth to smother guilty laughter. They moved on to the next Bosch, whispering to each other about it, and made it through the exhibit without getting in trouble again.

Enjoy what you have. It wouldn't be much of a struggle.

*

"I'm so full." Shifting in his seat after a delicious dinner, Santiago pressed one hand dramatically to his stomach. "If I eat anything else, I'll die."

"So dramatic." Lola set a plate of homemade *rosquillas* on the table. The scent of cinnamon and sugar wafted into the air, sharpened by a hint of lemon.

He straightened. "Never mind. I always have room for those."

Mariana leaned in for a closer look at the Spanish pastries. Powdered sugar dusted the little donut-like desserts, and their cute, asymmetrical ridges showed how Lola had hand-rolled the dough.

"Have you had these anywhere yet?" Maca tapped one, then popped it into her mouth. "Everybody's selling them this weekend, for San Isidro."

Mariana shook her head. "No, I missed them."

Maca shot her brother a dirty look. "Good job, Mr. Tourism."

Lola shrugged. "It works out for me. I make them the way my grandmother taught me, so they're different from

the fancy bakeries'. But you won't know the difference."
She grinned, a show of playfulness that echoed her
children's. "As far as you're concerned, these are the most
delicious *rosquillas* in the world."

With a laugh, Mariana took one, prepared to lie
through her teeth. The glaze smudged on her fingertips as
she bit into the *rosquilla*—and no lying was necessary.
Mmmm. The exterior crunched, but the inside was soft
and fluffy. Alongside the spices and citrus, the bittersweet
tang of anise added a twist she wouldn't like in anything
else, but for this pastry, it worked. "It's delicious," she
garbled, one hand over her mouth.

"She makes the best *rosquillas*." Santiago reached for
his third helping.

Smile brightening, his mom chucked him under the
chin. "I pay him to say that."

After the tasty desserts disappeared, he cleared his
throat and with a more formal tone announced, "I have
something I wanted to say. Or ask. While everyone's
here."

Maca's gaze flicked to Mariana's hand before she and
Lola cocked their heads, almost in sync.

Mariana wiped her hands clean, cheeks crawling with
heat. *Is this it? Wait, I should look at him.* She glanced his
way—and found him on one knee, looking up at her with
adoration. "Shit." She slipped to English in her surprise.
Forcing herself back into Spanish and the act: "Santi,
what are you…?"

"I know we haven't been dating for long," he told her,
heart-eyed, "but I think I've loved you for years. It only
took us meeting in person for me to realize I can't imagine
being with anyone else."

Proposal. Proposal. What do people in proposal videos do? With a gasp, Mariana covered her mouth with both hands. *Nailed it.*

Without looking away from her, Santiago reached into his pocket and pulled out a geometric wooden box, small enough for jewelry. Small enough for a ring.

She scrambled for something to say. Anything. But she could only stare as he flicked open the lid to reveal a simple gold band with a small round yellow citrine gleaming in the middle.

"Be mine, *dulzura.* And take me as yours." He caressed his thumb over the back of her hand, drew it to himself, brushed his lips against the ridge of her knuckles.

The kiss felt no different than any other touch, but it *looked* appropriately intimate. *Did Maca suggest that?* But then again, Santi had never showed any difficulty playing the part of the doting lover.

"I want—need—to stay by your side." Despite how intensely he declared it, Mariana could see the levity in his dark eyes, and it steadied her. "If you'll have me."

She blinked away imaginary tears. "Of course. Yes, of course."

Hoping it was a good move, she pulled him toward her and met him with a brief, chaste kiss. No sparks, but she didn't need them. Her fingers light on his jaw and cheeks, she met his gaze with all her affection for their friendship, from the silly argument that had brought them together to the dark nights they'd walked each other through.

"I love you." One way or another, it was true.

*

Carmen scowled at the camera. "I don't like this."

Mariana's heart plummeted at her mother's words. "Before I left, you said you'd give him a chance." She adjusted the laptop as if that might improve the Skype call. Beside her, Santiago took her hand to reassure her, but a muscle ticked in his jaw. Maca and Lola had conveniently disappeared.

Rafael leaned toward the webcam, brow furrowed. "This is all so fast."

"Dad, we—"

"I know you were friends before. But you only started to date, what, a month and a half ago? And suddenly he wants to get married?"

"That's what I want too." Mariana kept her tone even and warm despite her disappointment. "I want him to come be with me." It was truer now than she had expected it to be. And not only because of the inheritance—which her parents didn't know the condition of. "I *want* to marry him."

Carmen looked her over...and sighed. "I know you do. Bless your heart. But don't you think, if he liked you—?"

"I love her," Santiago said, less than patiently.

"Thanks for that 'if,' Mom." Mariana's cheeks burned. "Appreciate the vote of confidence."

Carmen crossed her arms. "Baby girl, sometimes you have to think with your head, not your heart."

"I *am* thinking with my head!"

"Did your head ever consider that he might be getting something else out of it?" She looked away. "Not everyone is out to get you, but not everyone is looking out for your best interests either. You have such a big heart, Mari—it can be easy for someone to take advantage of it."

Right now, that heart twisted with both indignation and conflicting loyalties. Feeling like an injured animal backed into a corner, Mariana struggled to keep herself from lashing out. In defense of Santiago, in defense of herself. "He's not like that. And you act like I can't take care of myself. I'm an adult—I need you to trust my judgment on this. *Please.*"

Her parents stayed silent for longer than she would have liked, but finally Rafael leaned back. "You're right. You're a good girl. We just don't want to see you hurt."

Santiago swallowed hard. "I would never hurt her."

"We'll defer to your judgment on this," Carmen said, ignoring him, "out of respect for you as an independent adult. I don't want this to come between us."

Mariana exhaled in relief, her breath shaky. "Thank you."

"But," Carmen added, "please remember you can come to us for anything. We love you no matter what."

Rafael nodded. "And since this boy means so much to you, we want to get to know him. When he moves here, you should both come over for lunch after church on Sundays."

"Definitely. That sounds great." She had to go, so she blew them an air kiss. "I appreciate you supporting me. I love you."

"Love you too," her parents said at the same time. But before she pressed End Call: "If that boy so much as looks at her wrong, I'm—"

She hung up. "I'm sorry, Santi. I thought they'd...be more reasonable." Emotion trembled in her voice. *Keep it together. Everything's fine.*

As long as her parents didn't bury her fiancé in the backyard simply for existing near their only child.

Everything's fine.

Chapter Eight

In Which Parents Are Hostile

JUNE

Santiago finished the school year at his current position, then packed up his desk and his apartment. Maca and their mother helped him squeeze as much as possible into his set of suitcases. Most of his stuff he left with them— what they needed they kept, and what they didn't they sold or donated. He put his clothes, his meager collection of books, and his more impressive collection of movies in checked luggage at the airport, with only his newly stamped passport in his hand and a backpack slung over his shoulder.

Maca had been doing better for the last few weeks— he suspected the "game" as well as the hope had improved her outlook—but tears gathered in her eyes as she hugged him goodbye. "Text me when you get there. Skype me every Saturday. Don't eat yellow snow."

"My little sister is so sage. Wise beyond her years." He tugged on her braid, and she yelped.

"I'm going to tell the government on you." She held both hands over her hair protectively. "Bully."

"Meanie."

"Jerk."

"Dummy." He pulled her in for a tighter hug, his eyes burning. "You're the worst. I'm going to miss you."

"I'm not going to miss you at all." When she pulled back, she swiped at her eyes and pushed at his chest. "Try to act like a good husband when you get there."

"I'll call you if I need any help figuring it out."

"What's sad is that I probably *am* your best bet. I accept gratitude in the form of cash, check, and gift cards." With a cheeky grin, she waved him off. "Go catch your plane."

He managed to sneak in a few catnaps during this flight. This *one-way* flight. The thought threatened to strangle him, but he smothered the anxiety. He was in this for real now; so was Mariana. No turning back.

When he walked out into the DC airport this time, he knew who he was looking for. His mind filtered everyone else out so that, like a magnet to iron, his gaze snapped directly to her. His entire body warmed, and a burden lifted he hadn't realized he'd been carrying. *There she is.* The delight infused into that single thought almost overwhelmed him.

How could he like being with her this much already?

She was beaming at him, though, so he pushed the concern aside to sweep her off her feet and spin her around before dotting a few silly, light kisses around her face to make her laugh. Nothing too serious or deep—he didn't want her to worry about appearances.

But when she held on tight and whispered, "I missed you," his insides twisted and melted.

I'm in so much trouble.

They stood by the conveyor for checked luggage. They stood and they stood and they stood until the belt transitioned into the next flight's cargo. Santiago shifted his backpack and stared. Maybe the airport had accidentally put his suitcases on the plane from Chicago.

"Is it not here?" Mariana looked to him in concern.

"No." A hot-pink luggage set rolled past. "Maybe this is the wrong conveyor?"

"No, it's the right one." She hesitated. "What do we do? I've never had luggage get lost before."

"I definitely have. We need to find the lost luggage people." He asked an airport employee where it was, and she pointed them in the right direction. He turned back to Mariana, who'd crossed her arms as if hugging herself. "You okay?"

"I should've been able to figure that out." Frowning, she scuffed one toe on the floor. "Sorry."

He shrugged. "We got it done."

"*You* got it done," she muttered, and he gave her a weird look. *What's wrong with that?*

*

Dust danced in the midday sunlight streaming into the Mitogos' dining room. Birds called to one another, their songs layering in natural harmony. In the late-spring breeze, leaves rustled on the oak tree outside the wide window. Santiago pulled out Mariana's chair for her, and when her parents sat without a word of criticism, he figured he must not have messed up too badly.

"So, Santiago." Rafael served himself a helping of salad. "Which would you say you like more—my daughter's money, or the green card?"

Mariana choked on her rice. "Dad!"

"I'm here to be with Mariana, not any of those things." Santiago went for a charming smile—and got icy stares in response. Oh. Not a great start. Still, he held on to the smile. "I always enjoy family meals at home. Thank you for inviting me to join you."

Mariana's father nodded stiffly. "Whether it was a good decision remains to be seen."

Stellar. Santiago shoveled some sweet potatoes into his mouth to stall for time.

"Lunch is delicious," Mariana interceded. "Thanks for cooking, Mom."

He swallowed. "Yes, it's delicious. Thank you." *Wow. Genius.*

Carmen looked him over, unimpressed. "We didn't see you two at church this morning," she said to Mariana. "Were you there?"

"We went to Mass in Fredericksburg."

Rafael coughed. "You went to Mass? As in Catholic church?"

Mariana rubbed her temples and sighed.

"I grew up Catholic." Santiago took a tiny bite of chicken. "I know your family usually goes to a Baptist church, right? We believe the same—"

"We only pray to God." Rafael stabbed his chicken with a fork that suddenly seemed too sharp. "So no, we don't believe the same things."

"Dad, stop it."

Santiago took another bite. Chewed. Swallowed. Considered throwing himself out a window.

"All your friends are at Trinity Baptist." Her mom, at least, seemed more concerned than angry. "You grew up going there. You're going to leave, just like that?"

Mariana pressed her lips together. "I can choose what church I want to go to."

Santiago took her hand, both to support her and to anchor himself.

Her parents glowered.

He released her hand. "Um, can I use the bathroom?" Mariana pointed him in the right direction, and he tried not to feel like a dog running off with its tail between its legs as he fled for a tiny respite.

"You can do this," he muttered to his reflection in the mirror. He splashed water on his face. "They need to get to know you. That's all. You can make it."

When he returned, he took his seat and summoned a pleasant expression. Mariana had sliced her chicken into miniscule pieces while he was gone.

"...and I think it's a bad idea," her mom was saying.

"Maybe we can alternate Sundays at the two different churches," Santiago offered.

"Perfect. Win-win." Mariana gave her parents an isn't-that-fair look, but they remained unmoved by the compromise.

Time to change the subject to something less incendiary. Santiago took a bite of salad and reviewed conversation starters he'd memorized for professional events. "Have you seen any good movies lately?"

Carmen shrugged. "We don't watch much TV."

He pressed on. "We watched the new comedy special on Netflix yesterday, and that was funny."

Mariana winced, and Santiago's stomach dropped. *Oh, no. I've made a mistake.*

"Secular comedy is so raunchy." Rafael scowled. "You enjoy that?"

"Some people don't mind consuming garbage." Carmen frowned at her daughter. "I would've thought better of you though."

Mariana pinched the bridge of her nose. "It's comedy, Mom. It's not supposed to be taken seriously."

"Anything you're putting in your mind should be taken seriously." Carmen spooned the last of her rice into her mouth.

Okay, so "no" to movies and "no" to comedy. There had to be something he could talk about, some neutral topic somewhere. "I'm looking forward to meeting more of Mariana's family. Do you have any other relatives in the area?"

Pain flashed across Carmen's face.

Mariana translated under her breath. "My mom's parents lived in Richmond, but they passed last year. My dad's family is in Colorado. We don't talk to them much anymore."

Great. Good job, me.

They fell into utter silence broken only by the clinking of silverware on porcelain. Finally, Carmen stood, holding her empty plate.

Santiago knocked his knee on the table in his rush to stand as well. "Are you done? Can I help with the dishes?"

She sidestepped him. "Guests don't help with the dishes."

Mariana glared at her. "Mom. I'm marrying him tomorrow. He's not a guest—he's family. He can help if he wants."

"I'm not opposed to him making himself useful." Rafael waved for him to...

Well, Santiago wasn't sure what all was encompassed in that wave. The full spectrum from *go ahead* to *go screw yourself.* He gritted his teeth and took Carmen's dish as well as his own to the kitchen. She followed him, silent.

As he rinsed a plate, he waited for her to say something, but it was dead quiet. He took the conversation upon himself. "You have a beautiful home. How long have you lived here?"

Mariana's mother side-eyed him as if he were plotting to uproot her. "About fifteen years."

He waited for her to expound on that timeline, or on their history with the house, or on *anything*.

Nothing.

He cleared his throat. "Did you live around here before then?"

"Yes."

Well, this was going great. Washing the other plate, he tried for a different approach. "Mariana's the best. What was she like as a kid?"

"She was a good girl. Always listened to her parents."
A quiet scoff.

I'm not touching that. "Did you take a lot of pictures
of her? My mamá has so many photo albums of me and
my sister, I never knew what to do with all of them." He
cracked a smile.

Carmen did not.

"Maybe sometime we can look at family photos?"

"Maybe." Translation: *no.*

Back in the dining room, Mariana hissed something
unintelligible but fierce. At a normal volume, her father
said, "Fine, fine."

Santiago slid the dishes into the dishwasher and
returned with Carmen to their seats.

"Thank you," Mariana told Santi pointedly.

Rafael grimaced like he was in pain. "You have...any
hobbies, Santiago?"

Besides fraud? "In my country, I coached a soccer
team for kids. We were number one in the region,
actually." Santiago showed them a couple pictures on his
phone. The little six- and seven-year-olds had been so
cute. "I miss that."

"Hmm." Rafael gave the photos a passing glance
before returning his attention to his meal. Having
expected them to be ignored completely, Santiago
considered this a success.

After putting away the leftovers, Mariana touched a
hand to her temple. "I've got a headache coming in. We'd
better head home."

Her parents frowned but didn't argue as they walked them to the door. "We'll see you next week," her dad said. "Text us if you need anything."

"Anything at all," her mom emphasized.

Doubting a hug would be well received, Santiago extended his hand to Rafael. "Thanks again for having me over. I look forward to getting to know you better."

Rafael squeezed his fingers into dust.

Clearly, the feeling is mutual.

Santiago thanked Carmen and shook her hand as well, and Mariana hugged both her parents goodbye. She slid into the car, and as they pulled out of the driveway, Santiago rubbed the bridge of his nose. "I think your parents genuinely still think I'm a serial killer."

She let out a tired groan. "That was...not the best meal I've ever had with them, no."

"Do you really have a headache, or did you just need a break?"

She gave a dry laugh as she turned onto the main road. "Fair question. But, yes, that did actually give me a headache. I need some ibuprofen and a nap ASAP."

He blew out a long breath. "A nap sounds amazing right now."

"Exactly."

When they got home, Mariana dropped her purse onto the floor and collapsed facedown on the couch.

Santiago poured two glasses of water and set one on the coffee table beside her with two painkiller tablets. "You should...hydrant." That wasn't the right word, but it was close, and he was exhausted.

She didn't bother to correct him. "We don't have to do anything else today, right?"

He slumped into the recliner. "I hope not." *I don't think I could manage it.*

"Good." After downing the water and the ibuprofen, Mariana turned onto her side so that she faced the back of the couch. "Naptime."

He settled in, eyes closing. "Sounds good to me."

A mumble of agreement came from the couch, but they were both already sinking into blissful sleep.

*

Mariana woke later than she had intended to, her grumbling stomach the alarm clock. With Santi asleep in the armchair, she pushed herself to her feet and tiptoed to the kitchen. She popped some leftover lasagna into the microwave and leaned against the counter while she waited, her emotions still turbulent from the disaster that was the family meal.

The recliner creaked as Santiago stirred. He stretched, then leaned back to look at her upside down. Voice sleep-hazy, he asked, "Is it time for dinner already?"

"Mm-hmm. You hungry?"

He dragged himself up to meet her and nodded. "Can we make macaroni and cheese? From the box?"

The microwave dinged. She ignored it. "I was gonna have some leftover lasagna, but if you want mac and cheese, sure, we can make that. I have a couple boxes in the pantry."

He lit up. "Really?"

"Yeah, of course." The excitement confused her until she remembered that box mac and cheese was an American thing. "Haven't you had it before?"

Santiago shook his head. "It's hard to find in Spain— it's only in special American stores, and expensive."

She laughed. "It's only eighty-nine cents here."

He struggled to convert that to euros. "That's not a lot, right?"

"Right."

"Cool. Cheap is the second-best price."

"Free is the best," they said at the same time, and Mariana smiled.

Abandoning the reheated lasagna, she bent to retrieve what she'd need to make the requested meal. The pot she filled with water and set on the stove to boil; the boxes she ripped open to pull out the fake cheese mix. She sliced up a stick of butter after she dumped the macaroni into the steaming bubbles. Once the pasta hit that perfect degree of tenderness, she shook it through a colander and then back into the pot to mix with the butter and the milk.

Santiago peered into the pot and saw the artificial orange. "Ooh. That can't be healthy."

"It's definitely not, but it tastes good."

She directed him to her designated mac and cheese bowls, patterned with yellow polka dots on the outside and a fat gray cat on the inside. She scooped an equal amount into each and handed one to him. "All right, time to try a classic American delicacy."

He held up one hand and set the bowl on the counter. "Wait. I need the full experience." He bolted to the bedroom, and before she could ask what the "full experience" was, he reemerged wearing an American flag-patterned hat, star-spangled sunglasses, and a red-white-and-blue T-shirt emblazoned with the word *MUR'KA*. "Perfect."

Mariana laughed so hard she planted a hand on the counter to keep her balance. "Tell me that's ironic."

He had the indecency to look slightly offended. "Of course not. I'm excited. And embracing your scarily patriotic culture."

She tried to keep a straight face and ended up snorting. "Oh, Santi, bless your heart."

"That sounds sarcastic."

She dissolved into giggles again.

He pushed up the patriotic sunglasses, which were dropping sideways off his regular glasses, and took his bowl of mac and cheese. "I bet I won't even like this."

They sat at the kitchen table for once, rather than on the couch. At the first bite, Santiago's eyes bugged.

He looked into his bowl in awe. "Until this day," he said reverently, "I was dead."

Mariana snorted and pointed her spoon at him. "I made two boxes, so there's plenty. No stealing mine."

"I would never dream of it," he lied as he dug back in. He eyed hers when she slowed down, and he downed half of what would have gone in the fridge as well.

Though his ferocity frightened her, she grinned. He ate twice as much as she did.

Her days of week-old leftovers were over.

Chapter Nine

In Which They Get Married

JUNE

Rain drummed on the courthouse roof as Mariana, Santiago, Mariana's parents, and Embry waited in the hall outside the courtroom. Dressed up in her favorite white sundress, Mariana bounced on the balls of her feet.

At least she wasn't alone. Santiago, spiffy in a deep-blue suit (his only suit), rubbed circles on the back of her hand with his thumb. Carmen and Rafael sat on a bench across from them, looking faintly ill, but at least they'd come. Mariana hadn't been sure they would.

A beaming Embry stood on her other side, clicking her heels against the floor, picking invisible lint off Mariana's dress. "You look so pretty, Mari! And you're getting *married*! I can't believe it." She hugged her. "You deserve the absolute best."

Mariana ducked her head. "Thanks."

A security guard opened the double doors to the wood-paneled courtroom, and they all filed in. The judge, an older white man with a trimmed salt-and-pepper beard, took his place in the center of the front of the room while the guests sank onto the wooden benches. When their names were called, Mariana and Santiago walked up to a podium with a microphone placed on it.

The judge peered down at them. "How're you two doing today?"

What did he see? "Good," Mariana squeaked.

Santiago beamed. "Great."

"Good to hear." They went through some preliminary necessities, and then the judge cleared his throat. "Please face each other as you make these vows to each other. Mr. de los Reyes, you'll go first."

Santi took both of Mariana's hands and looked her in the eyes. "Ready?" he whispered.

It's real now. There's no going back. She struggled to maintain eye contact, struggled to stay still. *Don't bounce.* Her feet itched to tap against the floor.

"Santiago de los Reyes Martínez," droned the judge, "do you take Miss Mariana Mitogo for your lawful wife, to have and to hold from this day forward, for better and for worse, for richer and for poorer, in sickness and health, until death do you part?"

Santiago nodded without faltering, emotion in his eyes. "I do."

Everything was going the way it should, but Mariana glanced toward the door and tried not to picture herself running away.

"Mariana Mitogo, do you take Mr. Santiago de los Reyes Martínez..."

Come on, come on, get it over with. She let go of Santiago with one hand and tugged on her skirt. Doubting, hoping, fearing, praying, tug tug tug tug tug.

Warm fingers closed over hers.

She stilled. Looked up.

Santiago smiled at her, squeezed her hands—and stuck out the tip of his tongue.

"Ha!" The sound burst from her, too loud, more anxiety than humor.

The judge stopped in the middle of his sentence. "Miss Mitogo?"

Oops. Mariana swallowed, cheeks burning. "Um, sorry, sir. Your Honor." *Get it together.* "You can keep going."

Beside her, Santiago snickered.

She squeezed his hand hard.

"*Huy.*" He shook her off with a grin.

"...death do you part?" The judge raised an eyebrow.

Throat closing, Mariana skated her gaze to Santi. He'd said his two words earlier, and now he watched her, still smiling. Still there with her.

Smooth your dress. Tell the truth. Run from the room and the courthouse and the entire charade.

She took a deep breath and slipped both her hands into his. "I do."

The judge folded his hands. "Do you have the rings?"

"I have them." Wedding bands in hand, Embry tiptoed up to the podium as if she might be reprimanded for leaving her seat. "You're doing great," she whispered, handing over the rings and then giving them thumbs-ups.

Mariana repeated after the judge, trying not to think too hard about the words: "I, Mariana Mitogo, give you, Santiago de los Reyes Martínez, this ring as an eternal symbol of my love and commitment to you." *Eternal-ish.* Swallowing hard, she slid his ring onto his hand. The silver gleamed in the courtroom lights.

Santiago echoed the same vow and slid a second ring onto her finger, the simple, slim gold band fitting perfectly against her citrine engagement ring.

"By the power vested in me by the state of Virginia," declared the judge, "I now pronounce you husband and wife. You may now kiss the bride."

Embry cheered and applauded from her seat; Carmen and Rafael golf clapped. Trying to ignore her parents and the nervousness buzzing under her skin, Mariana placed her hands on Santi's shoulders. She slid her palms over the heavy cotton of the suit and hesitated. *Does he initiate the kiss? Do I? Should we have practiced this? We definitely should have.*

He brushed his thumb against her cheek and gave her a little nod and smile.

Okay. Go for it. With an inhale, she kissed him, light and chaste. His fingertips ghosted at her hips before she stepped back and beamed at their audience. He laced his fingers in hers and raised their intertwined hands above their heads in celebration.

We did it. We're married. For real.

Mariana posed for a few pictures in a daze and then followed Santiago and Embry out of the courthouse, barely registering as they slid into the backseat of Embry's massive SUV. Her parents followed in their own car.

"Party time, y'all," Embry announced as she sped out of the lot. "I can't wait for you to see what I pulled off on such short notice. I put the 'honor' in 'maid of honor.'"

Mariana grinned. "Thanks again for hosting the reception. And for being so modest about it."

Santiago blew a raspberry. "Modesty is overrated."

"Thank you, Santiago!" Embry grinned into the rearview mirror. "See, he understands."

"Oh!" He held out his hand to Mariana and wiggled his fingers. "Give me your phone."

She handed it over. "The password is—"

"James Farmer's birth year, 1920, I know." He brought up her contacts list. "What am I listed as?"

That was a question? "Your name, genius."

"That's it? Boring." He searched himself and changed his contact information. "'Best Husband Ever.' Now that we're married, I can officially take that title." Then he handed her his phone. "Here, put your fingerprints on the auto-unlock thing."

Embry glanced back in surprise. "That's some true love, right there."

"Who can resist her?" Santiago smiled at Mariana, who ducked her head and input her prints before changing her own name in his contacts.

"I'm now 'Cutest Wife in History,'" she announced before trading his phone for hers. Moments later, an incoming text chirped.

BEST HUSBAND EVER: *You're doing awesome.*

CUTEST WIFE IN HISTORY: ♥

They pulled up to Embry's house, and she parked in the last available spot on the long driveway. Mariana's parents parked along the curb and went inside. A big sign took over the yard, topped with a eucalyptus garland: *Welcome to Mariana and Santiago's Reception.*

Santi got out on his side first and then helped Mariana step out of the car. Embry walked them to the front door, opened it for them, and announced, "May I introduce Mr. and Mrs. de los Reyes!"

The guests clapped as Mariana and Santiago stepped into the house. Embry had decorated in gold and greenery, with mini garlands draped along the back of every chair set out in the open space. A curtained photo booth stood in the far corner with a basket of props beside it. Hoops laced with greenery and fairy lights hung from the high arched ceiling. Across the way, the kitchen was laid out with champagne, a massive charcuterie board, aromatic barbecue, and more. At the bar, two empty crystal champagne flutes waited for the toast, and two tall chairs were wreathed with the words BRIDE and GROOM hanging from the back.

"Everything is perfect!" Mariana hugged Embry. "Thank you so much."

"Can we go get some of that food?" Santiago made lovesick eyes at the kitchen and then patted his belly. "Getting married burns a lot of calories."

Mariana's stomach grumbled at the spice of barbecue in the air. "We need to make our rounds first. But after that, absolutely."

He took her hand and swung it lightly. "All right, if you promise. I'll be sad if everybody but us gets to eat."

"I feel like it's illegal to let the guests of honor go hungry."

"If it's not, it should be."

Embry's housemate and friend, Rhiannon, appeared at Mariana's side, silently holding out two plates piled high with snacks. Her golden hair was pulled back in a complicated braid. Her crisp button-down shirt was all business for such a party.

Santiago lit up as he took a snack plate. "Thanks!"

Mariana beamed and took the other. "You're a godsend."

"I overheard you pining for the food. Congratulations on getting married." Her tone was even, calm. "I'm Rhiannon, by the way." She extended her hand to Santiago. He hugged her instead. She stiffened but patted him on the back. When he let go, she smoothed her shirt. "If you need anything, let me or Embry know."

Mariana swallowed her bite of pretzels. "Will do. Thanks for hosting, especially on such short notice."

"Of course." As the other guests' noise level rose, Rhiannon fidgeted with her necklace. "Don't let me hold you up. You have lots of people to talk to."

"You're not holding us up," Mariana protested, but Rhiannon was already edging toward the hallway. Then she disappeared, as quickly as she'd come. Mariana bit her lip and glanced at Santiago. "She gets nervous around people."

He shrugged. "She brought us food, so she's good in my books."

Mariana walked him to Embry's parents, Jamal and Connie. Their youngest daughter, Joy, munched on a bag of animal crackers beside them. Their teenage daughter was absent. "Charity couldn't make it?"

Jamal shook his head. "She's away at summer camp this week. She was sorry to miss this though."

Joy swallowed her mouthful of crackers and beamed up at Mariana. "You look pretty!"

"Aww, thank you, sweetie." Mariana spun in her white sundress so that the skirt flared out. "Thank you so much for coming. It means a lot to me that we get to share today with you."

"Oh, we wouldn't miss it!" Connie hugged her, then Santiago.

Jamal hugged him and clapped him on the back. "You have to come over for dinner sometime! We need to get to know you."

Mariana smiled and nodded, but her stomach sank at how openly they welcomed him. Why couldn't her own parents give him the same chance? She swallowed hard and mustered a smile. "That would be awesome. We'll have to schedule that in soon."

Clink clink clink clink clink. Someone tapped their glass, and then glasses were clinking all around the room. All eyes went to the newlywed couple. Mariana's throat closed. So many people watching her, expecting her to throw around affection as easily as the rest of them.

She forced a laugh and kissed Santiago, nothing more than a peck. Quick and minimal, like all their other kisses. Then she returned her attention to Connie and Jamal. "So when were you—?"

"Oh, boooo," Embry called from across the room. "A real kiss, you nerds!"

Mariana whipped her head back to Santiago, her pulse hummingbird-fast. A real kiss? He'd had plenty of experience with those, but she hadn't. What if it was unconvincing? Or too forward? What if it sent up fireworks that spelled out "green-card marriage"?

He plucked his bracelet nervously but gave her a small smile. His cheeks... Were his cheeks pink? Was he worried, too, or embarrassed?

Santiago inclined his head. Quietly: "Like Gothmog and Traylin, right?" Another couple from *The Frat House Gang*, the same fantasy show as the debatable Seraphina and Ainsley, but they had actually kissed on-screen. A relationship they'd both been fans of. A kiss she hadn't minded because it made sense.

That show had brought them together in the first place. Santiago's emphatic messages spelling out why he would keel over dead if his ships didn't end up canon. The dorky reminder cracked a small smile in return on Mariana's face, and she relaxed. It was just Santi. Even if she was about to kiss him, just Santi.

They kissed then, through their smiles. She tucked one hand along the back of his head and tugged him in, letting her lips linger this time. He was soft, gentle. He cupped her waist with one hand and the side of her neck with the other, and the pad of his thumb trailed along her cheek. A shiver ran down her spine. Something electric crackled in this kiss, and she found herself lingering, hesitant to break away.

His breath shook. Did he feel it too? He angled his head, so she matched the motion. Her fingertips trailed up the back of his neck and curled into his hair.

Then Santiago inhaled through the kiss, and something sparked like embers inside her. Heat that had nothing to do with embarrassment curled up her abdomen. Her fingers caressed down his jaw. "I...mmm." And she pushed harder for more.

He made a sound that might or might not have been a word as he pulled her flush against him with a smooth ease she couldn't have summoned if she tried. When he licked a thin line along her lower lip and then sucked lightly at it, she gasped—did the same to him, and his grip tightened. Hot butterflies tickled her stomach; her fingertips fizzled. Their glasses clinked together, but no way would she pull back to readjust. His tongue flirted again with the seam of her lips, playful and daring, and when she opened her mouth to him...

A wolf whistle cut through the haze of kissing Santiago.

"There are children here," someone said dryly.

Blinking, Mariana lowered to the flats of her feet, the phantom pressure of Santi's lips buzzing on hers. Her skittish gaze darted up to him—she wasn't sure what she was looking for—and found him as dazed and confused as she felt.

What, she wondered in equal parts amazement and horror, *was that*?

Chapter Ten

In Which They Share a Bed

JUNE

Since neither of them had the time or the money for a real honeymoon, they packed a lunch for a day trip to Washington, DC. Santiago bagged the sandwiches, filled two reusable water bottles, and ate an Oreo. In the interest of fairness, he gave Mariana a cookie too. Then ate three more. Nutrition.

"We can continue the sightseeing tradition!" She dropped the waters and sandwich bags into the back seat and tapped their first destination into the GPS.

He slid into the passenger seat. "I don't think two cities is enough times to make it a tradition."

"Rude. I can call it a tradition if I want." As she drove, she talked him through the history of the National Mall. Not a shopping mall, as it turned out. It took him an hour of chatter to figure that out, but he never had to ask, so he considered it an ESL success.

After eighty years of searching, they found a parking spot and headed straight for the Natural History Museum. Despite the heat, without thinking, he slipped his hand into hers. Their fingers laced together easily, the fit familiar, but parted for the security check—and the ghost of her touch lingered on his skin. He glanced down, half expecting to see a mark. A burn, maybe.

Nothing. Just a tingling where she'd touched him, and the wedding ring she'd slid onto his finger yesterday.

Weird. He shook off the thought, flexed his hand, and slung his arm around her waist. "Lead the way."

She beamed. "Okay, what do we wanna see first? Dinosaurs, mummies, creepy things that live in the ocean...?"

All great options, and those were only a few of the exhibits. "Sea monsters!" It seemed like a dramatic term. But Santiago gaped when they reached the giant mosasaur skeleton. "That...is a monster, yes."

Mariana laughed. "Some things should stay in the ocean. Thanks anyway, scientists." She lowered her voice to an ominous tone. "And think...we've explored more of our solar system than the ocean floor. What else is down there?"

"My hopes and dreams?" Santiago pulled out his phone with a grin. "We have to take a selfie with this thing." Tugging her flush against himself, he framed the shot and contorted his face into a terrified expression. She mirrored him, eyes wide and jaw dropped.

He snapped a few shots before flicking a glance at her—and his finger paused over the screen. Joy sparkled in her eyes, lit up her face. She snorted as she tried to smother her laughter, but she looked his way and it burst through. Shoulders shaking with giggles, she rested her forehead on his shoulder. Her breath warmed the side of his neck.

His stomach flipped.

No. I'm not feeling anything. Not like that.

But the flutter inside him whispered otherwise.

*

Given the high cost of, well, everything, they came back to the apartment at the end of the day instead of overnighting it. Mariana emerged from the bathroom to find Santi laying his blankets out on the couch in the lamplight. "No. We are officially married and you're already stiff and achy from cramming yourself on there the last couple nights. Come sleep in the bed."

"I don't mind."

"I watched you hobble through the National Zoo, Grandpa. If you don't sleep on an actual mattress, I probably will have to get you that Life Alert."

He made a face at her. "I'm only two years older than you. That makes you old too."

"Not yet," she teased. "And by the time I get old, you'll be ancient."

Two twenty-somethings were young by anyone's standards. But he did have several years of actual adulthood on her—as silly as he could be, he could fend for himself in the world. He knew how to do things, how to maintain a grownup life. He could go on dates, make more than one meal, talk respectfully to coworkers he hated. Even though she herself had been on her own for a while now, she was barely keeping her head above water.

And now that he was with her—living in the same small space, learning her habits with the intimacy of a spouse—he was going to discover every single way she failed as a responsible adult. She would no longer be able to cover up the worst slipups with a joke and an ocean between them. She had mentally prepared herself for awkward touches and pet names, for playacting and stretching the truth—not for that level of vulnerability.

Smile fading, Mariana took a step back. "You don't have to sleep in the bed. It's fine."

He shook his head. "No, I appreciate the offer. I'll probably take you up on it. Your couch is a little small."

She'd meant it when she said she was concerned about whether or not he could continue to sleep there, so she didn't rescind the offer. "I'm gonna brush my teeth and change into my pajamas in the bathroom, if you want to change in the room."

They almost collided as she left the bathroom and he entered. After a two-step dance and awkward laugh, they passed each other. On her way, she turned off the overhead light, leaving only the low glow of the lamp. She slipped under the covers on what was now her side of the bed and with a deep breath tried to settle. Habit urged her to roll over, to slant her body sideways across the mattress, but she couldn't do that anymore. Not as long as he shared her bed. She spent enough effort getting used to touch while she was awake—she wanted to at least have a break while asleep. At least there was plenty of space on her secondhand king-size mattress. And it wasn't like the visa investigation would see whether or not they spooned at night.

Probably.

The faucet turned off, and Santiago padded back into the bedroom; his weight sank onto the mattress and tugged at the sheets. His glasses clinked against wood when he set them on his nightstand. Worried she had been rude somehow, Mariana turned her head to cast him a small smile. "Sweet dreams, Santi."

He smiled back, the shadows under his eyes more visible without his oversized hipster glasses. *"Dulces sueños, cariño."*

The Spanish *sweet dreams* had been his send-off for years, but the new addition surprised her. They'd agreed to keep using cutesy Spanish nicknames for the romantic-language factor, but hearing it in an American context for the first time unnerved her.

Trying not to think too hard, she took off her own glasses, set them aside, and turned off the lamp. In the cavernous dark, every breath seemed to echo. Every movement reverberated through the mattress. She lay on her back...then on her left side...then on her stomach... then on her right side...then on her back again.

Maybe *she* should take a turn on the couch.

*

Her blankets were trying to pull away from her. Drowsily she clung to them, burrowing into her warm, soft cocoon. But they only jerked more insistently, and she didn't realize what it meant until a familiar male voice complained her name in a sleep-husky undertone. Well, she had fallen asleep at some point, against all odds. Unfortunately for him, that had involved stealing all the covers.

But if she gave them back, she'd be cold.

"Mari. Blanket."

She almost told him to go get some from the living room, but that was a lot of syllables, and marriage required compromise. With a long, low, unhappy groan, Mariana rolled over a few times, unwrapping half the sheets so that Santiago could use them. To cover himself he lay closer than before...and when she snuggled into her burrito, a solid, warm body grazed her back. Surprised, she wiggled away again—but he followed her. She tried to stay still and straight so she wouldn't bother him, and thankfully she slipped back to sleep.

She stirred again before the sun came up, barely awake, with one foot in her dream. But she did notice her personal heater—the back pressed against hers, with the blankets wrapped around them both. Contrary to the discomfort she'd expected, the presence reassured her, provided an anchor; and she dozed off thinking that maybe some touch while they slept wouldn't be such a bad thing after all.

Chapter Eleven

In Which They Have Their First Interview

JUNE

Santiago's first day of summer school started with coffee down the front of his shirt.

"I'm so sorry!" The woman who'd run into him covered her mouth with one dainty hand, the other clenching a now empty cup. "I can't believe—I wasn't looking where I was going. I'm so sorry!"

He yanked tissues out of his box of classroom supplies and mopped up the hot mess as fast as he could. The woman's strawberry-blonde hair gleamed. Her eyeliner was the slightest bit uneven, and her flowery full-length romper showed off her tall frame—topped off by a huge yellow necklace that he hadn't expected.

Mariana would like that jewelry.

"It's okay." It definitely wasn't. He gave up on his shirt, lifted his head, and extended his hand that wasn't full of coffee-soaked tissues. "I don't think we've met."

She shook his hand. "I'm Yelena Montalban. I teach tenth grade biology."

"Santiago de los Reyes. The new Spanish teacher. It's my first day."

With a groan she covered her face with her free hand. "Great. 'Welcome to the school, please wear my coffee!'"

"It could be worse." He tried to come up with an example...and only managed with a grin, "I didn't fall over and break my leg, right?"

She laughed and shot him a guilty look. "You can dump a drink on me tomorrow, if you want."

"Don't make offers you don't mean." He did need to figure out what to do about his shirt though.

Only once she was gone did he realize that he should have, on some visceral level, responded to the friendly, gorgeous woman laughing with him on the stairwell. Not that he ever dated coworkers, but his body should have acknowledged more than aesthetic appreciation.

Yelena should have set off every bell, but she'd barely registered as a blip on his radar.

Huh.

*

After a long day at work, Mariana blasted the radio on her drive home. She'd drop off her stuff, maybe change into something comfortable, and then go pick up Santi from the high school. She was tired just thinking about leaving the house again, but it was what it was. When she walked in the door, though, Santiago waved at her from his place at the stove, wearing her president-patterned apron as he stirred a steaming pot. "Hi!"

She couldn't tell by smell what he was making, but the more pressing question was: "How did you get home?"

"My coworker Yelena dropped me off on her way." He tossed some chopped vegetables into the pot and continued to stir. "You said you would go home before you came to get me, so I didn't think it would matter."

She shook her head. "No, it's fine. I was just surprised."

"Surprise!"

It shouldn't have been a big deal, yet irritation simmered in her gut. Sure, whoever Yelena was had saved Mariana a trip to the school—but how could he not let her know about the change in plans? If she had to chauffeur him everywhere, that was the least he could do.

"We need to get you a license." She went to the bedroom to fold the clean bedsheets before she said something mean. On her bed, her phone buzzed with a calendar notification. She checked... "Shit! That interview is today!" She threw her phone back down as if it had scheduled USCIS in secret, and she popped her head out of the bedroom. "Forget dinner, we don't have time for that. I need to put on fresh clothes, and we can heat up leftovers or something. I don't know—"

Santiago stirred feverishly. "What time—?"

"Half an hour!" The bedroom door slammed behind her.

A knock came from the front door.

"Oh, hell, no." She yanked an orange sundress off its hanger. "Get the door, Santi!"

In the kitchen, the serving spoon clattered to the counter. He bolted not to the guest but to her. "I need a better shirt—"

The door banged open and whacked Mariana on the temple. "Ow!" She reeled backward, her vision blurring.

He winced and pulled on a clean sweater. "Sorry."

Not acknowledging this, she twisted to zip herself up. "How can they be half an hour early? *That* should be illegal."

"Don't rip their heads off."

"I don't make promises I can't keep." She stormed to the front door, mad at herself and Santi and the government and her aching head and—

A willowy redhead beamed on the porch step. "You must be Mariana!"

Since when did federal agents wear rompers to interviews? Mariana reached for a smile and fell short. "You're early."

"Early?" The woman's brow creased, then smoothed when Santi emerged from the bedroom. "Hey! You left this in my car." She held up his wallet.

"Oh, thanks!" He reached over Mariana's shoulder and grabbed it. "Mari, this is Yelena. She's the one who gave me the ride home today."

Oh. *Oh.* Mariana looked at Yelena again, really looked, and her stomach sank. Long legs, gleaming waves of strawberry-blonde hair, a bright smile. Slim, graceful curves contrasted with Mariana's plus-size ones. Yelena leaned down and hugged her as if they already knew each other, no hesitation in the touch.

So this was the driver Santiago had chosen.

"Okay, thank you." Mariana touched the door handle. "We have an interview, so..."

"Oh, um, okay, nice to meet you—"

Santiago waved. "See you tomorr—"

Mariana shut the door, the buzz of anger fading into something more unsettling. Was that what he wanted—lovely and affectionate and normal? Was he waiting for Mariana to become someone like that? Or was he hoping for someone like Yelena to come along and share whatever it was that two people attracted to each other shared?

Another knock at the door.

Ugh. Mariana reopened it. "Listen, Ye—"

Not Yelena.

A balding white man in a business suit stuck out one hand. "I'm Craig Harrison. I'll be interviewing you today."

I would like to punch something. Mariana shook his hand too firmly. "I'm Mariana and that's—" She motioned for Santiago to *get over here right now.* "—Santiago."

The three of them sat in the living room, Mariana stiff beside Santiago, who rubbed the St. James cross on his bracelet.

Harrison cracked open his briefcase and took out an imposingly thick stack of papers. "Some of these questions you've already answered, and we're confirming. Others, we're looking for more information. Just be honest." He eyed them. "Lying during a federal investigation is perjury and will be prosecuted to the full extent of the law. Do you understand?"

Mariana swallowed. "Yes." Time for some creative truth-stretching. And perjury. *Shit.*

Harrison examined their paperwork. "So, when did you two meet?"

"Two thousand twelve," they chorused.

"And when did you meet for the first time in person?"

"Uh…" Mariana glanced at Santiago. "A couple months ago."

"April," he supplied.

"Yeah, April." *So far, so good.*

Harrison marked his paper with two flicks of his pen. "And why didn't you express any romantic feelings before this?"

"Why would we?" Mariana asked at the same time Santiago said, "We didn't want to get ahead of ourselves."

Oops.

Mariana hurried to cover the slipup. *Other people feel attraction.* "I mean, like he said. It's hard to be sure." Technically true. "And we didn't wanna risk it."

"We really value the friendship."

"You got married almost immediately after he arrived." Harrison indicated his copy of the marriage certificate.

Santiago took her hand. "When you know, you know."

Mariana smoothed her dress and nodded. It would be perjury to say aloud that she'd ever known.

Harrison wrote something on his paper. "Speaking of which, how is your sex life?"

She froze. "It's fine," she said at the same time as Santiago said, "It's great!" *Oh, come on. We can't catch a break.*

Harrison eyed them, his pen hovering over the notes. "Ms. Mitogo—"

"Mrs. de los Reyes."

"—how regularly would you say you and your husband are intimate?"

"Um." She glanced at Santi, scrambling for an appropriate answer. Were romance fanfics or sci-fi TV shows more accurate about sex? He widened his eyes at her as if to send a message, but she had no idea what that message was supposed to be. "A normal amount?"

"Can you be more specific?"

Once a week? Every day? What was the right answer here? "How is this relevant?"

"Every few days," Santiago blurted.

Harrison tapped the end of his pen against his knee and raised an eyebrow. "Please let her answer her own questions." He directed his attention back to Mariana. "It's relevant if you're lying about being in a genuine relationship and aren't actually involved. So, how regularly?"

She knew the answer now. "Every few days."

He scribbled something—maybe *couldn't answer on her own*—and flipped to the next page. "On another note, are you aware that Mr. de los Reyes regularly sends money to his mother and sister in Spain?"

Santiago startled, and Mariana squeezed his hand. "Yes, I'm aware."

"And how do you feel about that?"

She shrugged. "It's fine. I understand."

"So it doesn't bother you that he's not saving that money for your future together?"

Her mouth fell open. *What do I say to that?* "I mean... It's not..."

Harrison jotted something down. "Especially given *your* financial situation."

Cheeks burning, she squeezed Santi's hand so hard he flexed his fingers in protest.

"One hundred and eighty thousand dollars in debt, I believe." It wasn't a question.

Swallow me up, earth. She cleared her throat. "It's tuition mostly. And the credit cards are from a few years ago when I had to help my parents with their bills for a while."

"It's convenient that you two started a relationship soon after you found out about the inheritance." Staring her down, Harrison set his papers in his lap and waited.

Mariana picked at her hem. *Think of something!* "Life sure is funny like that." *Wow, great job.*

"We met in person before she found out about the inheritance." Santiago put his free hand on her knee; she started at the unexpected touch. "And we knew each other for so long before that. I mean, I saw her at the airport, and I knew." His gaze darted toward her as if he were embarrassed to admit it. "It all clicked."

That's some good acting.

Leaning back in his seat, Harrison crossed his ankle over his knee. "Do share."

Yeah, share. What was she supposed to follow that up with?

Santiago actually flushed. "I got off the plane, and there she was, waiting at the end of the hall for me. And

I...got the breath knocked out of me. She was so beautiful, and she was wearing this yellow dress that made her look..." He blew out a rough breath. "I was screwed."

Heat crawled up Mariana's neck and cheeks. *I looked...? No way.* He'd been upset when he saw her, not whatever this was. It was a good cover story; that was all. But he'd finally stopped rubbing his bracelet, and he now refused to look at her.

After, Harrison left with a warning that he'd be scheduling individual interviews.

Mariana hugged herself and turned on Santi. "Hey, what were you talking about? About seeing me at the airport?" *Please don't change things.*

He stuffed his hands in his pockets. "What about it?"

"You know what."

Santiago had referred to it during their fake asking-out Skype session, but she'd assumed he was playing the part. But to say it again? Like he meant it?

Shifting his weight, Santiago rubbed the back of his neck. "I mean, it was true. You're pretty, and I noticed. As a friend."

Heat burned her cheeks. She had to be sure. "Just as a friend?"

"You don't have anything to worry about." He inclined his head, brow furrowed. "Please don't worry, okay?"

She sighed and dropped her arms. "Okay. I don't want things to be weird, y'know?"

"I get it." He tapped his fingers on a chair. "It's why this whole thing works. We aren't weird."

"I mean, we're kinda weird, but in a good way." She ruffled his hair and sank onto the couch. "Also, that interview blew."

Santi scrubbed his face with one hand. "You're telling me. We have to be on such good behavior now."

"Uggghhhh." Her abdomen cramped at the stress of it all. "Why does this have to be so hard? Why can't we defraud the government and go on our merry way?"

*

Santiago pulled the blankets over his head when Mariana stumbled out of bed early in the morning. It couldn't possibly be eight o'clock yet. Burrowing further down, he relaxed to go back to sleep. She would come back to bed or make coffee, and she didn't need him to be awake for either of those.

Then she retched in the bathroom.

Jerking upright, he scrambled out from the twisted sheets and skidded to his knees beside her. "*Cariño?*"

Palms braced against the toilet bowl, she convulsed again with an ugly sound. Vomit splattered in the water. Tears gleamed at the fringes of her lashes. He rubbed her back and tried not to think about the smell.

Once she'd emptied her stomach, he handed her the tissue box so she could wipe her eyes and blow her nose. Miserable, she dumped the used tissues in the toilet, flushed it all, and pushed herself to her feet to rinse her mouth out at the sink.

"Are you sick?"

She didn't have any vacation time left, and he knew she had a lot of work to do, so if she'd come down with the flu or something, she was in trouble.

She shook her head, wan and drained. "I'll be okay in a few days." She skirted around him to start the shower.

He pivoted to follow her movements. "What was that, then?"

With a sigh, she turned to fix him with a flat stare. "I started bleeding last night."

"Bleeding? Are you hurt—?" The light turned on. "Oh."

Oddly blank, she shooed him so she could wash. He backed out, and she shut the door.

Should I do something? I feel like I should do something. But Maca didn't vomit during her time of the month. What would help?

Racking his brain for ideas, Santiago poured her a big glass of water, unfolded her softest blanket, found the ibuprofen, dug up a pack of mint gum, and plugged in the electric heat pad he used when his back acted up. The shower water turned off, and he grabbed a protein-heavy granola bar from the snack drawer too.

Mariana emerged from the bedroom wrapped in her fuzzy bathrobe, blowing her nose again. When he handed her the water, she downed it. He passed her the blanket, and she took it, but she edged around him, eyes skating by without contact. She curled up on the couch by herself, pulled the blanket up to her chin, and rested her forehead on her knees.

He watched her from the kitchen, at a loss. Though periods were universally acknowledged in Spain, the US could be squeamish about them, and he didn't want to embarrass her if she preferred not to talk about it. "Do you need anything?"

She shook her head. "I'm just going to rest. You can go back to bed; don't worry about it."

It wasn't a test—her eyes closed, and there was no judgment in her tone. Yet her brow crinkled in pain, her nails dug into her arms, and her complexion had lost its usual ebony warmth. He couldn't leave her to deal with this on her own, the way she had before he'd joined her here. The way she would have to again after they separated.

He brought over his pile of supplies and set it on the coffee table where she normally rested her feet. He turned on the hot pad and handed it to her.

She slipped it onto her stomach and managed a small smile. "Thanks."

I wish I could read minds. "Do you want a book? Or a movie?"

She started to reply, but then she gasped, scrunching up her face and curling in on herself. The fridge buzzed. No, wait—it was *her*, humming in pain through gritted teeth.

He refilled her water and, when the bout had passed, handed her the glass and multiple painkillers. When done, she set the empty cup aside and leaned against the back of the couch.

He touched her arm. "Does your head hurt?"

She laughed humorlessly. "Santi, *everything* hurts."

"Okay, then. Come here."

*

Mariana wasn't sure what she wanted: she didn't want him to see her in all her miserable cramping vomiting helpless glory, yet she also didn't want him to ignore her completely. But she didn't expect him to coax her to lay her head on the pillow on his lap. She held the heating pad to her lower abdomen, uncertain how to handle this development. Should she take the independent-adult route and insist on handling it herself, the way she always did?

Then he rubbed her temples with exquisitely gentle but firm pressure—a pleasant distraction from the pain—and handling it herself no longer tempted her, independence be damned.

When the cramps tore through her again, she stretched to different positions, trying to find an angle that made her not feel like a velociraptor was ripping her open. She ended up with her legs over the back of the couch, the only position that gave her any relief.

"Is this okay?" She didn't want him to feel weird. This was a new level of touch for them. "I'm not trying to..." *Start something? Be sexy?* God knew there was nothing sexy about this side of her life.

"I didn't think you were trying anything. I'm fine, but thank you for checking." He shifted his weight, settled in, and reached for the remote. "How do you feel about *El Ministerio del Tiempo*?"

"I might fall asleep," she warned him, though it wouldn't be because the show bored her. He had introduced her to the show back when she visited Madrid, and they'd started season two last week. "I'm exhausted."

He tapped the tip of her nose and smiled. "It's okay."

She smiled back, and this time, she didn't have to work for it. "You're the best."

"Remember that the next time I say something stupid." He found the current episode and clicked Play, his free hand tracing circles on her scalp.

True to her word, she drifted off within the first fifteen minutes. When she woke, he was still watching, although she didn't know if it was the same episode. Sleepily, she pulled her legs down beside her and curled into his side. Somewhere in the back of her mind, she knew she should pull away. It would be safer to keep her distance in such an intimate moment. But he draped his arm around her, easy as breathing, and she snuggled in with a contented sigh.

He's a friend. Her best friend. He was warm and sweet and safe, and she drifted back off, her pain fading.

Chapter Twelve

In Which Mariana Trusts Santiago with Her Work Feelings

JULY

Rain tapped on the windows, graying the afternoon sunlight in the kitchen. Santiago stirred a small pot of macaroni with milk, butter, and prepackaged too-orange cheese. Under his breath he hummed along with the Spanish radio station crooning on the counter beside him. The apartment was too quiet without Mariana around; music helped fill the space. Once the dinner mixture was a smooth yellow-orange, he sprinkled some salt on top and mixed that in as well. *Salt to taste*, the box said. He added another pinch.

He glanced at the door. Mariana should've been home by now. Was she working late? Why hadn't she texted him to let him know? Or had she gotten into an accident?

A car lock beep-beeped in the parking lot, and he peeked out the kitchen window. Outside, Mariana chatted into her phone as she slung her purse over her shoulder and tucked her lunch box into the crook of her arm. The rush of relief, of satisfaction, from her being home surprised him. He turned down the music, took the mac and cheese off the heat, and went to go greet her at the door.

The door opened, and she beamed up at him. "Hi, Santi."

She reached up, and he was already there, pressing a kiss to her lips that didn't last long enough for his liking. Her fingers ran through his hair, and he couldn't help the noise in the back of his throat.

A familiar, tech-tinny voice called out in Spanish, "Get a room!"

He pulled back. "Maca?"

Mariana laughed and waved her phone. "I called to see how your mom was doing, but we got to talking." Switching to Spanish: "I'll let you go, Maca. I can smell dinner."

"Okay, have a good dinner. Talk to you two later. Byeee."

"Byeeee."

"*Hasta luego, tonta*," Santiago added sweetly.

The call ended with a beep. Mariana slipped her phone into her back pocket and dropped her purse beside the couch. "So is that mac and cheese I smell?"

"It is. I added salt this time, so let me know if you like it better or worse this way." He hugged her from behind, and she leaned back into it with a smile.

"Will do." She kicked off her shoes, headed into the kitchen, and pulled two polka-dotted bowls out of the cupboard. She dished herself up a serving of macaroni and picked out a spoon from the silverware drawer. "Sorry I'm late. A meeting ran over the expected time." She ran her free hand over the small of his back, and his skin tingled under his T-shirt. "Ready to eat?"

"Definitely." He served himself, and they sat side by side on the couch. He switched on the television. "What are we watching today?"

"Ooh, how about that new spy movie on Netflix?" Mariana took a bite of her mac and cheese—and coughed sharply. With much effort, she swallowed. "Um, *cariño*, how much salt did you put in that?"

"Not a lot." Giving her a weird look, he tried it himself. He gagged and spat the mouthful out into his napkin. "Okay, maybe more than I realized."

"Maybe a little." She stuck out her tongue as if airing it out. "Box mac is pretty salty on its own. I don't know that it really needs any extra. Good effort, but I might have to go look for leftovers instead."

He sighed. "I'm sorry. It won't hurt my feelings if you do."

"Good, because that was rough." Mariana ruffled his hair and got up. In the kitchen she heated up some leftover empanadas, and she brought back a plate for each of them. "Here. You're welcome."

"You're wonderful." Santiago cleared his throat. "This failed experiment aside, I think we should make mac and cheese a weekly tradition. I'll make it—you don't have to. In fact, I *insist* you don't."

"I appreciate that, but no."

He pouted. "Come on. Imagine...delicious macaroni and cheese...with a normal amount of salt..."

"No." She stretched her legs across his lap as she stared down his puppy-dog eyes. "We cannot have mac and cheese every week."

Was this a budget thing? "Why not? It's cheap!"

"It's unhealthy!"

He dropped the pitiful expression. "I need to perfect my methods." After this too-salty attempt, he needed to redeem himself. It was a matter of pride.

She bumped her legs against his torso. "There's no method to box mac and cheese, Santi."

That sounds like a challenge. "I'm going to make the most delicious box mac and cheese you've ever had, and you're going to regret doubting me."

"So would you say I'll...eat my words?"

It took a moment for the pun to click; he groaned. "No, Mari, no."

She cackled.

"I'm going to pretend I never heard that, and press play on this movie." He stroked his palms over the crest of her legs, and she snuggled up against him.

The feel of her—of her with him—buzzed warmly in his body. After the cuddle-fest that had been her period, the last of her touch anxiety had disappeared. Now she rested against him easily, ran her fingers through his hair, let him hug her as he passed by. And he only itched to touch her more.

As if she could read his mind: "Maybe we should practice kissing."

Because it was bad? Or because she liked it too? Either way, he backpedaled. "What, because my sister's obnoxious?"

Mariana shook her head. "No. At least, not completely. When we tried at the wedding reception, too, it seemed like we kinda scared people."

Heat flooded his face. *Tried?* Clearly, she remembered that kiss differently than he did.

"I feel like there has to be some level of regular kissing that will convince an audience without grossing them out."

"Yeah." He tried to keep his tone casual. "We can practice being...regular." Maybe he would calm down. *It was just new. Now I know what it's like, and it'll be boring.* That had happened with people before, so it wasn't an absurd theory. But those men and women hadn't meant as much to him as Mariana.

She leaned forward, expectant. Gently he pushed her legs off his lap, and she adjusted to a better angle toward him. The first kiss had been a surprise, no time to think. This time, he absorbed the look of her. Out of her element but relaxed and trusting.

Regular kissing. He could do regular kissing.

He tilted his head and touched his lips to hers. Kept his hands to himself. Moved in an easy, slow pressure—he wasn't trying to tempt her to open to him again. A gentle, family-friendly kiss. Sinking into the feel of her.

Her fingertips grazed his forearm, and he hid a shiver. He could have stayed there forever, lost in the tender, simple intimacy, but he pulled back. He hoped his voice sounded normal when he said, "Not bad. We're convincing." Almost enough to fool himself. He couldn't get enough of her.

She nodded, but he couldn't read her thoughts through her expression. Evenly, matter-of-factly: "Should we practice deeper kissing too? In case it comes up?"

A simple question she meant nothing by—but he almost choked at the thought. The little noises she'd made at the reception, the way she'd felt pressed tight against him...

He wanted it.

Too much.

"No, we're good." He scooted back on the couch, away from her. "Anyway, this movie has been playing, but neither of us are paying attention to it. Let me rewind it." He scrambled for the remote and turned his whole body toward the TV, not inviting her to extend her legs over his lap like usual.

*

Thrown off-balance by his sudden retreat, Mariana struggled to find a foothold in the movie. She had liked kissing him...had liked it a lot. Definitely in the Top Five Things She Liked About Fake-Marrying Santiago.

But he had withdrawn.

He'd broken off the first kiss, with a clear but gentle reminder that it was practice for the charade and *only* practice. Like an idiot, she'd poked at the idea of doing more, and he'd bolted. Not that she blamed him. The terms of their arrangement had been rock solid. If any real feelings developed, both of them would end up hurt.

Still, she nursed a tiny wound: she wished he hadn't been so eager to flee the possibility of kissing her again. Was it that intolerable?

She tried to push aside the pain and move on, with limited success. The empanadas and spy movie helped, although he himself didn't, the way he kept space between them while they ate. It was so out of character it couldn't be anything but intentional.

A hint of that insecurity followed her to work the next day—and her stomach plummeted when she saw the short middle-aged woman setting up a laptop. Wan white skin, and mouse-brown hair in an outdated cut. Cheryl.

How had Mariana forgotten to mark it on her calendar? Cheryl only came into the office a few days a month because she usually worked from home, and Mariana always wrote herself a note so she could mentally prepare. And close her office door and wear headphones all day long.

As if she'd heard the plan, Cheryl looked up with a tight-lipped smile. "Good morning, Mariana. Good to see you."

Mariana mustered up every ounce of professional friendliness in her body. "Hi, Cheryl, how are you?"

"Fine. Lots to do for the James Farmer project proposal." The project Mariana had suggested for a new exhibit, as a change of pace to bring in new patrons. But the chilly look in Cheryl's eyes wasn't complimentary.

In response, Mariana maintained her Work Professional Smile. "I appreciate all the work you put in to help the team." Though she wouldn't mind if she never saw the older woman again, she had to admit Cheryl did know her job. She might not be enthusiastic—or friendly, at all, ever—but she got the work done.

"Morning, Cheryl." The secretary, Rosa, set her lunch in the fridge. "Morning, Mariana—I like your dress!"

Mariana lit up at the compliment. "Thanks!" She'd pulled today's ensemble out of the back of the closet; her mother had given her the sleek dress a few years back, but it hadn't fit well then. It reassured her to know it looked good on her now. But that wasn't the best part. "It has pockets!"

"What?" Rosa darted over, peering around the skirt for telltale bulges or lumps. "Where? Show me."

Delighted, Mariana slid her hands into the tiny seams on the sides, and they disappeared up to her wrists.

"Nice." Satisfaction seeped through Rosa's voice.

"Right?" This one fashion device—such a pleasant, useful surprise.

"That is a nice dress," Cheryl added. Trying not to let her surprise show, Mariana thanked her—and the older woman finished, "I try not to waste too much money on clothes myself. I prefer to spend it on more important things."

Rosa pivoted on one kitten heel and walked away from that.

Mariana sucked in a breath. First of all, she hadn't even *bought* this dress; it had been a gift. Second of all, that wasn't even the point! How sad would a person have to be inside to turn a compliment into a backhanded insult?

(Third of all, Cheryl's bland, old-fashioned wardrobe revealed it might behoove her to spend more money on clothes.)

Don't sink to her level, Mariana coached herself. *You have to respond, but don't sink to her level.*

"It is important for everyone to...budget appropriately." The words almost strangled her. "I need to get to work. I'll see you later." And she professionally speed-walked to her office, which, by the grace of God, featured a door. She closed it behind her.

Unfortunately, she did have to see Cheryl later. Mariana had a meeting with their manager, Joe, about the potential new exhibit, and since Cheryl was in the building, she'd help present the proposal in person. Omar would've been her preference as backup, but he had a mandatory meeting to attend, and when Cheryl had offered to help, Mariana hadn't felt like she could say no.

After making small talk with the boss, Mariana shared her screen and watched his nonverbals—brow crinkling or smoothing, eyes widening or squinting, shoulders tensing or arms folding. When necessary, she reframed the conversation around those changes, and by the end, he was giving the Slow Nod of Agreement.

"Sounds like a good idea," he said. "It's past time to branch out."

"Thank you." Mariana smiled. "We do need to diversify. History—"

"You know I've mentored Mariana, taught her the ropes and helped her find her place." Cheryl's dead, soulless face was earnest. "Isn't she articulate?"

What? Indignation strangled Mariana. "That's not—"

"I'm so proud to see my efforts coming to fruition. She's relied on me for a lot of the details, but she's coming into her own."

"And we appreciate your contributions in all those areas." Joe inclined his head. "This goes well, and it'll reflect well on you both."

Mariana gritted her teeth and fought to maintain her smile. Cheryl had sent her exactly two emails about her project, both of them passive aggressive, if not overtly racist. If that was mentoring and high reliance, she'd eat her own shoes. "Yes, I'm excited about where it's going. I've put a lot of work into it, and I can't wait to bring it all together."

Is it worth starting something? ...Yes. Yes, it is.

Once they concluded the call and shut off the laptop, Cheryl went for the door, but Mariana moved faster. "Hey—" She strained for professionalism. "What was that?"

The older woman looked down her nose at her—as best she could, being almost half a foot shorter. "We need to present a united front. This is a team, you know."

"Yes, it is." Mariana took a deep breath. "And I'm glad to have you involved. I just want to make sure that..."

How to phrase it? *Treat me like a human being?*

"...credit goes where credit is due, and everyone gets treated respectfully." *Articulate*, for God's sake.

"Don't you think you're being too sensitive?"

Don't I think I'm...? Mariana bit down on the inside of her cheek to keep from saying something that would get her in trouble. "I'd appreciate it if you didn't interrupt me, going forward. Or call me articulate. That's all."

"It's a compliment."

Ugh. Her jaw ticked. "It implied that you didn't think I would be."

Cheryl stiffened. "I'm not racist, if that's what you mean. I have a Black friend."

Don't flip. Mariana stayed on track rather than pointing out the issue with that statement too. *I shouldn't be responsible for correcting her in the first place.* "I'd still prefer you not call me it."

Cheryl gave a thin-lipped smile. "Okay, great." The office-friendly equivalent of a different two-word phrase.

"Thanks." Mariana couldn't summon a smile anymore. The smartest response was to take Cheryl's words at face value. But irritation sizzled under Mariana's skin. She might be young, but she wasn't stupid. This was *her* project. And to have to deal with microaggressions on top of it... Unfortunately, she was still working on the "keeping her emotions under control" aspect of professional life. *Get it together.* "I appreciate your support on this project." An intentional word choice—support was not leadership.

Cheryl nodded stiffly and left the conference room.

Great. That went well. Mariana went to her office and grabbed her mug from her desk before heading to the kitchen for a coffee refill that was feeling more and more necessary by the minute.

Omar was waiting for the microwave, Tupperware in his hands. He smiled at her when she came in. "How's your morning?"

She exhaled and stared down the sputtering Keurig. "It'll be better with some more caffeine."

"I feel that." He leaned back against the counter. "Hey, did the presentation go okay? Sorry I couldn't help you out today."

How much could she say? She considered him a friend, but he was also a coworker. Not only that, he had his life together. If she wanted to be a professional, she had to Be A Professional. Fake it 'til you make it. She gave her polite adult smile. "Yeah, Joe gave me the green light. I'm just trying to figure out how to get it all done."

Omar took her at her word and left with a congratulations.

Mariana shut herself in her office until quitting time, when she drove to the high school with a strangling grip on the steering wheel.

Santi shot her an odd look as he slid into the car, so she forcibly relaxed herself. But he knew. "Tell me what happened."

The simmering irritation exploded. "Okay, *so!*" Mariana relayed the story so quickly and aggressively she couldn't be sure he caught everything, but he made offended noises in support, and it felt good to yell the story at someone she trusted. He yelled with her, and by the time she parked in front of their apartment, he had her laughing.

That Saturday, she met with the lawyer, Fredrick Cho, to tell him she had married. When suspicion flickered in his eyes, she assured him, "We've known each other for years, and we love each other. We fit perfectly together."

And it was true.

Chapter Thirteen

In Which Family Meals Initiate Angst for Different Reasons

AUGUST

"...and the biography I'm reading about him is interesting, which bodes well. Bonus, it has a ton of info I can use for building up the exhibit, when we print the plaques and stuff."

Mariana tried to talk as much as she could through family lunch after church on Sunday. The less chance she gave her parents to talk, the better—they couldn't be rude to Santiago if they couldn't get a word in edgewise. So far, she'd gone through James Farmer's entire life story.

"Oh, and tonight we're having dinner with Embry and her family. That'll be fun. I haven't seen them since the reception. And while we're there, we're buying her roommate Rhiannon's old car. For next to nothing too—"

"Wait, you're what?" Rafael broke in.

Damn it. She'd hoped they'd leave that alone. As if it were no big deal, she pulled out her phone and showed them a photo of the gold sedan. "It's this old Subaru. Got a few miles on it, but it works great. She has a second car, and when I mentioned how I have to drive Santi everywhere, she offered to sell this one to us dirt cheap."

"Where are you getting this money? Your inheritance hasn't come in yet, has it?"

She shifted in her seat. "Um, no, it hasn't." Not that her parents knew why it hadn't come in yet, or what she'd had to do to get it.

"So why are you buying a car if you don't have the money?" Carmen gripped her fork and knife, glowering at Santiago across the dining room table.

"It makes sense." Mariana tangled her fingers with Santi's under the table. "I can't drive him everywhere. He's got his license now, so we can get a second car—and Rhiannon is giving us a serious deal."

"So *you're* buying it for him," Carmen said, "naturally."

Mariana sighed, her pulse quick in her throat. "*I'm* not buying it. *We're* buying it. We're already going halfsies on rent and groceries and bills, so we're just adjusting a little to fit in a cheap car."

Rafael stared at her, clearly willing her to understand. "You're paying more bills so he can have a car."

"No, the car is for both of us." Santiago touched his free hand to Mariana's forearm.

Her parents nailed him with such icy glares, he leaned back in his seat and took a long drink of water.

"I'm paying less to exist now than I was two months ago." She swallowed. *Why isn't this getting through?* "Santiago is paying his share of everything, and we need the car."

Her parents had a Silent Conversation Through Expressions before Carmen sank back in her chair. "If you're determined to do it, we'll help you out."

"Huh?"

Rafael nodded. "This is a tough time, and we love you. We might not agree with every decision you make—" A not-so-subtle dig at her marriage. "—but we're here for you."

"Oh." She glanced at Santi, whose eyebrows had shot up to his hairline. "Thank you."

After lunch, Mariana washed the dishes and Santiago dried. A sting in her skin made her wince, and she rinsed off the suds to find her middle knuckle had split in the hot water.

Santiago sucked in a breath and took her hand in his. He examined the tiny wound as if it were gaping. "*Dulzura*, let me take a turn washing."

The care in his voice, the endearment on his tongue, warmed her inside. She smiled at him. "Thanks, *cariño*, but I'm okay."

His thumb grazed the back of her hand before he released her, and she missed the contact. "Seriously. Here, trade places with me." Santiago's palms on her hips, he spun them in a half-circle so that he took her spot at the sink and she took his beside the oven. His fingertips lingered before he stepped back. "I need to run to the restroom. I'll be right back. Don't you dare stick your hands in that water while I'm gone."

She gave him a kiss on the cheek. He handed her the towel and headed to the bathroom.

In his absence, Carmen materialized at her side. "Mari, are you doing okay?" The question was quiet, inaudible to the men. "Really okay?"

Mariana scrubbed the water droplets off a serving bowl, irritated at what seemed like distrust. But when she turned to face her mother, she saw only genuine concern. Love doused her anger. "Mom, I promise, I'm happy. Santi and I love each other. I trust him—I wish you did too."

Carmen placed her hands on her daughter's cheeks and drew her down to kiss her on the forehead. "It's hard when it looks like someone might be taking advantage of my baby."

Mariana sighed. "I know. But he's *not*. Literally, right now, I'm drying dishes because he noticed the water split my knuckle, so he took my place as the washer."

Carmen was unconvinced. "You can tell us anything. You know that, right? The truth is the most important thing."

Was it, though? If they would only believe her if she said what they wanted to hear?

*

At home, Santiago started on twice-baked potatoes to bring to Embry's house as a side dish for dinner, and then he snuggled up with Mariana on the couch.

She rested her head on his shoulder and sighed, her legs tucked over his lap. "I hate that I can't tell my parents." Not the first time she'd complained about it.

"There's no good way to explain 'technically, yes, he's faking it but that's okay' without following up with 'we're both faking it.'"

Santiago stroked the curve of her shoulders, silent. Anything he said would inadvertently make it clear he was no longer sure how much he was faking.

He gathered—based on the blatant weekly lunch conversations—that the Mitogos didn't doubt *her* feelings, but *his*. Yet they gave him the evil eye when he did touch her or call her various terms of endearment, which came dangerously easily to him. He found himself looking for reasons to graze his fingers, his lips, over her skin. To whisper *cariño* and *dulzura* and *tesoro* and *amada* and see her eyes warm, her lips turn up in a smile. She no longer jumped at the intimacies, and it was all too easy to imagine she liked it, too, when she returned them in kind.

But there was only pain in entertaining that thought.

"Why don't we tell them, then?" He rubbed her shoulders. "Would that make you feel better?"

She shook her head. "My parents are honest to a fault—they're terrible liars. If they get interviewed, they need to be able to say honestly that as far as they know, we married for love."

"But they don't think that. They think I'm in it for the green card." And they weren't subtle about it either. Honest to a fault indeed. "So, either way, we can't count on them to say what we need them to say."

"If they don't know the truth, they can't out us for real. They only have parental suspicion." She sighed. "They're not like Maca, Santi. I don't trust them to lie for us."

"Whatever you think, *amada*. I'll follow your lead."
After popping the baked potatoes into the oven for the
second time, he video-called Maca, with Mariana tucked
under his arm. "*Hola, tonta.*"

"I don't like you," Maca told him in Spanish. "How
are you, Mariana? Has he driven you crazy yet?"

"Not yet. Give it another week."

"Hey!" He twisted to block Mari's view of the screen.
"I feed you delicious food! How can you treat me like
this?"

She pushed him playfully out of the way. "You feed
me box mac and cheese!"

"That's what you make?" Maca's jaw dropped.

"First of all—" He raised his voice. "—it's the most
delicious box mac and cheese ever. Second of all, she's
forgetting the *croquetas* and *cocidas* and paella and
empanadas—"

His sister scowled. "You're a terrible husband!"

"This is why I don't call you more! You're mean to
me!" He tossed his head to jerk out of Mariana's grip and
pinned her arms to the couch. "And you're no better."

She winked theatrically and blew him a kiss.

He melted. *God, she's beautiful.*

"Are you two always like this?" Maca made a face.
"My teaching worked too well. You're disgusting. You're
practically real newlyweds."

"We're just friends." Mariana protested more quickly
than Santiago thought was necessary. It wasn't *that*
horrible of an idea, was it?

Oh. Maybe he ought to be more defensive about it too.

"Yeah, come on, dummy. We've had over a month to get our act together—of course we're doing better." He struck a pose. "Acting!" *More or less.*

"Acting!" His beautiful, amazing wife threw out her arms. "I'm getting pretty good at it. It comes naturally to him though."

Maca shot him a pointed look. "Hmm. What talent."

He clenched his jaw and widened his eyes at her in the universal *shut up* expression. "I'm a talented man." And not having feelings for his fake wife in any way, shape, or form. No matter what his sister thought she saw.

When the washer beeped and Mariana left to change the laundry over, Maca leaned in close to her camera. "What are you doing?"

He squinted. "Talking to you?"

She made a choked noise in the back of her throat. "No, with *Mariana*, stupid! You act like that and she doesn't *know*?"

"Of course she doesn't!" he exploded. "What kind of person do you think I am? We're friends—she doesn't want any more!"

She pinched the bridge of her nose with a huff. "She's not that good of an actress, Santi. She likes you."

"That's not—" He strangled the air, trying to find a way to explain. "She's not romantic. She can flirt *because* it doesn't mean anything to her."

Maca said something, but the Wi-Fi stuttered, and he missed it.

"What?"

Pursing her lips, she shot him a dirty look that was not at all softened by pixilation and iffy Internet. "I said that if you don't tell her about your feelings like an *adult*, you're going to end up sad and alone." In a less serious tone she added, "And then you're going to come crying to me. I won't have any sympathy for you, buddy. You did this to yourself."

She wasn't wrong. But she didn't know how badly Mariana had reacted after the USCIS interview when she thought he was interested in her. How uncomfortable she'd been, and how terrible he'd felt for bending the truth to make her feel better.

He wouldn't risk losing her by trying to turn their friendship into real romance.

After the video call, they drove to Embry's house for dinner, with Santiago holding the twice-baked potatoes in a Tupperware container.

Mariana shifted in her seat before warning him, "I basically grew up with Embry and her family. They're like a second set of parents. So don't be offended if they're protective of me, okay? I mean, I don't think they'll be mean or anything—"

Like your parents? He didn't dare say it aloud.

"—but if it takes them a little while to open up, it's not you."

Okay, so prepare for dinner to be a reenactment of Sunday lunches, just with a different family. Fantastic. He forced a smile. "It's okay. I understand."

She mustered a smile in return. "You're gonna do awesome."

He had zero faith in that, but he said, "All I can do is my best, right?"

"I appreciate you sticking through all this. I think you're the actual best, and they'll agree with me once they get to know you."

He had the feeling she wasn't just talking about Embry's family.

Rhiannon opened the front door for them, pristine in a crisp blouse and pencil skirt despite it being a casual Sunday dinner. "Come on in. Dinner's almost ready."

Mariana high-fived Santi before stepping into the foyer. "Our timing is perfect, then! What are we eating?"

It smelled like pasta, and Santiago was down for that.

"Chicken alfredo!" Embry waved at them from the kitchen with her free hand, stirring a pan with the other. The open-concept layout made it easy to see her across the room. "Take a seat."

Before they could take a seat, Embry's father, Jamal, set aside his newspaper, rose from the couch, and enveloped Mariana in a huge hug. "Hey, my girl. How's your day?"

She embraced him tightly. "Better now that we're here."

When Jamal released her, Santiago stuck out his hand, preparing for his bones to be crunched again. Instead, Jamal batted his hand away. "C'mere." He hugged Santiago, complete with two manly back pats at the end.

The warmth, the openness, sent him spinning. He struggled to maintain a straight face. "Nice to see you again, sir." He hadn't visited with Embry's family since the reception, and this was the welcome he got?

"Oh, let me have a chance at them." Embry's mom, Connie, bustled out of the kitchen and wrapped both Mariana and Santiago in a warm embrace. "How was your drive? Oh, what's in the container?"

Santiago held out the Tupperware. "Twice-baked potatoes. I made them myself, but it was my first time with that recipe, so if they're bad—"

"Nonsense! I'm sure they're delicious. Besides, it's almost impossible to mess up potatoes." With a wink, Connie took the potatoes from him and set them on the dining table. "Do you cook a lot?"

He brightened. "I do! I love to cook. There's nothing like making a good meal for the people you love."

"Honey, we think the same way. I love my kitchen time too." Connie gestured toward the couch. "Sit down."

But Santiago edged toward the kitchen. "Is there anything I can help with?"

"Aw, thank you, sweetie. Sure, you can set the table. Mariana, can you show him where everything is?"

He half turned, and Mariana was at his shoulder, smiling. "Can do, Connie." She strode to the cabinets, counted out a stack of multicolored plates, and handed it to him. "Here's these. I'll get the silverware."

He walked the plates to the table, where Embry's sister Joy was already sitting, ready to eat. "What's your favorite color?" he asked her.

She sucked in her cheeks as she considered this serious question. "Yellow."

He found a yellow plate in the stack and placed it in front of her with a flourish.

Joy beamed, and so did Mariana as she added the silverware to each place setting.

Jamal sat back down on the couch, though he left his newspaper folded over. "So you like to cook. What's your favorite thing to make?"

"Don't say box mac and cheese," Mariana teased.

Santiago huffed. "Box mac and cheese is a gift. But if I had to pick something else as my favorite, maybe *cocido madrileño*? The English name is—well, I don't actually know. It translates to, uh, 'Madrid stew.' It has vegetables, chorizo sausage, chickpeas, and pork that cooks for over four hours, and then you eat it in several courses. So good."

"You haven't made that for me yet." Mariana nudged him. "Should I be offended?"

"I think so." Connie smiled as she tossed a salad at the kitchen island. "If your personal chef is holding out on you—"

Santiago grinned and laced his fingers with Mariana's. "I would never."

She smiled warmly at him, and he drew her closer without meaning to. *Holy shit, she's beautiful.*

"Hey now, save those looks for your parties of two," Embry teased from beside the stove.

"Yeah, yeah." Mariana led him back to the kitchen area, where they pulled glasses out of another cabinet.

"So, Madrid stew," Connie echoed. "Is that where you're from in Spain? Madrid?"

Santiago helped Mariana carry the glass cups to the table and placed them beside each plate. "Yes, I'm from Madrid. I grew up there."

"How are you adjusting to life in America? It's gotta be a pretty big culture shock."

"So far so good, actually." He missed Spain and his sister and mother, but it hadn't been too overwhelming so far. He was still in the honeymoon phase, according to Maca and the Internet. "We talk to my family all the time, so that helps the homesickness."

"Aww, that's good. I don't know what I'd do if one of my kids moved overseas." In the kitchen, Connie pinched Embry's cheek.

She swatted her mother away with a laugh. "Food's ready. Leave me alone so I can put it on the table."

"But now I'm thinking about you moving to another country!"

"No one's moving anywhere," Jamal grumbled with a smile. "Let your firstborn handle dinner."

Embry poured the chicken alfredo into a serving bowl and set it on a trivet, with the twice-baked potatoes on one side and vibrant green broccoli on the other. "Oh, while the water was boiling, I did one of those personality quizzes online and it said that if I were a fruit, I'd be a persimmon." Embry stuck a serving fork into a massive piece of broccoli. "What does that even mean?"

"You tell us," Mariana teased. "You're the one who took the quiz. It should've given the description at the end."

"Well, okay, yeah, it said I wanted to be special, but I think that's rude."

"What did you answer?"

"In the quiz? The normal things, I don't know."

Mariana inclined her head toward Santiago. "If I were a fruit, what do you think I'd be?"

He chewed his lip as he considered. "Mmm... pomegranate."

She wrinkled her nose. "A pomegranate? Really?"

He nodded and gave a little smile as he leaned in to explain. "There's a lot going on inside your head, you're a snack, and I'd stay in the Underworld for you."

Beaming, Mariana laced her fingers through his and rested her head on his shoulder—and the trust in the tiny movement buzzed through his body. Something deeper came over him, though he couldn't (or wouldn't) put a name to it, and he pressed a kiss to her temple. She shifted into him with a happy little sigh, and he sucked in a deep breath to avoid thinking about the sudden knot in his throat.

When they slid back into the car in the sunset after dinner, he left his seat belt hanging loose and leaned over the center console. "We should kiss." His hand was already tracing up her neck to up her jaw. Her heartbeat stuttered under his thumb.

But she met him in the middle, and he pressed his mouth to hers, a warm and tender but firm claim. She ran her fingers through his hair, and he shuddered. Maybe her friends could see from the house, maybe not. He didn't care. He kissed his wife, his best friend, and time stood still.

*

Mariana tossed and turned that night, unable to turn her brain off. When, finally, she slipped into sleep out of sheer exhaustion, the thoughts followed her. Hands on skin—twisted sheets and hot breaths—but more than that, cuddling under a blanket on a snowy day. Waking up intertwined or with their backs pressed together. Buying "from the both of us" holiday cards, receiving "to the two of you" cards in return. Friendly, easy Sunday lunches with her parents, no suspicion or dark looks or quiet questions. Warm honesty, openness, truth to it all, the scenes now overlaid with an overplayed love song from the radio.

The sound barely registered as the alarm. She squinted through the dark with bleary eyes. The man-size lump of blankets beside her groaned, though, and that pushed her to pull one hand out from under her pillow and fumble with her phone until the noise stopped. Blowing out a lungful of dry mouth, she shoved off the covers and slithered off the bed to pad into the bathroom, careful to close the door before turning on the light so she wouldn't blind Santiago.

Her husband.

The fluorescent lights above the sink gleamed off the citrine in her ring. *This is no dream*. Or nightmare, if anyone found out they'd lied—were still lying. Fines, *jail time*, not to mention Santiago would be deported with a no-returns policy. She'd never get her inheritance, never pay off those looming debts. Neither of them would benefit from being outed, hence the living arrangements, the sleeping arrangements, the method acting.

That was all it was: method acting.

If Embry or Omar held her gaze and grazed their fingertips over the small of her back as they passed, she would feel exactly the same. And, of course, she had to give as good as she got because if anyone noticed two madly-in-love newlyweds avoiding physical contact, someone would call bullshit, and the entire thing would be blown to bits faster than she could say "green card marriage."

Money. Money. Money, she chanted to herself as she brushed her teeth with more vigor than necessary. She was in it to win it—namely, by getting her $200,000—and that was all there was to it. Helping him, and helping herself. Just two friends being pals and getting the money they needed.

Behind her, the door creaked open and Santiago shuffled in, his hair rumpled and sticking out at odd angles. He covered a yawn with the back of his hand and waved a sleepy good morning with his fingers as he joined her at the sink. She passed him the toothpaste.

"Fhnnks."

She nodded with a tired half-smile.

If she liked the way they looked side by side in the mirror, the thought was purely platonic.

Chapter Fourteen

In Which Mariana Expands Her Vocabulary

SEPTEMBER

Summer faded into fall, the transition barely visible in the warm green of the South. The after-school mentoring program started up again, bringing Mariana to Santiago's school every Wednesday afternoon. On the first day, Embry's teenage sister, Charity, treated her to a rare hug and a "Hi, Miss Mitogo." She couldn't call her Mariana at school functions.

"I'm actually Mrs. de los Reyes now, not Miss Mitogo."

"Oh, right. You got married this summer. I remember. Sorry, I was at summer camp."

The next week, Charity returned, eyes wide and jaw dropped as she approached. Appalled or in awe, or maybe a mix of both. "Is the *Spanish teacher* your husband?" she demanded with no pleasantries. "Did you marry Mr. de los Reyes?"

Mariana choked on a laugh at the intensity of the reaction. "Uh, yes?"

The girl's mouth snapped shut, and she crossed her arms, muttering something.

"Didn't catch that."

Charity scowled. "He's cute. But I can't have a crush on him if he's your husband."

"Oh." Was that a compliment? "Thanks?"

"Yeah." Sullen as only a teenager could be, she stalked over to a cluster of girls her own age, some of whom Mariana knew, and told them something (*what could it be?*) that made them all pivot to gape at Mariana.

She smiled and waved.

Embry strolled over to take a seat beside her. "Oh, they finally figured out you took the cute new teacher off the market? How could you."

Mariana threw her hands in the air. "I have no idea what's happening. What did I do?"

Laughing, Embry shook her head. "I must've heard from three different girls last Wednesday how cute the new Spanish teacher is. More this week too. He has quite the fan club already."

"What?" An open grimace. "They're fifteen. What did they *think* was going to happen—he'd fall in love and wait for them to finish high school?"

Embry shrugged. "It's a tiny teacher crush. Mine was Ms. Takahashi in ninth grade English. Futile but harmless. You know how it is."

No...no, she didn't. Mariana's flustered frustration charred into embarrassment. Years ago, had her classmates pined for their teachers too? She'd never felt whatever it was these girls felt, young and green and premature as it was. Had she missed some kind of pubescent rite of passage?

Was that why, when it came to romance and sexual attraction, her ex had called her broken?

Unable to find this funny anymore, she excused herself to use the bathroom. Thankfully, none of her other kids brought it up, but she didn't sing along with the radio on the drive home, too caught in her own thoughts to enjoy any of the songs.

She pushed through the front door. "Is Maca still up?"

Santiago looked up from the stove, eyes big and hair mussed. "Probably. Why?"

She threw her purse on the armchair, throat thick with tears. Something delicious steamed from a pan on the stove, but her twisted stomach revolted at the idea of eating anything. "I need to talk to her."

Confused, Santiago gestured for her to join him. "Are you okay? Did something happen?"

"I...I don't know." She went to him for a hug.

"Do you want to talk about it?"

She shook her head. "I need to Skype Maca. She might be able to help." Later, she would talk to him, but she wanted to discuss it with someone who might be the same way. Santiago meant well, but he'd had several boyfriends and girlfriends over the course of their friendship. He'd never questioned her own lack of relationships, but still. He wasn't the same.

She took her laptop into the bedroom and closed both doors. Maca answered the video call after only two rings. *"Hola, hermana, ¿qué pasa?"*

Mariana struggled to find a good way to start the conversation. "I don't know," she tried, also in Spanish. "I didn't have..."

Something must have shown on her face. Maca gentled, leaned forward. "Hey. Did something happen?"

The question burst from Mariana's lips before she could stop it: "Did you have a crush on your teachers when you were younger?"

To her credit, Maca handled the odd subject with grace. "No, never."

Mariana mulled over the implications of this simple admission, then followed it up with a second question that revealed more than she would have liked. "What does a crush feel like?"

Raising her hands palms up, Maca pulled a rueful smile. "I couldn't tell you. I have no idea."

Mariana leaned back. "No—but—you told me how to act when I was dating Santi. Isn't that the same? Or similar?"

A shrug. "I know what it looks like. I don't know what it feels like. And God forbid anyone be able to describe it in a way that makes sense."

This is less helpful than I'd hoped. Looking away, Mariana rubbed her temples to stave off an oncoming headache. "I..." She trailed off with a wet sigh. *I what? Don't get it? Want to feel normal? Can't figure out what's going on?*

Maca waited for her to finish the sentence, but Mariana stayed silent. "Did something happen?"

Mariana related today's revelation that Santiago's students found him attractive, and then stumbled into her overall confusion. "I get why they find him aesthetically appealing, but they don't know him personally and it's going nowhere. How can they have a crush on him?"

Saying nothing, Maca nodded for her to continue.

Mariana took a deep breath for the courage to admit, "I don't know what that attraction is supposed to feel like, but it seems like I'm supposed to. It seems like everyone else understands without even trying. Like they found Waldo, and I'm running around just trying to figure out what he looks like!" She trembled with the memory that had shadowed the back of her mind for years. "My high school boyfriend told me I was broken for not feeling...whatever it is."

Deep sympathy showed in Maca's face, and she hugged herself. "No, of course you're not."

If anyone can say so from personal experience, she can. Probably overstepping the boundaries of their friendship but desperate for reassurance, Mariana continued, "You don't feel that stuff either, right?"

Maca nodded. "I don't feel romantic or sexual attraction at all, ever, for anyone. I'll flirt like a boss for fun, but I have no interest in kissing or dating or sex. I never have."

Mariana pressed her lips together. She hadn't even known it was an option; no one ever talked about it. The world seemed to assume that everyone had a Waldo point of reference.

"But it's not an all-or-nothing thing. Some people are grayscale about it. Like, have you ever wanted to kiss someone?"

Santiago. She very much wanted to kiss Santiago. "Mm-hmm."

Maca looked right at her but didn't call her out on who it might be. "Do you want to be with them more than other friends? Not to the *exclusion* of other friends, because that's creepy, but in a physically and emotionally close way? Like, extra special?"

Without the ambiguous "romance" terminology: "Definitely."

"But you don't meet someone and immediately think, 'Hey, I want to kiss them' or whatever?"

Mariana pulled a face. "Ew, no." She'd met people and known they would be friends, but she'd never wanted more than that right off the bat. Even when she'd found Santiago cute at their first meeting, she hadn't wanted to jump his bones.

"Okay," Maca hummed pensively. "For this...*person* you want to kiss..." This vague description sounded pointed to Mariana. Did Maca know? Given how quickly she'd figured out the relationship was fake—probably. "Did it happen fast, or did it take a while before you wanted to be Extra Special?"

"We were friends for years first."

"So it's, like, special best friends feelings? But also the desire for physical intimacy and being...partners? For life, or however long?" Maca grimaced. "Sorry, I'm doing the best I can, but I have no personal experience to draw from. Plus, it's past midnight here."

"No, I appreciate it. I'm sorry I'm keeping you up."

"It's okay." She thought of something and snorted. "Why am I the relationship advisor. I, the aromantic asexual. I give relationship and attraction advice. What saint decided that was my talent?"

Mariana laughed. "That does seem...odd."

"I'm going to start charging for my services," Maca warned. "Anyway, so you feel the things, but only after the strong emotional connection."

Afraid this was weird, Mariana scrambled for a clearer explanation. "Sort of like...pizza? If I never cared about pizza, but there's one particular pizza I became hungry for after I smelled it for a long time?"

"Okay, yeah." Maca stared up at the ceiling for a minute. "I think I might know."

Mariana sucked in a breath. Could there be a word for this? Could there be other people like her?

"Everyone experiences things differently, so the overall labels are only approximate, and someone else might identify the same but have different, uh, signs..."

"Of course, yeah."

Maca kissed her teeth. "It sounds to me like you could be demiromantic, demisexual—when you don't feel those attractions until you've established a strong emotional connection first."

That...that made sense. So much sense. But: "Isn't that being abstinent?"

Maca shook her head. "If you're abstinent, you feel the attraction and desire but choose not to act on it. If you're demi, you don't feel the desire *at all* until you hit that certain point."

This revelation almost knocked Mariana off her feet. This was a *thing*. She wasn't *broken* just because she didn't fit society's expectations. "Yes. That's it. That's exactly it."

Despite a smile, Maca covered a yawn with one hand. "I'm glad to help, but I work in the morning, so I need to sleep."

Once the video call ended, Mariana opened the bedroom doors to throw her arms around her husband. He hugged her back, though obviously confused. She didn't want to verbalize what had brought on the epiphany, why she realized she could want someone at all—he'd promised he didn't see her that way, so if she admitted he was the reason she knew she could have romantic feelings, it would make things awkward. Not that she wanted to be in an actual relationship anyway until she got her life together. She might have feelings, but she didn't love him, and that was for the best. Love had to wait until she got her life together, until she felt like an adult. Why bring someone into her life permanently if she wasn't offering them the best version of herself?

Still, she couldn't keep him out of the loop.

"The romance—dating—feelings. I'm not broken," she whispered into the crook of his neck. "It's okay that I don't get crushes. I'm not a freak. *I'm not broken*."

He kissed the side of her head. "I never thought you were, *cariño*."

Chapter Fifteen

In Which Santiago Starts a Team

SEPTEMBER

CUTEST WIFE IN HISTORY: *Hey, love of my life*

CUTEST WIFE IN HISTORY: *Guess what you get today*

BEST HUSBAND EVER: *A puppy???*

CUTEST WIFE IN HISTORY: *I wish. No, lasagna*

BEST HUSBAND EVER: *LASAGNA*

BEST HUSBAND EVER: *FOR REAL??*

CUTEST WIFE IN HISTORY: *I'm making it rn*

BEST HUSBAND EVER: *I will get home so fast*

BEST HUSBAND EVER: *Wait*

BEST HUSBAND EVER: *There's a yard sale*

CUTEST WIFE IN HISTORY: *Don't do it*

BEST HUSBAND EVER: *I'm doing it*

CUTEST WIFE IN HISTORY: *NO*

BEST HUSBAND EVER: *YES*

In the afternoon sunlight streaming through the kitchen window, Mariana stirred the meat sauce for tonight's lasagna and laughed at her mother-in-law's pun over video call on her tablet. "That joke actually works in English too. *Purr*-gatory."

"How's your béchamel coming along?" Lola peered at her screen. "I only see the meat."

"Béchamel?"

"The white sauce? Milk, flour, butter, spices?"

"Oh, my recipe doesn't have that. I make a ricotta cheese mixture." Mariana held that bowl up to the camera.

"We should trade recipes! Send me yours, and I'll send you mine, and we can make each other's over a video call. Actually, I think Santiago has mine. You should be able to get it from him." Lola's breath started coming short, and she had to pause to catch it.

Mariana stilled her stirring, her smile falling away. "Are you okay?"

Of course, she wasn't. Lola still needed her surgery, but they couldn't schedule it until they could afford a full-time caretaker for afterward. But they couldn't pay a caretaker until Mariana's inheritance came in—and they were still counting down the days until they hit that oh-so-important six-month mark.

"I know I'm a literal ocean away," Mariana continued, "but is there anything I can do? Anything at all?"

Lola mustered a smile. "I'm as good as I'm going to be, all things considered. But thank you."

A rhythmic bounce-bounce-bounce outside the apartment drew nearer until the door opened. One knee raised, Santiago snatched a soccer ball out of the air. Mariana set her stirring spoon down to applaud his feat of grace and dexterity.

He took a bow. "Thank you. Do you want to play later? I got it for a dollar at that yard sale."

"I'm garbage at athletics, but I'll play with you if you want. Come say hi to your mom."

He looked around. "Where is she?"

Mariana gestured to the tablet on the counter beside the stove. Santiago trotted into the kitchen and switched to Spanish. "Hi, Mamá! What are you and Mariana talking about?"

Lola smiled at her son. "Our respective lasagna recipes, currently. Do you still have mine?"

"I think I wrote it down in my recipe book, yeah."

While Mariana laid out the cooked lasagna noodles in the pan, Santiago bounced his soccer ball from knee to knee, showing off for his mother. And eventually, he got around to what he was even more excited about.

"I want to make a kids' soccer team. Like I had in Madrid."

His mom beamed. "Oh, that would be so fun!"

He'd searched the requirements online and found that to join the Northern Virginia Youth Soccer Association, he'd have to take a course in Fredericksburg to earn an American coaching license, plus get a background check done.

"Nice!" Mariana liked to watch soccer games, although she wasn't talented herself. "We don't know that many kids though. How are you going to get players together?"

She'd forgotten, however, that when he'd coached in Spain, Santiago's sheer persistence and enthusiasm had almost doubled the size of his team there. So, in the following weeks, he used that same focus and had spoken to his students who had younger siblings, to the families at Mass on Sunday, to the couples corralling their kids as they ran yard sales. With puppy-dog eyes and promises of head massages, he'd also convinced Mariana to ask around her parents' church.

Once he had scrounged up enough soccer-enthused children, he hit up the local association to join the tournaments and game schedules for the other teams in the area. He had more than enough players, and he'd managed to squeeze his team in on the very last day of sign-ups. When he came back out to the car, Mariana gave him a double high five.

"How about some coffee to celebrate?"

When they arrived at a nearby coffee shop, she looked for the restroom but stopped to tug at his arm. "Hey, if you order before I get back, can you get mine too?"

"Sure." He started to walk toward the register.

He trotted along to catch up as she rounded the corner to the self-checkout. "What about that dinosaur oatmeal you like?"

"Was it on the list?"

He screwed up his mouth. "No."

"Then we aren't buying it."

A baby in a cart, wearing green truck pajamas and with fluffy white-blond hair, stared at them as they passed. Mariana beamed and waved at him; the little guy grinned and waved both his chubby arms.

She cooed. "Aww, hi! You're a happy one, huh?"

He made babbling noises.

"Oh, you've got things to say! So talkative! Tell me more." She bent closer to listen intently. Santiago couldn't take his eyes off her. *So sweet.*

The baby burbled with delight at the conversation.

His mom laughed. "He's a talker, all right."

"Yes, you are, little buddy!" Mariana straightened and beamed at the mom. "He's absolutely precious."

Smiling, Santiago wiggled his fingers at the baby, who bounced happily in his seat, that fluff of blond hair bobbing with him. "What a cutie."

They continued past the mom and baby, and Mariana's purse sitting in the baby seat of their cart suddenly felt obvious. He wasn't in any position to have kids right now, but he wanted them eventually, and fake-marrying his best friend for two years wasn't getting him any closer to parenthood.

Unless...

He stared at the cart, imagining how Mariana would be with a child of her own. Of *their* own. Carefully dressing a little girl to go grocery shopping with them, caring for her chaotic curls, reading her picture books about history. Sweet and caring and utterly loving. His insides twisted. She would be a great mom, despite her worries about not being "adult" enough.

He'd looked up the usual questions for immigration interviews so he could prepare for the next one. They would likely ask about their future plans, their *family* plans, like how many children they planned to have. They hadn't talked about it yet, not in terms of what they'd say if asked.

This wasn't what they'd agreed to. They had a marriage of convenience, nothing more. But it was hard to imagine spending his life with anyone else, and the more he pictured it, the more he liked it—the idea of starting a real family with Mariana.

As they packed their groceries into the trunk, Mariana glanced his way. "You know that baby in there? I was thinking..."

His heart leapt. *She was thinking about me too?*

"The USCIS-interview people are probably going to ask about our plans for kids. And regular people will ask, too, more likely than not, because no one knows how to mind their own business."

Santiago glanced at her as he pushed some bags farther back. "What do we tell them?" Not that he'd been picturing a life together, a real life, creating a family. That was staying safe and unspoken.

She leaned against the left taillight. "Well, do you still want two kids? I mean, not immediately, but at some point?" He'd told her that long ago, back when he'd first started a soccer team in Spain.

He shut the trunk and nodded. "It was cool to have a built-in friend, even if we fought sometimes. And you want minimum two, right?"

"Yeah. I've always been jealous of my friends who have siblings." She flashed a playful grin. "Like you, ya jerk."

He grinned back, pushing aside the tiny disappointment that she hadn't been thinking of him the way he was thinking of her. "Then we can stick with the truth. We both want at least two kids. Easy answer."

It wasn't so easy to keep himself from taking her hand as she drove them home, as he stared out the window and pictured what their two kids might look like. What names they might choose. Which child might take after which parent more. Mariana as a mother, cradling babies of their own. How was he supposed to survive being married to her when it was so close to what he wanted, yet so far?

He was so caught up in the parental thoughts that it startled him when Mariana touched him on the shoulder. "Hey, we're home."

Indeed, they were parked in front of the apartment building. He blew out a breath and unbuckled his seat belt. "Sorry, I zoned out."

"You really did." Mariana laughed lightly. "What were you thinking about?"

You, and how much I want to make a family with you. "Um, my soccer kids. They're doing really well, and our first game is coming up this weekend."

"How's Embry's sister Joy? Is she doing okay for you?"

"Oh, she's been great. Yesterday at practice, she helped one of the other kids with his kicks. I almost died of cuteness." Which was true, but not what he'd been thinking about.

"Awwww." Mariana placed a hand over her heart. "Kids are adorable."

"Yeah, for real." *Well, honestly, I was thinking about yours. Ours.* He unbuckled his seat belt. To bring it up or not to bring it up... Then she was gone, walking around the car to get groceries out of the trunk.

Leave it alone. So he opened his door and helped with the groceries and applauded when she carried 300 bags at once, and he said nothing about the thoughts that followed him into his dreams.

*

Santiago had Monday off work, but Mariana liked it when he brought her coffee in the mornings, so he rose at the usual time and brought her a mug in bed. She smiled sleepily up at him, snuggled in the bedsheets. "M'ning."

His chest warming, he held her mug out of her reach. "Sit up, *cariño*."

With a grumble, she pushed herself upright. Only then did he pass her the life-giving drink. He climbed back into bed beside her to read, sneaking peeks at her as she slowly woke up. The light came on in her dark-brown eyes, her lashes fluttering with each creamer-laden sip. When she brushed away a stray droplet from her lips with her thumb, he snapped his gaze away from the lush curve of her mouth and back down to his book.

Eventually, she got up and started getting dressed, and he rolled onto his side to turn his back toward her. The soft rustling of her rifling through the closet's contents and slipping on her chosen clothes sent him dozing back off into sleep. He dreamed that she came back to the bed and slid under the covers with him, tracing her fingertips along the side of his face before leaning in and kissing him. He was aware it was a dream, and that had to be why he pulled her closer and swept his palms over all those tempting curves, licking deep into her mouth the way he hadn't since their unexpected kiss at the wedding reception, shivering at the noise of pleasure she made...

The front door slammed, and he jerked upright in bed, his book falling onto the floor.

Mariana stomped through the living room and into the kitchen, where she threw open the fridge and began shoving around its contents.

Santi poked his head out of the bedroom. *"Tesoro,* you doing okay?" The clock on the microwave read 7:55 a.m. She should've been at work by now.

"I'm gonna kick something!"

Yikes. "Is it a Cheryl day?"

"No. First, I spilled coffee on my dress and had to change, then I got halfway there and realized I forgot my lunch—but I can't find it! At this rate I'm gonna be late for work!"

He pointed to the yellow container sitting beside the stove. "Isn't that your lunch box on the counter?"

Mariana looked where he was pointing, then sighed. "Yep, that's it." She snatched it up. "Well, see you later. Hope your day is going better than mine." She didn't wait for a response, but strode back out the door. Moments later, her car revved and sped out of the parking lot.

Since I'm awake, I might as well use the time. He made his way around the apartment and made a list of the housework that needed to be done. Besides dishes, Mariana had forgotten to clean this week, so onto the list went vacuuming and laundry and dusting and scrubbing the bathroom and mopping the tile floor. All the things she hated doing, but they didn't bother him. He liked feeling like he was contributing. Since his touch sent budgets up in flames, she took care of the money, and he took care of the apartment. Plus, if he had time, he could have dinner ready when she got home, which always perked her up.

But first, the bathroom. He tossed the dirty towels in the washer, then grabbed the foaming bleach cleaner and set about scrubbing the toilet. Once the porcelain gleamed, he switched to a different sponge and wiped down the sink. He washed out the bath with the foaming cleaner. He spritzed the mirror with Windex and wiped that down. Then he sprayed the floor with a multipurpose cleaner and scrubbed that. Sparkling bathroom, check.

As he moved on to vacuuming, his mind slipped back to Mariana. The poor thing had had quite the morning. *Hopefully coming home to a clean apartment and a good dinner will cheer her up.* His heart clenched at the memory of how upset she'd been. How could he improve her day? A back rub, maybe?

His phone chimed with an incoming text.

YELENA MONTALBAN: *Would you and Mariana want to come to the gym with me? I have free guest passes with my membership.*

SANTIAGO DE LOS REYES MARTÍNEZ: *Mariana's working today, but I'm free if you're cool with just me.*

YELENA MONTALBAN: *Oh right, it's just a school holiday*

He texted back a thumbs-up, and she sent him the address.

Once he'd put the vacuum away, he changed into workout clothes and sent a quick *heading your way!* text to Yelena on his way out the door. He drove to the local gym, where she was waiting for him outside the front doors, her hand blocking the sun out of her eyes.

Santiago followed Yelena inside, and she punched her thumb toward the treadmills. "I was planning to run today. Is that good with you, or did you want to do something else?"

"Running works." He was out of shape, but he'd do his best. He needed to get back in shape if he was going to have a soccer team, after all. "What made you ask me, anyway?"

Yelena shrugged. "I do best when I have someone else with me. Usually, I go with my roommate or my cousin, but they're both out of town for a football game today. And I knew you were off work, for obvious reasons."

Santiago raised his eyebrows and smiled. "So I'm your backup?"

Yelena grinned. "Yeah, but, like, in a cool way."

They picked out two treadmills across from a TV playing the news. Santiago stuck his water bottle in the holder and started stretching. Once he felt sufficiently warmed up, he started walking on the treadmill.

Yelena jogged beside him, her strawberry-blonde ponytail swinging merrily. "Do y'all have a gym you go to?"

"We probably should, but no. Mariana and I aren't great about going to the gym."

"If you decide you wanna join one, this place is great. They have a lot of exercise classes, team and partner recreational sports, all that jazz."

"Do you play sports?"

"I play tennis here, and I attend about four different exercise classes every week." Yelena rolled her eyes. "Oh my God, there's this one girl who's in all my classes, and she drives me absolutely up the wall. Like, in spin class, she's so fast it's the worst."

"She's so...fast?"

"Yeah! I was the fastest person in the class before she joined, and now she's blowing me out of the water. Ugh!" Despite her words, a smile tugged at Yelena's mouth. "It's the first time anyone's been a real challenge here."

"Do I know her? What's her name?"

"I don't know. I haven't heard it yet, but I'm determined to find out."

"Okay, well, if you find out who she is, let me know and I'll wingman for you."

"Ha! I don't need a wingman. I need to get faster so I can be number one again." She slowed down and took a swig from her water bottle. "Besides, what kind of wingman would you be? I don't think I've heard how you and Mariana got together, so you might be worse than me."

"Me and Mariana? I'm the romantic one between the two of us. I mean, that's how we met."

"Yeah? What's the story?"

"Did you ever watch *The Frat House Gang*?"

She laughed. "Oh my God, yes. That show was the best. Agrok was hilarious."

"Okay, well, you know Seraphina and Ainsley?"

"The bard and the hometown carpenter, yeah. Unpopular opinion—they were totally in love."

"*Thank you!*" Santiago threw his hands in the air and almost tripped over his own feet. "Sorry. Anyway, I had a blog back then. And I posted venting about their love, and it was all in Spanish about a show in English, so I expected to fly under the radar." He shook his head, smiling despite himself. "One of my otherwise quiet followers came out of nowhere to yell at me. She sent me a private message with 'FIRST OF ALL'"—he made air quotes—"in all caps and lectured me about how I didn't appreciate their friendship."

Yelena grinned. "That's amazing."

He couldn't wipe the smile off his face. "We debated back and forth forever. I never convinced her. She cared so much." Even before he'd known her name, he'd known her vibrancy.

As the conversation had continued, he learned more about Mariana, agreed to disagree for the sake of talking to her about other things too. He offered to switch entirely to English, but she wanted to practice her Spanish, so they shifted back and forth between the two. Eventually, they told each other their names. They introduced each other to more shows, more books, and even when *The Frat House Gang* ended, they intertwined further.

They sent postcards, birthday gifts, Christmas letters for years. They spoke every day by text, weekly by video calls. Then he'd seen her in the airport.

"I knew it was her." He stared at the treadmill control panel as he remembered, smile growing stupid with affection. "She was the most beautiful thing I'd ever seen."

Yelena watched him with a wry smile. "You've got it bad. It's adorable. Okay, I will officially allow you to be my wingman."

After they finished working out, Santiago bid Yelena goodbye and grabbed a peanut butter and chocolate smoothie from the gym snack bar before heading out. He raced home, showered, and started on *olla podrida* for dinner. The beans and the pork had been soaking overnight, so the next step was to season and cook the beans. He diced the onion, garlic, and half a green pepper, and stir-fried them with some bacon. In a large pan he cooked the other meats and the rest of the vegetables. The meat needed to cook a few hours, so he let it sit while he got back to cleaning.

By the time Mariana got home from work, the apartment smelled like spicy stew. Santiago was folding laundry on the couch and looking up puns on his phone that might make her laugh. When she walked in the door, he beamed and minimized the dad-jokes website. "How was your day? Did it get better?"

She sighed and dropped her purse. "Not at all, but dinner smells amazing. Thank you for doing that. How was your day off?"

"I cleaned, mostly." He cleared a space on the couch and motioned for her to come sit in front of him. "Come here. I'll rub your shoulders."

"Oh, man, you really are the best husband ever." She sank into the cushion and smiled in relief as he began to massage her tense shoulders. "Thanks, *amado*."

"Of course." He gently rubbed under the edges of her shoulder blades. As an afterthought he added, "I also ran to the gym with Yelena. You remember her? From work."

Mariana stiffened under his touch.

He immediately lightened his massage. "Sorry, did I hit a knot?"

"No, you're fine. Yeah, I remember her."

But she was still tense. Why? Maybe she wished he'd waited until she could go too.

Guilt flashed through his chest for not including his best friend. "Sorry I didn't invite you to come with us. We went around noon, and you were at work."

She shrugged. "It's fine. Whatever."

Hoping to soften her up, he gently rubbed her neck.

She sighed and hung her head. "That feels so good. You have magic hands."

He squashed down the thought of how else his magic hands could make her feel good. "I ran on the treadmill. That part was horrible. But it was nice to hang out with Yelena outside of work. She's cool. You'd like her."

"Mm-hmm."

He wasn't sure if he was allowed to share about Yelena's hate-crush on the other woman in her classes, so he skipped over that. "And the *olla podrida* will be ready soon. I haven't made it for you before, so you'll have to tell me if you like it or not."

Mariana flashed him a smile. "I'm sure it'll taste great, as long as you didn't pour thirty pounds of salt onto it like that one mac and cheese—"

"It wasn't thirty pounds! It was just a little too much!"

"Yeah, and Gothmog was a *little* obsessed with impressing Traylin."

He stuck out his tongue. "So what happened today? Tell me everything."

She sighed and rolled her shoulders. "You already know I spilled coffee on my dress and was late to work because I forgot my lunch."

He massaged her upper arms. "Right. Go on."

"My boss dropped a bunch of work into my lap this morning that was due by the end of the day, as if I didn't have anything else to do. Then a meeting ran long, so I didn't get to eat my lunch until almost two. *Then* the intern accidentally deleted all my updates to this one spreadsheet where we manage all our museum exhibits and restoration projects, and tried to play like I hadn't updated anything in the first place. And *then* Cheryl called…" She trailed off into a sigh. "Right there."

Santiago circled his thumb over the knot, working it out without pressing too hard. "Well, I can tell you something that might make you feel better."

"Yeah?"

"Yeah. You should wear glasses while doing math." He paused for effect. "It improves division."

A surprised laugh bubbled out of her, and she twisted to grin at him. "Did you look up puns just to make me feel better?"

Absolutely. And I'd do it again in a heartbeat. "I would never. But I've got another one if it did help."

She rested her head against him. "It did."

"My friend suspects I'm stealing her kitchen utensils. That's a whisk I'm willing to take."

Mariana laughed again. "Beautiful." The smile lingered on her lips, and he beamed, the light in her face warming him from the inside out.

*

Saturday morning was the first game of Santiago's season. Across the soccer field, he shouted encouragement and direction at the kids barreling toward their opponent's goal. From her folding chair on the parents' side, Mariana cupped her hands around her mouth and cheered them on.

It meant so much to her that he'd had a good turnout for the first game—it was easy enough to drop children at practice once or twice and pick them up afterward, but something else entirely for the parents to take over an hour out of their Saturday to sit and watch and cheer when they could be doing something more important.

People always say that time with your kids is the most important use of your time. She wanted kids of her own, but how would she handle that kind of emotion? As she watched the players run around, all knobby knees and pudgy legs and baby faces, her chest ached with the desire to have a child of her own to cradle and coo over and raise into a respectable human being.

Without conscious thought, her gaze darted to Santi, and unbidden, she pictured a tiny version of him in her arms, all messy hair and impossibly dark eyes and silly sense of humor and maybe her own round cheeks. The tiny thing would almost certainly have bad vision, given the genetics. A tiny toddler in glasses.

She was staring at Santiago.

With a quick shake of her head, she looked back to the game in time to see the ball sail into the goal. Santi's kids leapt into the air and shoved one another around in celebration, and she jumped out of her seat to add a whoop to their noise. The parents around her yelled in support as both teams trotted back to the center line for kickoff.

The now-offense apparently felt they had a point to prove. In the onslaught, one kid took a cleat to the calf and skidded across the grass for several yards. Though he made no sound, he struggled long enough to get up that the ref blew her whistle. As the designated team "medic," Mariana grabbed her first aid kit, rose from her folding chair, and hurried over to where Santiago was helping the boy to his feet—two scraped knees and a monstrous bruise already forming on his leg. Once he was seated on the bench, Santiago sent a replacement onto the field so the game could resume, and he shot her a glance before returning his attention to the game.

She knelt in front of the boy. "That was quite a tumble, bud."

"It's not that bad," he sniffed, but his eyes gleamed with restrained tears, and he'd skinned his right elbow too. Thin lines of blood were forming at all three wounds. *Sana, sana, culito de rana.*

"Yeah, you're gonna be fine." She patted him on the arm and fished through her kit. "Let's get you taped up so you can get back out there."

Nodding, he extended his arm and legs. When she swiped an antiseptic towelette over the first scrape, he yelped and gritted his teeth. "I hate that."

"You did it, though!" She gave him a high five. "We got that out of the way, and it's smooth sailing from here. Ready for the next one?" She waited for him to clench his tiny fists and nod stiffly before moving on.

Once she'd gently cleaned the dirt and grass off the wounds, she smoothed bandages over them and declared him good to go. "Let Coach de los Reyes know if your bruise hurts worse, okay?"

The boy nodded and darted off to beg to play again.

Kids.

These weren't hers, though—she had to remember that. They weren't hers, and Santiago wasn't hers, and she had no chance of having a child anytime soon, not until the visa police stopped watching them with suspicion and she and Santi got the amicable divorce they'd agreed upon. Not that it mattered, of course. They'd still be friends. She swallowed and looked away from her husband as he ruffled his thick black hair and called out to the distracted goalie.

They won the game 6–5, with only one more player who needed scrapes cleaned up. Mariana and Santiago passed out Capri Sun pouches and oversized Rice Krispies treats to all the kids, who were grinning from ear to ear with the high of their first victory. As the kids dispersed, a few stray parents came up to thank him for starting the team. He beamed and thanked them in turn for their support. When the field had mostly emptied, he wound his arm around Mariana, pulled her close, and pressed a kiss to her temple.

"Thanks for being here."

She closed her eyes and smiled, threading her own arm around his waist. "Anytime. It was fun."

"If the historian thing doesn't work out, you could try out nursing."

That made her laugh. "Yes, my ability to apply Neosporin and Band-Aids definitely qualifies me for hospital work." She thumped him on the side. "You stink, by the way. We need to go home so you can shower." Sweat darkened his shirt from pregame practicing, following the kids up and down their half of the field, and jumping and cheering.

"What, you don't like my manly fragrance?" He stretched dramatically, opening his armpit.

She bent backward to avoid the stench. "Put that thing back where it came from or so help me...!" Her awkward movement loosened his grip, and she tripped away from him before using the momentum to flee.

"You can't outrun me!" His cleated footsteps tore up the grass behind her. "I play soccer!"

"Yeah, but I'm motivated!" And she did manage to stay ahead of him for thirty seconds, zigzagging back and forth to throw him off, before he caught up. His arms looped around her waist, and he tugged her back into himself. She thought they'd fall over, but instead, he spun her around so that her feet actually left the ground, and he took a few extra steps to slow before he set her down. Rather than let go of her, though, he pressed closer to smear his sweaty shirt against her tee.

She wiggled in a fruitless effort to free herself, panting from the sprint even as she laughed. "Now I reek, too, you jerk."

He buried his face in her neck and took an exaggerated whiff. "Ha-ha, perfect. That means you can't complain now."

"I can and I will." She reached up to muss his hair. "Let me go, Stinky, or you're gonna be walking home."

"Well, that's mean." He released his grip on her, and although she wanted to air out, she almost leaned back against him. Grinning, he changed the subject. "Can we get lunch on the way back? I'm starving. You have starved me."

He was starving her, too, but in a completely different way. She tried to focus on the actual request. "Didn't we already go out to eat this week?" They'd merged their bank accounts for appearance's sake, but in reality, they went halfsies on rent and bills and groceries, and they'd agreed on certain rules to avoid overspending. *Agreed* here meant that Santi tried to find loopholes and she tried to close them.

"No, that was Sunday. Spanish weeks start on Monday. So it was last week." He smiled winningly.

"That's not how the budget works." She rolled her eyes.

He shrugged, undeterred. "It could be."

Biting her lip, she came up with a compromise. "Okay, how about this... We get a large fry on the drive back, and cook a healthy dinner when we get home."

"Now we're talking!" He high-fived her with an open smile and followed her to the car.

While they sat in the drive-through, they played rock paper scissors to decide that Santiago would pay for the treat that day. Mariana, as the driver, handed the takeout bag to him for safekeeping and pulled back onto the main road.

"Ready?" He picked out the crispiest fry (her favorite) and placed it in her open mouth so she could keep both hands on the wheel. The delicious taste of potato and salt flooded her tongue, and she hummed in appreciation. Once she'd chewed and swallowed, he offered her another.

She could've waited ten minutes and eaten when they got home, but something about the intimacy of sharing the side dish on the road warmed her heart. The gentle way he offered each fry, the warmth of his touch when he brushed a crumb off the corner of her lips. Gradually, he upgraded to offering two at a time, then three. Then, while her mouth was full, her nerd of a husband accidentally shoved another handful of fries in.

Her cheeks bulging, she tilted her head back in a futile effort to let gravity sort out the overabundance of fries. "Help!" she garbled through the food, trying to chew with little success.

"Sorry! Here, I got it." He reached over and took the wheel for her so she could focus on not dying by fry overload.

Finally, she managed to choke them down, and she smacked him playfully. "Thanks for that."

"I thought you wanted more!"

She eased to a stop at a red light and mock-scowled at him. "What part of 'my mouth is full' did you interpret as 'please put more fries in here'?"

"I'm sorry. Please forgive me and my overambitious fry-dealing." He took her hand and kissed her knuckles. Her cheeks heated at the intimacy, at the way his lips lingered on her skin, at the way it felt like everything she knew it couldn't mean.

She ached to kiss him, but she wasn't ready, was she? It couldn't happen yet. She wasn't together enough. But she couldn't pull away either, not when he was so close and so dear to her, and maybe a small kiss wouldn't hurt. She leaned across the center console, and she lifted her hand to bring his mouth to hers, and before she knew what she was doing, her lips grazed his. His palm came up to cup the side of her face, holding her close, and her lips parted as she—

The car behind them honked.

Mariana startled out of the kiss. Green light. *Oh.* Face hot, she waved sorry and sped up too fast to make up for being distracted.

But what a distraction it had been.

Chapter Sixteen

In Which Santiago Goes All Out

OCTOBER

Tree frogs called to one another in the darkness outside, stars gleaming against the clear, ink-dark sky. In bed, Santiago worked on lesson plans by the light of his bedside lamp. Mariana had turned hers off hours ago and was now passed out, snuggled up like a burrito in the covers. Only one hand poked out, her fingertips lax on Santi's side as if she'd fallen asleep making sure he was still with her.

How can she breathe under there? Tenderly he lifted the comforter off her face. Her full lips were parted, their curve hinting at a smile. Still asleep, she nuzzled her face into the sheets and sighed. Her fingers curled into his T-shirt.

He liked what they had—whatever this was. Not lovers, but not simply friends either. No friend he'd ever had would've sacrificed as much for him, and for his family, as Mari had. She treated them like they were her own mother and sister.

And no roommate would ever measure up to her. Sure, he and Mariana each had their pitfalls in terms of adult living. He couldn't maintain a budget to save his soul, and he refused to give up his weekly mac-and-cheese night. But she balanced him out, and he was learning how to work with her lack of interest in housekeeping and cooking, even enjoy them in a playful sense.

It warmed him to ease her out of bad moods and make a real dinner instead of her frozen meals and surprise her with a clean apartment when she'd forgotten to clean it herself. In fact, it was becoming easier and easier to imagine doing this long term. To stay with her longer than the visa supervision required—longer than friendship required, even. To introduce her as his, and mean it.

He could have stared at her for years, savoring the sweetness. And a *sappy* slow smile worked its way across his face while his insides warmed to bursting. He wanted to bottle this moment, save it for the times when he doubted his life choices. Because this woman—flaws and all—this woman made him want to stay right here with her for the rest of his life. She was a house in a storm, a peaceful recharge where everyone else drained him. He might return to Spain one day, but he wouldn't enjoy himself without her at his side.

This realization hit him like a punch to the stomach, knocking the breath from his lungs so that all he could do was stare at his best friend nestled in bed beside him.

He loved Mariana.

And he wouldn't be able to live with himself if he let her go without having done everything in his power to win her heart in return.

*

On Monday morning, Mariana walked into her office and stopped short. Resplendent red roses bloomed beside her computer.

Santi?

He hadn't said anything—they hadn't conferenced on the flowers as part of the charade. And these couldn't have been cheap. She would have helped pay for them if she'd known.

Cheryl stopped in to drop off some final paperwork for the James Farmer exhibit, and she pursed her lips at the bouquet. "How...extravagant."

Mariana couldn't disagree. Yet the sumptuous colors and soft petals and sweet smell enveloped her in a reminder of her husband all day long, and she warmed with pleasure that he'd thought of her—well, of the gesture for her as his temporary wife.

She asked him about it at dinner, and he nailed her with the dimples. "I thought you would like them."

Her skin buzzed even though he couldn't mean it the way it sounded. "Her" as his convenient wife, not "her" as *her*. And she wasn't interested in making this an actual relationship anyway. To press the point home for herself: "I'll go halfsies with you on it. How much was it?"

He laughed and leaned over to kiss her on the temple. "No, *cariño*, it was a gift."

"But I—"

"*No.*" The word was warm, fond. But an unreadable emotion flickered in his eyes. "And you're not allowed to bring them home either. You spend more of your day at work, so if you leave them there, you'll see them more."

Now *that* rationale she could get behind. "Can do."

The surprise roses, she understood. They shouted for attention in her office, so she could write off the romance as being for the benefit of their audience. She couldn't do that for the carton of her favorite ice cream that appeared in the freezer, or his unprompted offer to massage her shoulders, or the lingering compliments murmured so low and husky her pulse jumped.

The attention seemed unnecessary given that it was only between the two of them...yet she didn't tell him to stop. "Do you know why he's going all out?" she asked Maca during their next one-on-one call.

Maca shrugged and blinked at her innocently. "Couldn't tell you. My brother is an unknowable force of nature."

*

"I know exactly what you're doing!" On camera, Maca jabbed her finger toward Santiago.

He feigned confusion. "Doing what? I'm sitting here, talking to you."

"Yeah, right." She called him a string of unflattering names unfit for polite company, or even moderately impolite company. Once she finished, though, she smoothed back an errant curl and, of all things, grinned. "It took you long enough."

With a sigh he admitted defeat. "Just say it and get it over with."

She flicked the back of her index finger out from under her chin. "I told you so!"

"Yep. Thanks."

"I told you you liked her. Right from the beginning."

"I remember."

"Mariana told me about the roses. Way to go for the most cliché option. You should have called me for advice sooner."

He rolled his eyes. "She loved the roses. You're not the only person in this family who knows how to flirt." At least, that had been the case before Mariana turned him inside out.

Mock-pensively Maca tapped her cheek. "That's funny; I must have dreamed the time I had to pull you into the bedroom and tell you how to flirt with your girlfriend."

Ignoring this, he moved back to the topic at hand. "So, yes. I love her. I want her to love me. I thought it was only fair to tell you."

*

"I will tell you—" Maca leaned toward her screen as if to let her sister-in-law in on a secret. "—that he is not subtle. What's there is what's there."

"Oh." Mariana deflated. "I see. So, if it looks like he's stepped up his acting, that's what it is."

"Or..."

"Not that it matters." Mariana straightened her necklace. "I decided a long time ago that I'm not dating until I have my life together. So really, it's all moot."

Maca stared at her in abject horror. "Is this a test from the Lord?"

*

"What exactly are you going for?" she asked her brother.

He knew the answer to that question at least. "I want her to fall in love with me." He ran a hand through his hair. "This way, she'll know how I feel. Eventually."

She rubbed her temples. "And you plan to throw romance at her until she figures it out? The other person I had to pull into a bedroom and tell how to flirt?"

"...Yes." It sounded ridiculous when she said it like that.

She put her head in her hands. "You two morons are going to kill me."

*

"He's a good guy," Mariana sighed. "For real, he's amazing. It's not his fault that I'm...that I started..." She trailed off, unable to voice the thought.

Unfortunately, Maca's eyes gleamed with interest at the unfinished idea. "It's not his fault you what?"

"Nothing." Mariana hastened to move on. "My point is, I'm not ready for a relationship."

The deflection was not subtle. "If you started..." Maca pointedly trailed off. "...then you should tell him."

Stomach clenching with anxiety, Mariana looked away. "I can't tell him. My life isn't together enough to add a real relationship to the mix."

"Maybe if you talk to him, you'll figure it out."

"I can't. It would be too much."

Maca threw her hands in the air. "Fine! Do what you want! Don't blame me if you two never resolve this."

Still, the attention was sweet. The next morning, Mariana checked her work voicemail with a smile on her face as she fingered the petals of her bouquet. Three messages. One from Cheryl, demanding why she hadn't picked up the phone, belatedly adding that she'd emailed a form for Mariana to sign. The second from Omar, confirming their meeting that afternoon. The third... Her smile faded.

Her boss's voice was cold, even through the distortion of technology. "I was reviewing the exhibit spreadsheet, and the Farmer exhibit is going to run us over budget if you can't find a way to cut costs. The interactive part will have to go if you can't."

How had the costs run up that much? In her estimates before they started, there had been plenty of room. Wiggle room, even. She'd planned the extra space just in case— How had they run through it all already? All of it and then some?

"Cheryl pointed out that having a section just for kids excluded the adults, and we don't want to alienate any visitors."

Mariana almost choked. The interactivity wasn't excluding adults. Adults could use it just as much as children. The goal was to help people interact with history in their own way, on their own terms. But Cheryl thought interactive exhibits were "childish," according to their last meeting, because she didn't like them and had decided somewhere along the line that because she was an adult, all other adults shared her opinions.

She called Cheryl back first, since she had two orders of business to discuss. "I signed the form and sent it back your way. But why are you telling Joe that the interactive section is kids-only?"

"Because it might as well be." The older woman sniffed. "No self-respecting adult participates in interactive exhibits at museums."

"I do, and my husband does," Mariana pointed out.

"As I said."

Ooooh. This woman. "I know plenty of adults who take part in those exhibits when given the opportunity." Mariana forced her voice to stay calm and even. "It's not exclusive to children. It helps all the guests see the exhibit from a more personal perspective. It makes it real."

"If you say so."

"Next on my to-do list is talking with Joe about why we should keep the interactive section in the exhibit. I'd really appreciate it if you had my back on this."

Cheryl cleared her throat. "I can keep my opinions to myself, if that's what you're asking. But I thought everyone's input mattered. Not these days, I guess."

"Thank you." Mariana let Cheryl go and called Joe. "Hi, I wanted to follow up on your call about the Farmer exhibit. Why are you looking at removing the interactive portion? It's not kids-only, it's open for everyone—"

"It's a financial thing." He sighed. "Another project is eating into your funds."

A fist closed around her throat. Her plans, up in smoke. "But we had a budget—"

"It's just the way it is right now. Everything's communal."

How had that happened and no one told her? No one had warned her that her first major project was being dissolved for someone else's use? *Everything's communal, my ass.* She'd bet her next paycheck that if she asked to use another exhibit's budget for her project, the lines would suddenly be hard and fast. But she couldn't say that to her boss. She fanned herself with one hand. "So what can I do to keep the Farmer exhibit as planned? How bad is it?"

"Listen, Mariana, you're down a thousand dollars."

Her jaw dropped. Her hand stilled. An entire grand was gone?

"Cut costs somewhere else or lose the interactive station. Those are your options. If you can't do it, tell me, and I'll hand leadership of the project over to Cheryl. She has more experience with this sort of thing."

Right. She was totally about to give Cheryl her hard-earned first major project. But how was she supposed to come up with that kind of money? Run the world's most historically accurate bake sale?

The problem shadowed her all day. When Mariana got home, she threw some vegetables and meat and broth in a saucepan and then moved on to procrasti-baking double-chocolate-chip cookies, which she was elbow-deep in when Santiago walked in the door.

"It smells like diabetes in here," he said happily. It took her a second to decipher his Spanish pronunciation of the cognate.

She waved him off. "If you don't want to die of sugar overload, I'll eat them all myself."

"Oh, no, I'll eat them. When will they be done?"

She made it through dinner without bringing up the work issue, but when the cookies came out, she broke down.

He tapped his fingers against his cheek and muttered about her boss and Cheryl. "That's unbelievable. Of course, you should keep the interactive part. I will fight them."

She laughed. "Thanks, *tesoro*."

"You'll fix it. Don't worry, *amada*. Here." He handed her cookie after cookie ("for medicine"), and she reached over the table to shove one in his mouth too.

Though the problem still loomed, he made it seem smaller, more manageable, and less personal. Less like a personal failure. When they relocated to the couch for a movie, she draped herself over him for cuddles and tried not to think about who would force-feed her cookies after a hard day at work once she was a divorcée living alone.

*

Santiago chatted with Yelena in the teachers' lounge while fresh coffee dribbled into the pot. Inexplicably, no one else had lined up for caffeine in preparation for the after-school meeting in ten minutes; last week's memo called it a "motivational" event.

"Absolutely no chance that he's good?" he begged.

Laughing, she shook her head, then smoothed back a strawberry-blonde curl that had bounced out of place. "I wish. That speaker has said the same thing for the last two years' meetings, and it wasn't helpful the first time."

Santiago covered his face with his hands and groaned. "I'm missing fresh lasagna for this."

She sucked in a knowing breath. *"Mariana's* lasagna?"

She'd gotten an earful the first time Mariana had made it—and the tantalizing smell of the leftovers had backed him up. He heaved a regretful sigh. "It tastes best right out of the oven. I'll have to reheat it—she's eating before she goes out with one of her friends."

Yelena clicked her tongue. "That sucks."

They sat together in the back for the meeting, pretending to take notes on the monotone, repetitive speech until, finally, the teachers were dismissed. Casting each other relieved grins, they made a beeline for the exit. Yelena was faster, though, and made it out before him.

Coming into the apartment, Santiago accidentally hit Mariana with the door. Her yelp had his hands on her before he realized what had happened, looking her over for injury. "I'm so sorry, *querida*, are you okay? Did I hurt you? Are you bleeding?" His worry drummed a fast heartbeat.

Once she'd recovered from the surprise knock, she smiled and ruffled his hair. "I'm fine. It bounced right off my hip." She glanced toward the open door. "It's cold out. I'm not paying to heat the entire street."

He apologized but grinned, nailing her with the dimples she liked. "Come closer—the neighbors are home."

This required no further explanation. Without hesitation she stepped into the doorway and pressed up on her toes to kiss him hello. Out of sheer habit and definitely for no other reason, he licked into her mouth. The taste of chocolate ice cream left no question as to her dessert choice for the day. She grazed her nails against his scalp on her path to cup the back of his neck, and he shivered.

When she pulled away, he almost tugged her back in for more, but the scent of dinner drew him inside.

"Lasagna's on the stove," she said, "and it's only been out of the oven a few minutes."

His jaw dropped in a delighted open smile. "You waited for me? You're the best wife ever."

She winked and blew him a playful kiss. "You bet, *lindo*."

On his way to steal an oversized slice of her perfect meal, he glanced at the fridge calendar he never used. She'd changed the picture—oh, it was October now, that was why. The fifteenth was blocked off in hearts and flowers. He squinted at the note scrawled in the middle: *25 years old!*

Mariana's birthday, barely a week away. He'd confirmed with her parents that they were treating her to brunch, so dinnertime was all his, and he couldn't wait to see her face when she saw where he was taking her. He'd been squirreling away money for a nice dinner in the city, at a restaurant she stared at every time they passed it. The best part: she didn't suspect a thing.

A message in Spanish from Maca popped up on his phone.

BABY SISTER: *Got a second?*

Concerned about the serious tone—namely, the lack of a joke or insult—he replied quickly.

SANTIAGO DE LOS REYES MARTÍNEZ: *Yeah, what do you need?*

She didn't redirect their conversation into a video call, which eased a little of his worry. If anything serious had happened, she would want to look him in the technological eye.

BABY SISTER: *My lease is almost over, and rent is going up. Mamá and I are looking at places closer to her rehab center.*

They wanted to move? How soon were they thinking? Could they even afford it? He chewed the inside of his cheek and hesitated over his answer.

SANTIAGO DE LOS REYES MARTÍNEZ: *When will that be?*

BABY SISTER: *Next month.*

BABY SISTER: *Some flats over there are available and less expensive than the one we're in now. We'd save money on rent AND on traveling to her rehab sessions after the surgery.*

She followed that up with a string of currency emoticons and two hands as if throwing the money in the air.

He appreciated the heads-up about the future change, but was it a heads-up or a request?

> SANTIAGO DE LOS REYES MARTÍNEZ: *Will you need help?*

Maca stayed silent for long enough that he wondered if she'd left the conversation.

> BABY SISTER: *With moving costs and the security deposit, it would take us a while to build up the funds.*

So, yes, they could use help.

But would he? Could he still take care of Mariana if he sent them extra money?

He'd keep sending his usual amount, of course. He would check with Mariana about potentially sending more. If she didn't mind, some of his current budget from each paycheck could go toward the security deposit for his mom and sister. He would remain able to pay his half of all the monthly bills so Mariana never had to front a bill for him. And he already had the money set aside for her birthday plans, so she wouldn't suffer a loss there either. She would remain happy, healthy, and safe in every way he could protect her.

First and foremost, he would protect her.

> SANTIAGO DE LOS REYES MARTÍNEZ: *Don't worry. I should be able to send extra money.*

Chapter Seventeen

In Which Santiago Takes Mariana Out for Her Birthday

OCTOBER

Hopping on one foot, Mariana pulled on her turquoise heel. The new shoes and the new dress—a V-neck cocktail dress, white on top with a yellow-flowered skirt that swirled when she moved—flattered her curves and made her dark skin glow. Probably too summery for mid-October, but she didn't care. She loved the outfit, and she loved how she looked in it, so the world could deal.

Santiago was getting ready in the bathroom, and although she was free to join him, she didn't. She finished up her makeup in the bedroom, then perched in the living room armchair to wait. He hadn't seen this outfit yet—not even on the hanger, much less on her—and she wanted him to have the full effect. She wanted to see the look on his face when he saw her completely dolled up.

Despite being determined to wait on an actual relationship, she wanted him to find her beautiful. Sexy, even. Wanted him to want to run his hands over her body and back her into the bedroom and...

Wait. What now?

Startled by the revelation, she slipped off her perch—and almost twisted her ankle pivoting on the slim heel. She stumbled into a turn but caught herself, arms thrown wide, and of course that was when Santiago stepped into the kitchen and saw her. He stopped short. The look in his eyes was worth every minute of prep.

"You look amazing." The words came out huskily.

She took a step toward him; her breath shivered. He'd taken the time to tame his hair into The Swoop, and the plum button-down... "You clean up good too." Her grin belied the heat inside her.

"We should head out, or we'll be late." They had dinner reservations in Fredericksburg, but he hadn't told her where, just that it was fancy. That likely meant midrange fancy, like Red Lobster or Olive Garden, and they were dressing up for the fun of it. He helped her into the passenger seat of his car, and as he pulled out of the parking lot, he rested his arm over the back of her seat. "How was work? Any progress on the interactive exhibit issue?"

She beamed. "I got some of the contractors to give me a discount to help counterbalance the money that went to whatever other project took my funds. It's not the whole amount, but it's enough that I can keep the interactive part."

He high-fived her with one hand, keeping the other on the wheel. "Good job! I knew you could do it."

The sun had already set by the time they pulled into the restaurant's parking lot, but Mariana gasped. Warm light glowed through the windows of the extravagant interior—and she recognized the swank, even without the lit-up sign reading *1776*. Her jaw dropped with a giant open grin. "Here? No way!"

He beamed. "You've never been here, right?"

"No, I haven't." She wriggled in her seat. "Oh, my gosh. I'm not... We can't... The budget, *cariño*." The protest came out sad and half-hearted. She would have never asked for this place because it was so far out of their league, and she loved that he had thought to bring her here.

Santiago touched a finger to her cheek and turned her head to face him so he could kiss her, lightly enough that their glasses didn't clink together. "No budget. This is on me." He paused, then stole another quick, smiling kiss. "Happy birthday."

Without meaning to, she hummed in pleasure, the sound almost a purr. She considered kissing him longer, but they had a reservation, and she was wearing lipstick, so she let him open her door and took his proffered arm. He walked her to the door, her hand curved into the crook of his elbow. As close as she was, she savored how good he smelled. *So* good.

Maybe she could smudge her lipstick on his mouth once they left the restaurant. For the charade, of course—didn't couples usually get extra intimate on birthdays? It was irrelevant that his smell and his hair and his clothes and his face and his personality made her want to cuddle up close and run her hands all over him. For the first time *ever*.

202 - | Ivy L. James

The hostess asked them to sit as she verified their table was ready. Mariana warmed all over at his thigh pressed against hers and his arm draped behind her shoulders. She didn't *lean* against her fake husband as they waited for their name to be called. That would be too much. But if she didn't move away when he sat closer than he needed to, that was fine. Friends being pals. Plus, marriage.

The hostess finally led them to a secluded two-person table framed by low-burning candles and rich scarlet curtains. At the slight lead of Santi's hand on the small of her back, Mariana slipped into a plush black leather seat, brightening at the deep cushion. He sat across from her, and the same surprised delight crossed his face.

"These *chairs*, right?" She felt like royalty. Their half-price kitchen chairs and thin Craigslist sofa didn't come close.

"*Yes.*"

She laughed. "Are we cheapskates?"

"No," he insisted with a suppressed smile. "We're *frugal.*"

"We'll go with that." She ran her hand over the silky black menu cover with its classic gold-plated label and then opened it to look over the selection that, on any other day, would make her wallet burst into flames on the spot. "How are there so many options, Santi?"

"Aren't fancy restaurants only supposed to offer, like, five things?"

"How do you even pronounce these things? What are these, Italian? French? I don't know either one." She squinted at the pasta section. "Tell me not to get the mac and cheese."

"Mari." He looked at her solemnly. "Don't get the mac and cheese. You should try something fancy and new, and besides, it won't be as good as mine anyway."

"An excellent point. Thanks, *tesoro*." She stared at all options. "I think I'm gonna go with the duck. That sounds appropriately fancy and new, plus I think I can say it right." She tried to wrap her tongue around the sounds of *magret de canard* and grimaced at her own attempt. "Nope. Do you think I could pretend I don't speak English so I look less pathetic?"

"No, I think he heard you talking to me when he came up."

"How inconvenient." When the waiter returned, Santiago gave him the orders without missing a beat, passed him both menus, and took her hand. Her fingers curled around his.

He drew her hand toward him and, with exquisite tenderness, pressed his lips to her knuckles.

Her gaze dropped, and she smiled. "Thank you so much for this."

"I'm glad you're here with me. I'll have to fight off the other people to keep you—you look beautiful."

Warmed, she tried not to wish he meant it the way she did when she replied, "You look perfect too." She could have looked at him for years. His hair, his dark eyes, his shoulders. She'd sneaked glances during the car ride, in the sparse light of the streetlamps. Now, with the candles' glow on his soft edges, and his tawny complexion set off by the resplendent environment, she couldn't take her eyes off him. She didn't need to ignore his physical imperfections; she *liked* them. He was stunning.

If only he truly saw the same in her.

She was finding it more and more difficult to find the line they'd drawn between charade and reality. The touches, the kisses, the terms of endearment all felt too honest, flowed too naturally from her. He had stepped up his acting to match—but that hurt as much as it helped, a bittersweet reminder that he could turn off the scene as easily as he could turn it on. For every wall her growing feelings swept aside, his remained tall and strong and unaffected. An act, the way it had been. The way it ought to be.

She didn't, couldn't, begrudge him his lack of real romantic feelings. It was easier that way, since she wasn't looking for anything more real than what they had now. No, she appreciated the intimacy of their married life; and when the inevitable divorce separated them, she would learn to live without him at her side. She'd had a life before him. She'd have a life after him.

Even if that life would feature a Santi-sized hole in her chest.

"Mari?"

She ripped her gaze toward him, embarrassed that she'd fallen so far into her thoughts. "Sorry, I didn't hear you. What did you say?"

He tilted his head and gave her a quizzical look.

Oh no, did my face do something? If he found out how she was beginning to think of him, want him...

He didn't ask if something was wrong, though, so either he hadn't seen anything betraying in her expression, or he was letting it pass. "I was thinking out loud about what it would be like to come here as, um, usuals?"

"Regulars," she supplied.

He beamed. "Yes, regular. Outside of the cost. Do you think the waiters give them special seats? Do they show up in exercise clothes sometimes, just because no one is going to turn them away?"

She tapped her bottom lip as she considered this. "What if they learn what each chef's food looks like, pick a favorite, and refuse to eat anyone else's food?"

Sticking his nose in the air with a haughty expression, he shooed at an imaginary plate. "Susan would never arrange her mixed vegetables like this! Was this Jordan? Take it away!"

"If Taylor called off tonight, I'm leaving!"

They barely cut off the running impersonations before the waiter came back with their fancy platters. He set them down with a *bon appétit* and then disappeared to help other guests (who might or might not have known who had cooked their food). In sync, Santiago and Mariana turned their plates toward each other. He cut off some bite-size pieces of his steak and scooted them onto her plate, and she spooned over a few slices of duck for him.

He took a deep breath, as if preparing himself for the food experience of his life. "This looks so good. Thank you for having a birthday so we could eat here."

She laughed. "You're welcome. Anything for you." She sliced her food into neat little chunks, and then stabbed her fork through two pieces and ate them both at once.

"Classy," he said through a mouthful of steak.

Placing one hand over her heart, she whispered, "This meal is a beacon of hope in a world of bitter darkness."

He was already on his third slice of steak. "I will never eat anything else ever again," he garbled, pointing emphatically at her pieces with his fork. He added some description of it she couldn't quite decipher but sounded almost blasphemous.

So she tried it, of course. "Santiiii, that's so good! Ugh."

"Right?" He took a bite of duck. "This is delicious too!"

Having eased the edges of their hunger, they slowed to smaller bites, if not less drama. Why tone down happiness for the sake of adulthood?

"Taylor did a great job tonight," Santiago purred before sipping his water.

"Um, excuse me, do you *see* these garnishes? They're curling counterclockwise. This was clearly made by Susan. Get it together."

"I would know Taylor's artwork anywhere, you...monster!" Pretending to ruffle his cloth napkin in a huff, he shifted in his seat, and his foot nudged hers under the table. He didn't seem to notice—he probably thought he'd brushed against a chair or table leg. She nudged him back.

His lips and eyebrows quirked upward, and mischief gleamed in his dark eyes.

She pointed her fork right at him, widening her eyes. "No. Do not. We're out here being fancy adults, and you cannot—"

He bumped the toe of his shoe against her ankle and grinned.

"First of all, don't scratch my new shoes. Second of all, we're not playing footsie." Still, a smile tugged at her own lips.

Another nudge.

This was ridiculous, but she wasn't going to let him have the last word (or nudge) either. Pursing her lips, she crooked her foot to nudge back at him. Both of his feet trapped hers, so she brought up her free foot and knocked one away. He took a nonchalant bite of steak, the picture of indifference, while his toes poked fiercely at her struggling feet. When he caged her against the table leg, her jaw dropped in playful offense.

"That's so illegal!"

"Someone's a sore loser." He blasted her with his dimpled grin, so at ease with the world and with her that she almost broke inside with wanting to keep him.

Maybe once she had her life together... Maybe this really could work.

Chapter Eighteen

In Which They Get Damp (and Not in the Fun Way)

NOVEMBER

> BEST HUSBAND EVER: *My after-school meeting was canceled. Yesss*

> BEST HUSBAND EVER: *It's getting late. Are you okay?*

> CUTEST WIFE IN HISTORY: *Sorry, just saw this*

> CUTEST WIFE IN HISTORY: *Go ahead and eat dinner without me. I probs won't be home till seven*

> BEST HUSBAND EVER: *I miss you [unsent]*

Rain slammed against the apartment roof and windows as Santiago stood over the stove, watching his *fideuà* finish cooking. The whistling wind kicked droplets inside when the front door opened.

"Something smells weird." Mariana shoved the door shut behind her and shook her rainboots off onto the floor. "Not the food, whatever it is. That smells delicious. But there's something else."

Santiago had smelled it too when he'd come home. Vaguely familiar, but he couldn't name it. He pulled the collar of his shirt to his nose and, only half joking, sniffed. "It's not me."

"Okay, good." Coming over to stand with him, Mariana rested her head on his shoulder.

In reply he pressed his cheek against the side of her head. "How was your day?"

"It sucked. It was a meetings day, and I couldn't get any work done until my boss's boss finally let us go around three. That's why I had to stay so late."

"That does suck. If it makes you feel better, I'm making *fideuà* for dinner. It's almost done now." He hadn't started cooking until five-thirty to ensure the pasta-and-seafood dish would be fresh when she got home.

Her lips curved. "You waited for me."

Of course I did. "I had a granola bar while I was waiting, but yes."

She kissed him on the cheek, and he melted. "Let me run to the bathroom," she said, "and then I'll be ready to destroy that *fideuà*."

He missed her when she stepped away, his side suddenly chilled. She closed the door behind her, and he spooned *allioli* onto the center of the noodles. Within seconds, Mariana opened the door again and popped her head out.

"*Cariño*, you didn't dry the floor after your shower. I almost slipped."

What? He gave her an odd look. "I didn't shower yet."

"Oh." She hesitated, her gaze moving from him. "Weird. I'm gonna check the toilet then." Porcelain clattered as she lifted the top, then replaced it with a "huh," and the plunger squelched. Then came the sound of her sweeping something around, probably a towel, wringing it out with a splatter in the tub, and dropping it into the laundry hamper. The sink water ran for a minute, accented by the squeak of the hand soap dispenser. She emerged wiping her hands on her pants and pulling a confused face. "It looked fine."

"Huh. Okay." Santiago trusted her judgment, and if he noticed something the next time he used the bathroom, he'd take a look himself and let her know. She took a bowl of *fideuà* and sat beside him on the couch, entwining her legs with his in a way that heated him inside, and they didn't think of the water again.

Until in the middle of the night when they woke up to a flooded apartment.

*

Rain battered the shadowed street outside. Wind howled through the trees in the dark. With only a porch light to work by, Mariana hefted her filing box for taxes and immigration and other government documents into the backseat of her car. Once her hands were free, she dialed their landlord for the second time in as many minutes, shoved her phone against her ear, and willed him to pick up. She ran back inside to get out of the downpour, almost colliding with Santi, who was balancing two bags full of who knew what. His soaked hair and pajamas clung to him, rainwater gleaming on his skin and speckling his glasses. She felt just as waterlogged, though she'd put her glasses in her purse so they wouldn't get rained on. She would be all but blind either way; this method offered slightly better visibility.

When the landlord answered the phone, Mariana didn't bother with idle pleasantries. "The apartment's flooded. Three inches at least."

To his credit, he got right down to business. He relayed the details to the contractors and assured her they'd be there early in the morning. But two people couldn't live in three inches of standing water, and he had no alternative accommodations to offer. Tightly, she thanked him and ended the call so she could call Embry.

Embry answered the phone in a mumble. "Hullo?"

"Hey, girl. Our apartment got flashflooded, and I was wondering if we could crash at your place."

"Oh, nooo." Embry's voice crackled over the line. "I wish you could, but I'm actually hosting some of my cousins from out of town this week. They're in the guest bedroom and on both couches. I have no room."

"Shit," Mariana whispered. Then, louder: "That's okay. Figured I'd ask. Thanks anyway."

Santiago weaved around her with another bag full of their stuff. As he passed, he mouthed, *Are we going to Embry's?*

Mariana shook her head no, and he muttered something that the thunder overtook.

"If it were any other time, absolutely. I'm sorry." Embry's voice went out for a minute, then came back. "Are you okay? Is there anything I can do?"

Mariana sighed. "Not really, but thanks. Time to make the call."

"Oof. The parents?"

"The parents."

"Good luck."

"Thanks. Talk to you later." Mariana ended the call and dialed her mom's cell instead. *I might have better luck with her than with Dad.*

Carmen's voice was threaded with tiredness, but more alarmed at the late hour than anything. "Mari? What time is it? Are you okay?"

"We're fine, but all this rain flooded our apartment. We don't have anywhere to go. Could Santiago and I come stay in your guest room until we figure out a more permanent living situation?" Mariana crossed her fingers for luck. *Don't turn this into a fight, please don't—*

Rafael's voice came over the line. "Santiago doesn't have a friend he could stay with?"

"Dad!"

"What? I'm just asking. He might not feel comfortable here."

"He'll feel comfortable if you *make him* feel comfortable."

Carmen took the phone back. "Of course you two can come stay with us."

Mariana's breath escaped her in a rush. "Thank you."

Santiago finished loading up the necessities while she finished the call and draped a few towels over the driver and passenger car seats. He met her in the doorway, shadows from stress bruising his eyes. "Are we going to your parents'?"

"Yeah." She scrubbed at her face with her free hand. "Ready to go?"

He didn't answer. She didn't blame him.

*

Waterlogged and exhausted, Santiago wrenched his cold, stiff fingers off the steering wheel once he'd pulled into the Mitogos' driveway. Mariana shivered beside him. Despite the heaviness of his limbs, he reached into the backseat and pulled out two full drawstring bags, one of which he dropped into his wife's lap. "Here's the overnight bags."

"Thanks for packing these." She gave him a tired high five. "All right, let's get inside. I'm ready to get clean and go to bed."

Please, God, let it be that easy. Her parents might've agreed to help them, but he doubted he was suddenly going to get a warm welcome into their house.

Her dad opened the front door, a few towels tucked in the crook of his arm. They ran for the porch through the rain, stopping to drip on the welcome mat before stepping inside. Rafael handed them each a towel and closed the door behind them. "The guest room is ready, and we set some blankets on the couch for you, Santiago."

And there it is.

"Excuse me?" Mariana eyed her dad. "We can both stay in the guest room. It's not a twin, is it?"

"Well, no—"

"Then we'll both fit, and Santi doesn't have to sleep on the couch. That thing is *old*."

"Your mother and I thought he would be more comfortable if—"

"No way. He has a bad back! And it's not like we're going to do anything."

Santiago studiously dried his hair.

Rafael looked his way and frowned. "Surely a gentleman wouldn't mind letting you have the—"

"Dad!" Mariana scowled. "I'm exhausted right now. I really don't want to have this argument with you. Santiago and I can share the guest room. We. Are. *Married*."

The guest room was neat and ready for them—well, for Mariana—with a midnight-blue comforter flecked with gold and two golden pillows. Much fancier than they usually lived. But after absorbing the fanciness, Santiago noticed something else about the bed.

They were used to a king mattress.

This was a full.

Mariana closed the bedroom door behind them and, turning so her back was toward him, peeled off her soaked pajamas. He spun away on reflex; months of living together had done away with the "I'll change in the bathroom and you'll change in the bedroom" awkwardness. Once they'd both showered and changed into clean, dry clothes, they were forced to acknowledge the size of the bed. Or rather, the lack of size.

He tapped his lower lip. "Well."

"Hmm."

"I can sleep on the floor."

She shook her head. "No, you can't."

"Why not?"

"Number one, hardwood floor is the actual worst to sleep on." She planted her hands on her hips. "And number two, you'd have to hire your own personal chiropractor, with your old-man back."

Those were, unfortunately, decent points. Still, he crossed his arms in his best imitation of belligerence, even as a rainbow unicorn stared at him from the front of her sleeping shirt. "I'll go sleep on the couch, then. Like they wanted."

"You are not sleeping on the floor *or* the couch!" She huffed and looked away in thought. Absently, she tugged at her oversized shirt. He struggled not to stare at the curves now more clearly defined. They both picked at the edges of the sheets without actually turning them over. Mariana opened her mouth to say something, then closed it.

"Well," said Santiago to the wall, "it's a small bed."

"Yep," she said to the pillow.

Best to get it over with. As quickly as he could: "We could spoon."

She jerked back, eyes flaring, and he tried not to overthink the negative response.

"To save room." He gestured to their limited space.

After a pause, she nodded jerkily. "That's true, I guess." She summoned her dignity and relaxed. "So how do we decide who's, uh, Big Spoon?"

Rock paper scissors.

Which was how Santiago found himself curled up into Small Spoon and tucked into her, every inch of her curves pressed into his back. It was possible he had underestimated the concept of spooning with Mariana.

No matter how hard it would be, he would keep his hands to himself. This was going to propel him to sainthood.

She shifted behind him, trying to get comfortable, and he gritted his teeth. Then she tentatively slid her arm over his torso and tucked her calves between his. The graze of skin on skin tingled all the way up his body. He reconsidered if sainthood was worth it.

He thought she pressed a kiss against his shoulder through the thin fabric of his shirt—but she had no reason to do that. It must have been another unintentional touch while she adjusted.

"Sweet dreams, Santi," she whispered, her breath warm on the curve where his shoulder met his neck.

"*Dulces sueños, cariño*," he whispered back.

She sighed, and when she inhaled, so did he. His breathing evened out, slowed to match hers. His limbs sank heavily onto the bed. As antsy as the pleasure-pain of her touch made him, he was *so* tired. And she felt *so* good, all snuggled up against him.

His eyes drifted closed. The last of the tension left his body. He melted into the most peaceful sleep he'd had in years.

But going to sleep had nothing on waking up. Not with her leg curved over his thigh, and her face nuzzled into his neck, and her hand on his stomach *under his shirt.* Groaning low in his throat, he wriggled gently to disentangle them—he was good, but he wasn't *that* good.

Instead of helping him, though, the movement only stirred Mariana from sleep. She mumbled something incomprehensible and shifted closer to him. With a yawn, she tilted her head to squint blearily, her shirt twisted, her cheeks creased from sleep.

"Need up?" Her sleepy hands skated over his arms and shoulders and hair. Staking a claim, if unintentionally. And he leaned into the touch.

"No, *cariño*," he whispered, settling back down, turning so that he faced her. *So she'll go back to sleep,* he lied to himself while he traced his fingertips over her soft, round cheeks.

Her lips had dried a little, and she had a hint of morning breath; he could taste it in his own mouth too.

And yet...he couldn't take his eyes off her.

He adored this look, her rumpled and sleepy and smiling like she belonged there with him—and it was all too easy to imagine waking up to this every day for the rest of their lives. A tangle of limbs, or two backs pressed together, or toes touching. His hand found the side of her neck; he scratched the sensitive skin under her earlobe the way she liked, and she made a soft noise of approval.

He ached to tell her he loved her, though he couldn't risk losing her by doing so. Staying silent, he skimmed his fingers over her beautiful ebony skin and let them come to rest on her full lips.

Her breath stuttered.

She was definitely awake now, but she wasn't pulling away.

Perhaps it was her quiet allowance that pushed him, or the freedom in early morning shadows. He moved slowly, his intentions clear so she could duck away if she wanted to. But she didn't duck away. She met him in the middle, and she didn't ask if it was practice when he kissed her, lingering and chaste. She ran tired fingertips through his mussed hair, and he sighed.

Because she didn't ask, he didn't have to lie. This was not practice. This moment was for him, and for her, not anyone else. Just this once.

Chapter Nineteen

In Which an Interview Enlightens Mariana

NOVEMBER

Santiago and Mariana parked in the driveway beside a small house tucked up against a copse of trees. The black door and window shutters emphasized the cream walls. "Oooooh." Mariana craned her neck to look into the fenced backyard big enough for a dog to run around. *I like it already.* "It's cute!"

Santi texted the landlady that they'd arrived, then tucked his phone into Mariana's purse. "It's small for a house."

"That's probably why we can afford it." *Will it be as cute on the inside as it is outside? Please, God, don't let it be a trash can.* It would be awesome to have a standalone place rather than sharing walls with strangers. And she'd feel so adult, living in an actual house. She wriggled in her seat. "I'm so excited."

The landlady pulled up beside them in an SUV. She waved to them through her window before getting out.

They met her at the front step and shook hands while Mariana admired her box braids spun up into a giant bun.

"Nice to see you, Rachonne." Santiago knew her better, as the mom of one of his soccer kids. "Thank you for showing us the house."

"Happy to help." She unlocked the door and opened it for them. "After you."

Mariana stepped into a small living room that opened into the kitchen. The shag carpet, though outdated, was clean and soft underfoot. A gray sectional couch hugged the wall across from wires where a TV would hang. She suppressed the urge to flop onto the furniture.

"The last tenant left the couch and the kitchen table." Rachonne indicated an oval wood table with three chairs around it, each sporting a brightly colored cushion. "You can keep them or get rid of them. I don't really care either way."

"Cool." Mariana tugged on Santiago's hand. "We wouldn't have to buy new furniture to replace the sofa and stuff that the flooding ruined. At least not right away." *Oh! I almost forgot my paper.* She'd printed a list off the Internet of questions to ask and things to look at when viewing a house. First on her list—

Santiago stepped in. "Have there been any major repairs?" Moving into the kitchen, he tested the cabinet doors.

There went items one and five. *Guess I have to skip ahead.* Also on the list: *check appliances.* She opened the fridge and was rewarded with a blast of cool air, plus ice in the freezer. The stove and oven heated up right away.

But Santiago got his answer (a replaced roof a few years back) and moved on to ask about local traffic, blowing through another question on Mariana's list before she could prove she'd prepared for this. Prove she knew things too. She went for number seven: "How's the water pressure?"

Santiago, standing by the sink, turned on the faucet. Water rushed out and gurgled down the drain. "It's fine here. We'll check in the bathroom too. How old is the fridge and everything?"

The simple answer stung. She could've checked it herself, but the list said to ask. And he hadn't paused to see if she had another question. He kept *talking*, and he kept asking the questions she wanted to ask, so when he did yield the floor, she scrambled to find something new. She'd wanted to feel competent, and instead, she felt...trivial.

As they toured the house, though, she fell in love with it. Pets were allowed, which made her and Santiago slap a double high five without looking. No dishwasher, but a tiny kitchen nook perfect for morning coffee. Only one bathroom, but extra-deep closets. On paper, it was imperfect, but it was precious, and she loved it despite the flaws.

When they pulled out of the driveway, he hummed in indifference.

"You didn't like it?" She flipped through the pictures she'd taken on her phone. "I thought it was super cute."

He shrugged. "It was fine. I liked it about the same as the apartments we saw yesterday. The best part of it was that we could have a dog."

That part did rock, but calling it the *best* part was pushing it. "Those apartments were so cookie-cutter. This place has personality!" At a stop sign, she showed him a selfie she'd taken with the coffee nook. "C'mon, you don't see it? It could totally be us."

"You really want to live without a dishwasher?"

"Hand-washing some dishes won't kill us." She brought up a photo of the double bathroom vanity. "The sink is big enough for us to brush our teeth together. The apartments' weren't." Such a small thing, but she looked forward to it every morning.

He glanced at the picture before pulling out onto the road. "It's nice, but I'd take a single sink if it meant lower rent."

Sure, the rent for the house was a little more, but not by that much. Did he not see any of this? Was he even listening to her preference? She went for the direct route. "I like this place better than the apartments. I love it. This would be my choice."

"I'm not opposed." He glanced her way, no change in his expression. "I think we should consider all our options."

But I like THIS option. Picking at her lip, she stared out the window on the drive back.

When they got back to her parents' house, Mariana started cleaning up in preparation for her USCIS individual interview. Carmen and Rafael were at a small group for church. In their absence, Santiago clanged around the kitchen, stress baking before the federal agent's visit; the dishes quieted only when he called his sister. Mariana listened from the living room as she folded the clean clothes that had been waiting in a pile, but he didn't have the call on speaker, so she only heard his half of the conversation.

Mariana waited for him to discuss the apartments and the house. He asked about Lola, and about Maca's jobs, and about the caretakers they were interviewing. He talked about school, and about soccer, and about something funny Yelena had said at a teachers' meeting. Fiddling with mismatched socks, Mariana waited.

"The deposit?" The refrigerator door opened and closed. "Yeah, it sounds bigger than expected. Still, it might be worth it."

She perked up. Bigger than expected, but worth it? Was he leaning toward the house, then? She hugged herself. If he hadn't cared either way...did that mean he was doing that for her?

Pots and pans rattled in the cabinets, and one clattered onto the stove. "I'm putting away extra money for it... Yes, obviously I'm thinking of her."

Smiling, Mariana went to the bedroom, slid the folded clothes into drawers and hung dress clothes in the closet. It shouldn't have been such a big deal, but he was choosing her, choosing the house he might not have chosen for himself, choosing the house *to make her happy*. Money was hard for him, a difficult part of adulthood, but he was going to manage it for her. The same way he'd managed to stock up on her favorite ice cream and send her roses at work. To make her happy.

"No, it shouldn't be a problem. I have a budget these days. Sometimes I even stick to it." He paused, then laughed. "Oh, thanks a lot. No, I'm not giving her my phone. The recipe for these brownies is on here." He raised his voice. "Mariana! Maca's going to call you!"

She stuck her head out into the hallway. "Tell her I'll call her after my interview!" Federal Agent Harrison would be there in an hour, and she needed all sixty minutes to get her head in the game.

Talking herself up, she sifted through her clothes for a nice dress. "You got this. You got this. You're a grown-ass adult." She carefully applied lipstick and eyeliner. "You got flooded out of your apartment and you're living with your parents, but you're a great pretend wife, and you're gonna rock this interview. You're—"

She accidentally stabbed herself in the eye with her mascara brush, and the pain startled out her less positive side.

I'm doing this in my parents' house. Because I live in my parents' house now. I'm homeless, and I have to do this interview instead of using the time to get closer to having a place to live.

When Harrison arrived with a gust of cold autumn air, Santiago left his desserts out for them and disappeared into the guest room. Mariana and Harrison sat at the kitchen table. He took his time settling in, looking around the kitchen and living room. She sliced up two brownies and stress ate them both bit by bit. *Please hurry up and get this over with so I can go back to my fake-married life.*

After thirty years, he pulled his papers and a tablet out of his briefcase. "How's your day going?"

Ugh. She dug deep for professional diplomacy for this person who could ruin her life. She was not particularly successful. "I'm stretched thin right now," she ground out. "We're trying to find a place to live—ASAP—and instead, I'm here with you, answering questions about how many times a week I have sex with my own husband."

He was unfazed. "And I appreciate your time. Are you doing anything fun after this?"

"Tonight, we have an office party to go to for Santi's work." *Fun* might be a stretch, but there would be snacks, so she was down for it.

Another note. "Tell me about the move. Where have you looked so far?"

Not like she spent all her time thinking about it or anything. She gave him an overview of the places they'd looked at, and he latched onto a piece of data about the house and one of the apartments.

"Two bedrooms? That would be...comfortable."

She was many things, but not stupid. "We'll keep sharing a bedroom. They just have a decent price and are available immediately."

"What would you use the second room for?"

"We aren't sure yet. Library, office, storage, exercise room..." Despite herself, she laughed. "That last one's optimistic, but we like to think the best of ourselves."

"Not a nursery?"

That question threw her off. Her carefully neutral expression slipped. "Maybe someday, but not right now." Not that she hadn't thought about it. Every soccer game ached in her chest—the kids loved him, and she... "It's too early."

He stared at her, eyes narrowing as he analyzed this development. "Do you want children, Mariana?"

Her jaw clenched even as she told herself not to react. It was useless to lie about this though. Better to be truthful about everything except the Big Lie. "Yes, I do. Eventually." With her husband, not that he was allowed to know that.

"Does Santiago?"

Not with her. No matter how many bedrooms they got before the divorce. "Yes, eventually. He's great with kids, but right now, he's focusing that on his soccer team."

"How many do you plan on?"

"We both want at least two, whenever we get there."

He made a note and, instead of pressing the issue as she'd expected, moved on. "Are you aware that his mother and sister are planning to move as well in the near future?"

"They are?" Mariana shifted in her seat. "Um, no, I didn't know that. That must be a new thing."

"Actually, it's been in the works for about a month now." Harrison scrawled something on his tablet as if he hadn't knocked her off her seat.

A month, and neither Santi nor Maca had thought to tell her? Mariana rubbed at the pressure in her brow. *He must've forgotten. There's a lot going on; it's fine.* Except it wasn't fine, not really. Communication was a basic part of adulthood, especially on such a big subject.

"I assume, then, you are also unaware that Santiago is paying for that move."

"He's...?" Her throat closed, and her fingertips stilled. The security deposit. *Bigger than expected.* The two of them were living in her parents' house, trying to scrape together the funds to find a new place to live...and he was *paying for his mother and sister to move out of a two-bedroom apartment?* "I... No, I didn't know that."

Why hadn't he told her? How could he send that much money off to Spain instead of putting it toward their own needs? Dear lord, they needed every penny they could scrape together. And he hadn't even told her himself. She had to hear about it from the government agent investigating him.

Harrison tapped his pen. "Yes. Apparently, rent is about to go up, and his sister feels their mother would do better elsewhere."

Obviously, I'm thinking of her. His mom. He'd been thinking of his mom.

Of course he needed to put his family first. Santi's first priority was, and always had been, his family. He'd agreed to this marriage in the first place because he needed to provide for his mother and sister. But he hadn't told Mariana that the situation had changed, that he would be sending them more money for their own move. He hadn't told her, and he hadn't conferenced with her on the logistics of it, even though managing a budget was one of the adulthood tasks she could actually do with some degree of competence. Had he even thought of her?

Was that why he'd dismissed Rachonne's house? Mariana might like the place, and if he hadn't sent away his extra money, they could've afforded it, but when it came down to it, he'd pick what his family wanted—and his family wanted a different apartment.

It came down to priorities, and she came last.

She blinked back the burning in her eyes and swallowed hard. "I can't argue with that," she lied.

Chapter Twenty

In Which Mariana Misunderstands At Least Two Things

NOVEMBER

While Mariana interviewed with Harrison, Santiago plotted his outfit for the evening.

Despite all the chaos in their lives (or because of it), he couldn't wait to take Mariana to the high school faculty office party. She deserved to relax and have a good time. Plus, he could use the public view as an excuse to kiss her and touch her as much as possible.

Tonight, he wanted her to find him attractive. He'd seen something flicker in her gaze before—when he'd gotten his hair cut for his interview, when he'd dressed up fancy for her birthday dinner. He wanted to see it again. And now, he could bring together all the things she'd reacted to, and maybe, just maybe, he would push a button to help her think of him differently. It required some effort, but if Mariana so much as looked at him for more than two consecutive seconds, it would be worth the inconvenience.

He picked out the crisp black button-down shirt that had once made her (and several of his married coworkers) do a double take, and he fussed with his hair until it swished in fashionable waves. After the interview ended, when he emerged from the bedroom to get her approval, he flashed the grin she'd once described as "blinding."

She didn't smile back.

He faltered. "Are you okay?"

Her cool gaze skated away from him. "When were you going to tell me that you're paying for your mom and sister to move?" Her jaw ticked. "I gotta say, I didn't love getting that sprung on me when I'm supposed to be talking about what a great pair we are and what a healthy relationship we have."

"I told you about that." He couldn't remember when, exactly, but surely, he had.

She scoffed. "No. You didn't. Because I might be reeeeal understanding about a lot of stuff, but that's some next-level shit, sending them the money *we need* for what's basically a convenience to them."

I didn't know things would be like this. He leaned forward, stuffing his hands in his pockets. "They can barely afford rent already. What was I supposed to do, let them get run out of their home because they can't afford a cheaper apartment without my help?"

"Now is not the *time*, Santiago!" Her voice cracked. "I don't know if you noticed, but we *do not have a home*. We are living with my parents, who only recently learned how to hold a civil conversation with you, and I haven't received my inheritance yet. We need to find somewhere to live, right now, immediately, and that requires you contributing, which you can't do if you send your family all your money!"

"I didn't know this was going to happen. Maca asked me way before we needed a new place to live."

She glowered. "Right. It's been how long that y'all didn't tell me about this? A few weeks? A month? That makes me feel lots better, thanks."

"*I thought I told you.*"

She planted her hands on her hips. "How much is it?"

"What?"

"How much money did you send them?"

Oh. Looking down, he shifted his weight and muttered, "Two thousand dollars." A paycheck and a big chunk of his newfound savings.

She fell silent. When he looked up, her eyes were squeezed shut and she was pinching the bridge of her nose, her jaw clenched. "That's so much. *So* much. How could you...?"

It dawned on him, then, what he'd done without meaning to. Instead of keeping her happy, he'd hurt her. Instead of keeping her safe, he'd put their living situation in jeopardy. It had been unintentional, but it had happened, and now he had no idea how he was going to fix it. "I'm sorry. I really thought I—"

"Don't." She sighed and dropped her hand, refusing to look in his direction. "I'm gonna go get ready. Please...give me some space."

We're still going to the office party? He wasn't sure why, but he'd take it. She couldn't give him the cold shoulder in public.

The drive to the school was utterly silent. When they pulled into the parking lot, she took a deep breath, looked at him for the first time in half an hour, and plastered on a smile. "As far as anyone in there knows, we've never fought a day in our marriage."

He forced a smile in return. "Who fights? Not us."

When they arrived at the party, they were immediately greeted by the eighth-grade English teacher, who was so friendly Santiago wondered if he'd had something to drink besides soda. After a quick escape, they were pulled aside by a string of his coworkers, most of whom asked the same questions and made the same jokes about newlyweds. Ironic, since this was the least newlywed he'd felt in their entire marriage. He didn't see Yelena, though, which surprised him—she hadn't been thrilled about the office party itself, but she'd told him she wanted to say hi to Mariana.

As he glanced around, he found the refreshments table and brightened. "Snacks! Do you want some?"

Mariana glanced at him, then at the food, and genuine appreciation warmed her smile. Not much, but a little, and he lived for it. "Snacks do sound good, actually."

Thank God I managed to get that right, at least. He weaved his way through the crowd as fast as he could, reluctant to leave her side for long. Balancing two small plates in one hand as he stacked desserts, he heard a familiar voice.

"If you take the last blonde brownie, I *will* rip it out of your hands." Yelena's smile merged playfulness and a touch of real competition.

Grinning in return, he set down the plates. "I'm glad you finally showed up." Finally, a friend who didn't want to kick him.

"I'm fashionably late." She popped a cheese cube into her mouth.

He slipped into casual conversation with her for a minute or two. Or ten.

*

Laughing at the principal's boring joke, Mariana shifted her weight and casually scanned the room for Santi. He'd left to raid the refreshments so long ago—how bad of a line could he have gotten stuck in?

Despite her bad mood, she hadn't anticipated how much she liked joining him at his work party. Not only did he look fantastic tonight, but most of his coworkers had said, "Oh, *you're* Mariana," usually followed by a variant of "He's always talking about you," which warmed her. Every time he brushed against her, that skin burned. He might not have told her everything, but as he'd taken her around to meet people, she'd felt *his*. Like he wanted her there, like he was proud to be hers too. Even when they were fighting, she wanted it to be true, because he was what she wanted.

Where is he?

She sucked in a breath, her stomach plummeting.

He was leaning against the wall by the snack table, talking animatedly with Yelena and hitting her with his full-power grin. With the dimples she'd come to think of as reserved for herself alone. She hadn't realized how...close the two of them were. Yelena smoothed her gleaming strawberry-blonde hair and leaned forward to laugh with him about something. He watched her intently. He never so much as glanced toward the wife he'd left in the company of strangers.

They were close enough to kiss, and he didn't step back.

A lump rose in Mariana's throat. In the weeks of romancing, she'd let herself forget one important truth: Santi hadn't married her because he loved her. He'd been forced into a corner, and he'd agreed to marriage *because* he didn't love her, because he would *never* love her, and he knew that was the only way it would work.

At some point, she had forgotten to pretend. More important, she had forgotten he *was* pretending.

It was all a lie, a pretty lie. Always had been.

And she, in months of stupidity, had fallen in love with him.

Ashamed of her own gullibility, Mariana swallowed her tears. She *would not* cry here. "Excuse me for a minute." With her head high, she went to collect her husband.

When she drew near enough to hear their conversation, the sound of Spanish slapped her in the face. It wasn't as though she thought he only spoke his first language with her—that would be ridiculous. But it was one of the things that had cemented their friendship. To hear him easily, intimately bonding over it with someone else...

Get it together. She lifted her chin against the tears rising again. *Put up some walls and handle this like an adult. We were never actually a thing. He didn't even tell you he was sending his mom and sister extra money.*

But that didn't mean he could flout her in public.

Teeth gritted, Mariana sidled up to both of them with a smile. "*Hola, tesoro.*" Her heart broke as she caressed the small of his back with well-practiced ease. She tried not to notice his surprise. "*¿Qué pasó? Te extrañé.*"

Santiago kissed her on the cheek as if nothing was wrong, but the warm, familiar touch was too much. She pulled away, averted her eyes so he wouldn't see them watering. It wasn't his fault he'd stuck to the original agreement.

"Mariana! It's awesome you're here." Yelena touched her on the arm. "Are you fluent in Spanish too?"

Mariana shrugged with a modest smile. "I'm proficient. It helps that I live with my tutor."

He wrapped one arm around her and beamed. "Cutest student I've ever had."

The false words stabbed her chest. Her smile didn't waver. "Do you speak it well yourself?"

Yelena laughed wryly. "If I mix up 'embarrassed' and 'pregnant' one more time, Santiago may decide to switch schools. Or professions. There's a reason they pay me to teach biology and not foreign languages."

"If it makes you feel better, biology is a foreign language to me."

A brilliant smile scrunched up her nose. "Sadly, that does make me feel better. Thanks."

"Do you like it?" Mariana asked. "Biology, I mean. Or teaching in general. Either one."

"Yes to both." Yelena nibbled on her blonde brownie. "Biology has always been my favorite science, and it's so satisfying to see the light come on for a student."

"I feel that. I love putting together exhibits for our museum attached to the Historical Society, getting to share the information in a way that makes sense."

Yelena beamed. "Right! Santiago mentioned you worked there. When I was growing up, I used to love when we'd take field trips there for history classes. I still visit the museum sometimes. How long have you been there?"

"Almost five years now. It started as an internship for college, and then they kept me on full-time after I graduated."

"That's awesome! Whatcha working on these days?"

Despite herself, Mariana smiled. "I'm actually heading up a new exhibit on James Farmer right now."

"Oooh, cool! I'll have to come check it out once it's up and running."

Someone called for Santi. He handed Mariana a sweet tea and a plate of snacks and pulled her away with a promise to catch Yelena again later.

"She's cool, right?" He sipped his Coke.

Mariana wanted to disagree, but Yelena was sweet and friendly and willing to laugh at herself. *Even WANTING to dislike her, I can't manage it.* She chanced a glance at him, assuming his attention would be elsewhere. He was looking at her, though, which somehow worse. She looked away. *I can't blame you for being interested in her.*

"Yeah," she said finally. "Yeah, she's cool."

When they got back to her parents' house, Mariana flopped onto the couch and stretched out, taking up the full space, keeping him away from her. Brow creased, he was forced to perch in an armchair. "Are you feeling okay?"

I feel like punching something. "I'm fine, thanks." Mariana took a deep breath and opened up housing websites on her phone. "I'm gonna look at houses. Well, apartments, I guess." The pointed amendment went unacknowledged. "You don't have to sit here with me."

He ignored the dismissal and pulled out his own phone. "I'll help look."

Her jaw ticked, but she didn't argue.

"We don't have to still pay rent on the apartment, do we?"

She double-checked their lease. "No, we don't. Which is great, but we still have to find a new place."

So they looked through apartments in the area, but as they read the details of the entries, it wasn't only rent they needed to agree on. His fingers tapped on the keyboard. "How long do we want a lease?"

She glanced up from the screen. "A year is standard."

He shifted his laptop to show her what he was looking at—some landlords offered lower rent rates for longer terms. "It might be smart to go longer." He grinned, showing off his dimples.

Don't react. "Two years would probably be safe. Even three could..." She trailed off. They'd said, what, three years to get him the longer-term green card and to ward off suspicion? Two and a half, now. *We'll be divorced by then.* Her chest twinged, and she averted her gaze. *Pull it together.* "No. Three would be too long."

No more sharing a bathroom. No more shoving fries in each other's mouths while driving. No more tangling their bodies together while watching movies.

They'd been long-distance friends before. They would be long-distance friends again. And she would survive... but something inside her would break.

"Oh." He managed the same neutral tone. "Well. Right. Divorced people probably don't live together."

"Probably not." Her voice remained even, betraying nothing, and she looked back to her phone. "We can do a two-year lease if we find a good place. But honestly, my main concern is finding somewhere to live that isn't my parents' house. If that means a shorter lease, so be it."

He made a low noise of agreement. After fifteen minutes, though, he broke silence. "We don't *have* to stick to being married only three years."

She half turned, not quite looking at him. "That was the plan."

"Yeah, but we're having a good time, right?"

Yeah, we are. That's the problem. Mariana scuffed the toe of her sock on the floor. "I don't think it's a good idea."

"Wait, what? Why not?" He scrubbed a hand through his hair. "We have fun. We like each other. We could go longer."

She shrugged without looking at him. "This was never supposed to be a long-term thing. The longer we wait, the more complicated the divorce will be."

"It doesn't have to be complicated."

"It will be though." She picked at some lint on her leggings. "All our stuff will be mixed together. We'll have stuff we bought together, so we have to decide who gets what. Plus—" She cut herself off.

He straightened. "Plus what?"

Plus, I'll keep loving you more the longer this lasts. Finally, she met his gaze, and she shut off the pain. "Plus, we still have to decide how we want to play the divorce. My vote is we don't have a big fight or anything, we just say we realized we work better as friends. Which is true."

He flinched.

"So we can pretend to be lovey-dovey for another six months or so, and then we start winding it down. And we don't need to keep practicing. I've got it." Practice. Method acting. The way it should have been, and it was her fault she'd let the lines blur so much. Now, though, she couldn't un-blur them. Her only solution was to redraw them, to build them back up into walls.

He sank back, stunned. "Practice doesn't hurt."

False. It was already hurting her. "I said I've got it. You and Maca trained me well, and now I can handle myself, like an adult. You haven't noticed?"

"Of course I noticed. You've been doing great."

Doing great? Her stomach turned. "Then trust I can do my job." The *job* of kissing him, touching him. Right. As if her hands on his skin were that much of an effort. But she wouldn't take it back. She needed the space.

He rubbed the cross on his bracelet. "You don't have to say it like that."

"Like what?"

"Like it's painful." Looking up at the ceiling, he scratched the back of his neck. "Look, there's something I think you should know."

She stiffened. *Please don't.*

He took a deep breath. "I think I'm in love with—"

"Yeah, I know." She couldn't bear to hear it out loud.

He paused, his cheeks darkening. "You do? How long have you known?"

She shrugged and inspected her nails, but her hands trembled. "I suspected for a while. Only realized it for sure tonight." Her first time seeing the two of them together when she wasn't cockblocking.

"Oh." Examining her, Santiago bit his lip. "Does it bother you?"

She dug her nails into her palms as if that might take the sting out of his words. "You know what? It kinda does. We had a plan. This was supposed to be simple." Things had stopped being simple a long time ago.

"I know, I'm sorry. I didn't mean for it to happen."

Rubbing her temples, she sighed. "I don't blame you. It's understandable."

He laughed.

What the hell?

"Sorry, I thought you were—never mind." He cleared his throat.

"Just keep it to yourself. And for the love of God, don't try to actually start something." There was no surer way to out themselves than for him to start up an affair right under her nose.

"It really bothers you that much?" He fidgeted with the end of his sleeve, eyes downcast. "Should I not have told you? Did you not want to know?"

Of course I don't want to know. I don't want it to be true. "You know what I would've liked to know? I would've liked to know about you sending your family $2,000," she snapped because it was easier to be mad about that than about him wanting someone else. "A heads-up about *that* would've been nice."

He reeled backward, wounded and confused. "That's not what we're talking about right now."

"Isn't it? It's what *I'm* talking about." And it was for the best. She didn't need a relationship at all, much less with someone who would rather be with someone else, someone who couldn't be bothered to include her in his life decisions. She needed to be an adult, and that meant standing up for herself and pushing back when someone tried to walk over her. Even if that someone was Santiago.

"I don't think you—"

She waved her hands to shut him up. "Well, I do think. And I'm so done. There's nothing you could say to me right now that would make my mood better—besides, maybe, 'I'm leaving for the night.'"

He winced.

"I don't have anything else to say to you. It'd be best if you went to bed. I need some time to myself."

Santiago left with one last lingering glance. She took ten minutes to gather herself, to keep herself from kicking something. Finally, she followed him into the guest room, but she said nothing. He sat upright in bed, his lesson plans spread out on his lap. She flipped off the overhead light, bathing them in lamplight, and she tugged down the sheets on her side. After setting aside her glasses, she rolled over so that her back faced him.

"*Dulces sueños.*" No term of endearment.

She didn't respond for a full thirty seconds. Finally, she shoved out the words: "Good night."

She hugged the edge of the bed, leaving a sliver of space between them that gaped. What she demanded but not what she wanted. Her every cell pulled toward the pressure of his weight, toward his heat and solidity. Two bodies on the small mattress, closer than they were used to, yet too far apart.

He set his work supplies on the floor and turned off the lamp.

With the room doused in darkness, she itched to roll over and reach out and find exactly where he lay, to graze her fingers over shirt and skin. It felt wrong to be separated. She missed curving herself around him, tucking her arm and leg under his, falling asleep to the rhythm of his breaths. She missed him. And despite everything, if he shifted closer, her hastily reconstructed walls would collapse. Despite everything, if he shifted closer, she wouldn't have the strength to resist pulling him all the way in. She wanted to kiss him until he forgot any other woman existed, until his mouth and his hands made her forget all the stress and exhaustion and hurt from today. She wanted to keep him.

But he didn't shift closer, and she didn't reach out.

Chapter Twenty-One

In Which Santiago Reconsiders His Life Choices

NOVEMBER

Santiago woke up cold and alone.

The curtains blocked out the sunshine; the closed door muffled any noise from the rest of the house. He turned off the alarm, pushed himself up to a sitting position with a groan, and smoothed one hand over the sheets. Cool and flat, without even the impression of Mariana on the mattress. *She's been gone for a while.*

This was exactly what he'd feared would happen if he told her how he felt. He'd been right to put it off as long as he had; he'd lost her, and it hadn't been because he lacked time or money or an emotional bond. He wasn't what she wanted. She'd been all too clear about that. Maybe today he could backtrack and reassure her that nothing would change, that he was as much her friend as ever, that she had nothing to worry about.

He pulled on a sweater and jeans and went to find her, to repair the damage from yesterday. The *snickt* of the door shutting behind him was swallowed up by the clatter in the kitchen. Mariana's mom stood at the sink, washing dishes.

Santiago joined her and pulled a towel off the oven. "Good morning."

"Morning." She handed him a plate. "Can you dry that and put it away? It goes in the second cabinet to your right."

He knew where all the dishes went, after months of Sunday lunches, but he kept that to himself. "No problem." He slid it into place, then dried and rehomed the bowls she'd already washed. "How did you sleep?"

"Fine, thank you." She passed him a saucepan. "How about you?"

A follow-up question? He almost tripped over his own feet. "Uh, good, thanks." It took him a second to remember that he had a pan to put away. "Do you know where Mariana is? She got up before me today."

"She's sleeping on the couch."

No. He couldn't help himself; he turned to check. Sure enough, one dark arm hung out from under a pile of blankets. He swallowed hard. *She left me?*

Carmen passed him a handful of silverware. "So, tell me. Why is she there?"

"I..." His heart squeezed. "We went to bed together. I didn't know she left."

"Hmm." She eyed him. "It wasn't because you argued?"

Oh, no. Had she heard? Did she know—? Had she figured it all out? He searched her face for some sign...but there was nothing. Just concern. A genuine question.

He hesitated. *Would it look bad to say we did argue?* He couldn't afford to give Mariana's parents any more reason to dislike him, but he didn't want to lie. "We had a disagreement," he admitted, against his better judgment. "I think the stress is getting to us."

To his surprise, she nodded. "You have a lot going on."

"And she had her individual interview yesterday. Mine is today. They couldn't reschedule either of us." He scoffed and toweled off a pot she handed him. "Our lives aren't complicated enough right now, apparently."

Carmen screwed up a wry smile. "That's the government for you."

Was this...a conversation?

Against all odds, she kept talking to him, and at one point, he made her *laugh*. Out *loud*. Before he could pass out from sheer shock, Mariana's drowsy "good morning" came from behind him. She slid into a chair at the small kitchen table. A pillow crease bisected her cheek, and her eyes were at the half-mast that didn't fade until twenty minutes after waking. An irrepressible lopsided little smile tugged at his mouth as she stared off at nothing. She looked soft in the mornings, sleepy but sweet, despite her quietness today.

A spatula tapped him on the shoulder, startling him out of his reverie. Mariana's mother was watching *him* for some reason (why would anyone look at him when they could be looking at his wife?), her eyes warming and creasing with an almost knowing smile.

"You'll do."

He wasn't sure what she meant he would do, but he got the impression it was a good thing. Still, what did it matter if he'd alienated the love of his life?

*

After breakfast Mariana volunteered to make a grocery run, avoiding Santiago on her way out. She parked in the back of the Food Lion lot and sat there for half an hour, resting her forehead on the steering wheel and trying to breathe.

I'm going to have to face him eventually.

She couldn't wrap her mind around it. How could he send that much extra money without telling her even in passing? That was the worst part—that he hadn't told her. If he'd told her himself, she might've rationalized it with him. Now, though, it only felt like he didn't care enough to keep her in the loop. Like their life together meant nothing if his family beckoned.

She pressed her lips together against the sickness in her stomach.

And the other thing he'd admitted... That had almost been worse. Making eyes at another woman in public, and then: *I think I'm in love.* At least he'd been honest about that, hadn't waited for her to catch him redhead-handed. Not that it made it hurt any less. She'd fallen for him, and he...well, he remained standing.

She kneaded her thighs with her knuckles. *It doesn't matter anyway.* She wasn't ready for a relationship, wasn't ready to give herself to someone. When she had a career position, when she paid off her loans, when she liked cooking, then she would reach the Adulthood level that would make her a good partner. She would finally have her life together, and she would find someone else who had their life together, and that would be that.

This plan was what she'd decided a long time ago, and it was what she was sticking with. She wasn't about to change just because she'd found someone who made her wonder if she could have a partner even when her life was a mess. The logic had carried her through years of singleness. It made sense. So why wasn't she happier about it?

When she got back home, an unfamiliar car was parked in the driveway. The interviewer. Santiago was seated at the kitchen table with a federal agent she didn't recognize, a short, older brown-skinned man with a receding hairline. As she put away the groceries, she pretended not to notice the questions about their future kids ("at least two") and his relationship with her parents ("they haven't threatened to kick me out of the house, so it's going better than I expected!"). Her cheeks burned when Santi described their sex life as "generous."

The agent tapped his pen on his stack of papers. "Tell me about when you first realized you were in love with Mariana."

She dug her nails into her palms and retreated to the bedroom. Some lies she didn't need to hear. She turned on some music to block out the conversation and picked up her copy of James Farmer's autobiography, one finger tapping anxiously on the cover as she read.

After his interview finished and the agent had left, Santiago poked his head into the room. "Hey."

She didn't look up from her book. "How was it?"

"Not too bad, I think." He edged his way in. "Can we talk?"

No. "Fine." She stuck a bookmark between the pages and looked up at him. "What?"

He shut the door behind him. "About the security deposit. I'm sorry. I should've checked with you, and I didn't."

"I don't understand how that happened." She scowled. "If it happened so long ago, what? Weeks went by and you didn't even think to let me know? Much less include me in the decision in the first place."

"I promise I meant to. I thought I did. With everything going on, it must have slipped my mind." Carefully, he perched on the bed by her feet. "It's shitty, and I get why you're mad. You have a right to be mad. But I don't want this to come between us. It was a mistake, and I'm sorry."

She swallowed. *I don't want this to come between us either.* Her anger shivered, cracked like a tooth breaking to reveal the pain at its root. "You hurt me. I hate feeling like you didn't think of me. Like I wasn't important enough for you to talk to me about it."

He raked his fingers through his hair. "That's not it at all. You're so important to me. I *hate* that I hurt you." His hand dropped, leaving his waves disheveled. "And about the other thing..."

I think I'm in love.

Looking away, he scratched the back of his neck. "I didn't mean to upset you. We're still friends. Nothing has to change."

"It's not like you can help it." She bit her tongue to keep from saying something stupid, like *If I were ready for you, I would have fought this*. "You can talk to me about anything, you know you can. But...I would rather you didn't talk to me about that." She had no interest in hearing Santiago moon over another woman.

His lips pressed together, just for a moment, but then his expression smoothed over. He nodded. "That's fine. Whatever you need."

With a sigh and a small smile. she patted his pillow. "Come here." He scooted up the bed to sit beside her, and she rested her head on his shoulder. "What are we doing about the money? For real. Are we gonna have enough?"

He blew out a breath. "Maca asked me about sending more money."

Mariana startled. "San—"

"I told her no." He shifted to face her. "What I have is yours. It was wrong of me to send them extra money without checking with you first. Whatever I have, it goes toward our life together. And if you like Rachonne's house, then I'll do whatever I can to get us that house."

Oh my God. She beamed. "You mean it?"

"Absolutely." He passed her his phone: his money and bank accounts were listed out in a spreadsheet. "I'm trying to get better about budgeting. Can you take a look?"

She warmed at the question, at his trusting her. "Sure, let me pull up mine for reference." She brought up her own banking app—and the six-figure number in her checking account blurred her vision. A lump formed in her throat. "Santi. Santi! It's here!"

He straightened up beside her. "What's here?"

She shoved her phone in his face.

His jaw dropped, and he shook his wrist. "Damn!"

"Yeah!" She pulled her phone back and cradled it like a baby. "I can't believe it actually happened. It didn't feel real. And now here it is. Two hundred actual thousand dollars."

He clapped with each syllable: "Pay! Your! Loans! Pay! Your! Loans!"

"Holy shiiiiit." She sucked in a deep breath, then blew it out all at once. "Okay. Here I go." First on the list: her Visa. "Make Payment, yes." Her fingertip hovered over Current Balance.

Adulthood, here I come.

Her Visa balance plummeted to zero. Next her MasterCard, then her undergrad loan, then grad school, then her car.

$0. $0. $0. $0. $0.

She burst into tears.

I can't believe it's over. The huge burden lifted from her, leaving her so light the room spun around her. Swaying, she caught herself on Santiago, who pulled her in for a hug. She clenched her fists in the back of his shirt as she cried on him.

Once her tears had waned, she sent him his chunk of the money. They stared at his phone until it chirped to alert him to the income.

She nestled into him. "Can you send it over now? What time is it in Madrid? It's gotta be late..." Quick mental math...well, not so quick.

He grinned and sent the money to a Dolores Martínez Rubio—it took Mariana a second to recognize Lola's full first name in the banking app—and ran a hand through his thick, wavy hair. "Should I call her? It's past midnight for her."

Mariana waved this off. "Call her, call her, call her!"

Before he could bring up the phone number, Skype sang with an incoming call from his mom. Santiago accepted the call, and Lola's tear-streaked face filled the screen. "S-S-Santi—" And then she dissolved into incoherent Spanish, wiping her cheeks as she sobbed. When he tried to respond, his voice cracked, and he broke down, too, covering his face with his hand as he wept. Tears filled Mariana's eyes, and she started crying again. Santiago grabbed a few tissues for himself and then passed her the box. She dabbed at her eyes. The only sound in the room was three people's happy sobs.

Lola was finally going to get the surgery she needed. She would have a full-time caretaker to make sure she recovered safely. She was going to be okay.

Chapter Twenty-Two

In Which the Light Comes On

DECEMBER

Winter storm clouds obscured the setting sun, streaking their new house in blue-gray. (Mariana still couldn't believe they had a house, even if it was rented.) Silvery rain tapped hard against the windows and roof. She swirled her afternoon coffee in her mug at the kitchen table. Beside her, Embry sipped her own, rocking her natural hair. Santiago had left ten minutes ago to catch a movie with a friend, so it was a girls' night in.

"What's in the oven?" Embry took in a deep, happy breath. "It smells amazing."

"Lasagna. Surprise?" Mariana gave her a sheepish thumbs-up. "I can make exactly one thing well, so that's what we get."

Embry pointed at her. "I love your lasagna. Don't even."

"Yeah, but it's..." Mariana sighed. *Might as well put it out there.* "I feel bad. Like if I were more of an adult, I would know how to cook more things. Or I'd like cooking in general. I'd take either." She set her mug down and rubbed her temples. Lightning lit up the windows.

A rueful laugh. "And I wish I remembered to do laundry before I run out of underwear. Sometimes we gotta take the hand we're dealt and hope to God we find someone else who likes to do the other stuff."

Wait...what? "You forget to do laundry?" Mariana leaned in, uncertain if she'd misunderstood. "But you're...an adult. Like, an adulty adult." Embry was thirty-two years old, went to the gym regularly, and was never late to the mentoring program.

"Oh, I forget all the time. I hate doing laundry, so I put it off forever." Embry laughed. "Adultiness is relative. I'm low on shirts, but I always fill up the car before the gas light comes on."

"Ooh. Nice." Not a joke.

"You don't like to cook, but whatever. You're good at other stuff. Embrace what you're good at."

Thunder cracked. The lights flickered. What was Mariana good at? The answers came more quickly than she expected. *I can stick to a budget. I wash the bedsheets every week. I always remember to bring team snacks to the soccer games.* For the first time, these felt like genuine victories, not mere attempts to make up for her shortcomings. She was good at adulting on some things, and not as good at others. And maybe that was okay. "How come nobody talks about this?"

Embry shrugged. "Nobody wants to admit we're all bullshitting our way through life. We really are though."

"What?" *How dare the world have misled me like this.*

"Oh, yeah. I'm totally guessing half the time."

Mariana's jaw dropped.

Embry toasted her with her coffee mug. "Cheers to no one knowing what they're doing."

"Cheers to that." Still appalled, Mariana clinked her mug to Embry's and took a relieved sip. *We're all making it up as we go, and that's okay.*

Then she choked on her coffee.

Because all this time she, like an idiot, had pushed away love due to those pervasive feelings of insufficiency, of inadequacy. As if she'd only deserve someone—as if she'd only deserve *Santiago*—once she'd reached some invisible threshold that was forever out of reach. A threshold that, it turned out, no one ever quite reached.

Good job, dumbass.

Her phone chimed from her pocket, a phone call. Caller ID: *Best Husband Ever*. Why was he calling? He should've been at the movie theater by now. "Hey, everything okay?"

The line was mostly static, punctuated by thunder. Santiago's voice crackled in and out. "With the...in the road...I didn't...accident...into the...stuck there."

Her entire body lit with fear. "You were in an accident? Are you okay?"

"I...my head but—" Thunder drowned him out. "—the car."

"Where are you?"

Static. Then: "Richmond Road."

She yanked on a jacket. "I'll be right there."

Lightning flashed as Mariana ran out the door with an apology and the promise of a rain check. Her umbrella blew inside out and she abandoned it beside the door, pulling her hood over her head to protect her hair from the rain. Water blurred her glasses. She slid into the driver's seat of her car, wiped the lenses clear, and peeled out of the driveway, thunder rumbling with the engine.

Rain grayed out the windshield as her wipers thrashed back and forth to clear it. She passed a minivan crunched against a guard rail, an ambulance wailing in the distance. Her skin buzzed with anxiety. Was he okay? If he'd hit his head, he could have a concussion or worse. Was he bleeding? Was he trapped?

He's going to be okay. He has to be.

She was his best friend. She was his wife. She loved him with everything in her. And she was going to find him, no matter how dangerous the drive.

The traffic light ahead turned yellow, red. She eased to a stop, giving the car in front of her extra space. Foot on the brake, she texted Santiago.

CUTEST WIFE IN HISTORY: *I'll be there as soon as I can.*

CUTEST WIFE IN HISTORY: *Are you hurt?*

No response. The light turned green. Her wheels skidded on a sheet of water, then lurched her forward. She hissed out a breath. Only ten minutes away.

The car skidded again—swerved toward the oncoming traffic. "Oh, f—" She jerked the wheel and barely missed an SUV. Her pulse pounded triple-time in her throat. Lightning shot across the dark sky ahead, followed by a crack of thunder. Trees stretched over the road, their branches shaking and snapping in the wind. She clenched her teeth and gripped the wheel harder.

He has to be okay.

She slowed when she turned onto Richmond Road, searching for his car along the long country road. Everything was muddled with rain and dusk, with no lamps to help her. Squinting down the street, she struggled to make anything out—but then she saw it. Red hazards flickered from afar, on and off and on. A familiar gold sedan. Her foot went too hard on the gas, almost sent her careening off the road, but she steadied the car and pulled in behind him, barely avoiding the lake of rainwater crossing the highway.

From up close, it looked bad. The tail end of his car hung out onto the shoulder, while the front tipped into the ditch that had flooded onto the road. The light inside the car was on, revealing empty seats. Her chest seized. *Where is he?*

Santiago sloshed around the side of the car, his hair plastered to his head, his sweater and jeans heavy with rain. He held up one hand to block his eyes from her headlights. "Mariana?" Even at a shout, his voice barely carried over the wind and rain.

With a sob, she burst from her car, ran to him, and threw her arms around him. He stumbled but hugged her back as she held on as fiercely as she could. The storm and his clothes drenched her, but she wouldn't, couldn't, let go.

She dragged him into the backseat of her car so she could hear him, feel him. "Are you okay?" She pulled back to inspect him. "Does anything hurt? You didn't hit your head, did you?" She ran her fingers over his skin, checking for blood, appreciating the feel of him so close when this car accident could've ended so much worse. Her thumb traced over his temple, her fingers lacing into his wet hair. *He's here. He's alive.*

He shook his head. "I'm fine. A little whiplash maybe. The main problem is that I'm stuck." He gestured to the ditch.

Mariana wiped rain from her glasses. "I have some traction tread things in my trunk. We can stick them under your wheels." Her lips and hands trembled. "Are you really okay?"

He cupped her face in her hands and kissed her on the forehead. "As far as I can tell. Are you?"

"I—" The words choked off at the lump in her throat. Her vision burned and blurred. She pulled back to wipe at her eyes. She meant to say something general, maybe *let's get the treads*, but she couldn't let go of him. *It could've been so bad, I could've lost him, he could have died, and he wouldn't have known that—* "I love you."

He sucked in a breath, but he played along, as if she were only practicing saying it. "Yes, I know. Let's—"

"No." It would be easy to back off, to pretend it had been part of the act. But she was done acting. Cold rain poured onto the windshield and roof. She lifted her chin, despite her jitters and her tears. Her voice faltered, but she pushed the words out. "I *love* you, Santi."

*

Lightning lit up the clouds, punctuated by thunder. The wind whistled around the car as Santiago stared at his wife and struggled to grasp her words. She couldn't be serious... Could she?

"I don't care if you want Yelena." Dripping and shivering, she set her jaw. "I—"

"Yelena?" Why would she ever think he wanted Yelena?

Lips pressed together, Mariana jerked her head away. "You forgot all about me at the work party after she showed up."

Emotion thickened his accent, made him search harder for the English. "We are friends. Only." This seemed the most important thing to get out of the way.

Poor use of pronouns. Mariana leaned back, eyes flaring with uncertainty and hurt. "I know we are, I just— I thought—"

"No!" Pressing a hand over his eyes, he tried to slow his breathing. His heart, unwilling to cooperate, smashed out a frantic beat. He scrambled for words that dissolved on his tongue. "It's not... I can't..."

She said nothing, but he heard the wounded inhale. He dropped his hand, and the pain etched on her face punched him in the gut.

No no no no no. He wanted to charm her, to romance her, to make her understand how much he loved her. Why couldn't he make his words work for him? "I don't want to..."

"Santi." Her voice broke on the single word.

Come on, come on, come on. Desperate to get out something that made sense, he went with the quickest coherent sentence he would think of. "*I love you.*"

*

A wet noise strangled in the air—and it had come from her own throat.

"I am no actor." Those big dark eyes pled with her to understand.

Her pulse battered against her ribcage, her throat. "No, you... Yelena and... You said you wanted..."

"I want you."

She choked on her own breath.

Santi's hands stayed at his sides, but his fingers curled and uncurled, maybe buzzing with the same frantic energy in her own. "I have wanted you since the restaurant," he pressed. "Since the dinner with Embry's family. Since the...almost since the beginning. I don't want anyone else, and if I see you want someone else, I think I'll break apart."

Her head spun.

He leaned forward. "*Cariño*, I don't want to act with you anymore— I haven't been acting. Not for a long time. Everything has been real for me."

"It's been real for me too. That's why seeing you with her..." She averted her gaze and ignored the squeeze in her stomach at the memory. "That's why I was upset. I didn't think... You looked..."

"I told you, no. It was not her." He brought one hand up, caressed tentative fingertips over her forearm.

Despite the cold, she burned where he touched her, and her face warmed, but she didn't move away.

"There was never anyone else."

When she dared to flit her gaze up to his face, she saw earnestness in his eyes, determination in the set of his jaw. Hope bloomed somewhere inside her. "Yeah?" This reply was sadly insufficient for the explosion of thoughts and colors whirling in her head.

He cracked that dimpled grin for her. "Yeah."

"There was never anyone else for me either."

His smile widened, and both hands drew upward to graze the sensitive insides of her elbows. A slight tug toward him without really moving her. He watched her with such intense focus that she grinned nervously.

"You okay, Santi?"

He considered this, his eyes never leaving her face. "Can I kiss you now? Not for practice?"

Her heart seemed to expand, to squeeze past her lungs and ribs to fill her whole chest. This time when he tugged her, she was already coming toward him, and then his mouth found hers, the taste of him both familiar and new. She parted her lips out of habit, her body sizzling at the memory of their other kisses.

His tongue swept boldly over the inside of her lower lip. She didn't realize she'd reached up until her fingers clenched in his thick, wet hair. Pulling him closer, she pressed up to feel more of him against her. His touch felt impossible, or impossibly satisfying, and she ached for it. Her husband, her best friend wanted to be with her. Wanted *her*. He knew her inside and out, and he loved her despite it all—or perhaps because of it all.

He was hers. She was his. After so long pretending, this was finally real.

Chapter Twenty-Three

In Which They Explore

DECEMBER

The bedside lamps cast warm shadows around the room, the curtains hiding the stars outside. Mariana snuggled up against Santiago in bed, her cheek against his heartbeat, their legs tangled together. He was all warmth and familiarity, and she ran her fingers through his hair as she caught him up on her day—the first day her James Farmer exhibit went live for the public.

"We had so many first-time visitors!" She beamed. "It was amazing."

He high-fived her. "That's my girl!"

"Even Cheryl said it was a good turnout. If she had something nice to say, you know it must be true. And she didn't even turn it into an insult."

"Cheryl can kiss my ass," he said sweetly.

She giggled. "The interactive section I had to fight for went over really well. I had five different families thank me for adding in something to spice things up."

Content, she caught him up on all the details of the exhibit, reveling in the success...and then cleared her throat. "There was something else I wanted to talk to you about."

He propped himself up on one elbow and dropped his chin into his palm. "Go for it."

You have to talk about this. Openness is part of being in a healthy relationship. Even if it might be uncomfortable. She traced one finger down his arm to steady herself. "I'm demisexual."

"Right." She'd told him a while ago, but they hadn't discussed it in detail.

"So I don't feel attracted to someone unless there's a strong emotional bond first. Which we have. And obviously I'm attracted to you." Smiling, she ducked her head. "A lot."

He grinned. "And I couldn't be happier about it."

"I love kissing you—not right now!" She tapped him on the nose when he leaned in. "And I'm interested in experimenting with touching. But as we go, I don't know what I'll be down for, so please be patient, okay?"

"Of course." He sobered and placed a light kiss on her forehead. "To be honest I don't fully understand what that feels like, but I accept you, one hundred percent. I'm happy to do or not do whatever you need."

Anxiety needled her. "And you'll tell me if it's not enough for you?"

He kissed her again, on the lips this time. "You're enough for me." His hand skated over her curves, tracing her body reverently before dipping under the waistband of her pajama pants. Then lower still. "Can we experiment with this?"

Santiago's fingers moved, and she gasped at the surge of pleasure.

He paused. "Bad?"

Oh lord. She had to catch her breath. "Good. *Good.*" It took all her self-control not to cant her hips into his hand.

His lips moved to her neck. With a lingering kiss, he caressed her in lazy circles, and she melted under him. *I deeefinitely like this with him.*

"Oh, I've wanted this," he whispered against her skin, his mouth trailing down to her clavicle. "You feel so good."

Warmth spread through her body as he worked her over, his touch somehow both soft and firm. "Mmm." She gave in and arched against his kisses.

He moaned. "Yes. God, yes." But he pulled back.

Why? She opened her eyes. "Santi?"

Gaze hazy, he urged her to sit up for a moment. "Shirt?"

It took a second for the word to process, but she peeled off her tank top and tossed it aside, leaving her in a bright yellow bra. She licked her lips and waited anxiously for any sign of mixed feelings, but his laser focus on the curves of her breasts suggested otherwise.

"You okay?" His voice was rough.

She nodded.

"Okay if I touch you?"

She nodded again, expecting his hands, but he bent his head, and it was his mouth that traced the scalloped edges of her bra, kissing along her exposed soft skin. She murmured and arched again, looking for more. Her breasts felt bigger, too full, needing to be touched.

His hands smoothed around her bare sides, onto her back, until his fingertips found the bra clasp. "Can I take this off?" he whispered.

"Off," she panted, "take it off."

It took him two tries, but he unlatched the bra, and the straps fell down her arms before he drew it all the way off and dropped it near her shirt. Then his mouth was on her nipple, hot and wet and sucking, and she gasped. *Yes.* She threaded her fingers into that hair she loved, and she clutched him close, the pressure of his tongue both easing and stoking the fire inside her. "Oh. Ohhh. *Santi.*"

He made a satisfied noise in the back of his throat. "Yes?"

"Yes. Yes, yes, yes. Keep going."

His hands skimmed over her waist, down her hips, and trailed under her pajama pants again—with a gentle tug. "How about these come off too?" he suggested with no pressure in his tone.

If less pants meant more Santi, she was down for it. She raised her hips from the mattress, pulled the pants off, and tossed them to the side. "Done," she managed. "And yours?"

"I can do that." He yanked his sweater off over his head in one efficient, male motion. It fluttered to the floor, but she didn't see where. Her attention was otherwise occupied.

She ran her hand over his rounded stomach, over the wiry hair on his chest. "You're so handsome."

He bent and kissed her, his tongue exploring her mouth as his hands explored her body, caressing down her sides and fingering the lace edges of her matching yellow panties. One of his legs slid over her body, and then he eased himself on top of her, still kissing her, touching her everywhere except where she wanted him most.

She shifted underneath him, tilting her pelvis into him and finding a tent in his sweatpants that fit perfectly against her. She ground against his erection, and the friction sparked the most intense pleasure yet. Sighing with gratification, she canted her hips against him, over and over, wetness slick on her underwear.

He groaned at the contact. "*Cariño*, I would die to be between your legs right now."

She hesitated. "Maybe not yet. But...can I see you?"

His Adam's apple bobbed. "Sure. Whatever you want." He slipped his sweats off, and his cock thrust toward Mariana through the opening in his boxers, thick and veined with a slight curve. He waited for her, didn't move until she gestured for him to come close again. He climbed back onto the bed, and she settled beneath the comforting weight of him with a smile.

"Give me a kiss," she demanded playfully. He lowered his head and devoured her mouth, and the flame in her abdomen lit higher. She ran her hands over his back and then into his hair, gripping hard enough that he moaned. "Do you like that?"

"I do. It feels..." He trailed off into another sigh when she pulled at his hair again.

She arched her hips up into him, reveling in how good he felt pressed against her. She couldn't imagine being with anyone else this way. The way he'd touched her... "Will you touch me again?"

"Sure." He skimmed his fingertips along her sides to tickle her.

She yelped and squirmed underneath him, but his weight held her down. "No fair!"

Santiago grinned. "You didn't say where. Or how."

Swatting his tickling hands away, she glared up at him. "You know where."

He shrugged. "I'm not a mind reader."

She huffed. "My *clit*, you monster. Aren't you supposed to make this easy for me?"

"Easy, no. Fun, yes. And don't I do a great job?"

"Debatable."

"You hurt me. So mean." His hand slid beneath her underwear, fingertips sweeping over her mound to circle over her clit the way she'd liked before. "But you're so sexy, I might forgive you."

Her breath hitched at the intimate touch. "Sexy?" No one had ever made that connection with her before.

"Definitely." He licked up the side of her neck and nibbled on her earlobe. His hand that wasn't pleasuring her slid up her body to massage her breast. "I've wanted to feel you and taste you for months now. Your body is the ultimate temptation."

Flushing, she hummed in appreciation and tilted her hips to maneuver his touch into the right spot to make her— "Ohhh, yes. There." Her head fell back against the pillow, and her whole body arched.

He lowered his mouth to her ear. "You're so wet. After you come this time, I'm going to taste you, lick you up, and make you do it again. I want to feel you come against my mouth."

"That's—Santi, shit—" She pushed toward the pleasure coiling in her center, hot and demanding. Sensation, desire, pulsed within her, barely out of reach. She could have sobbed.

Speeding up his circles, he took her mouth, his tongue teasing hers and exploring her mouth. She fisted one hand in his hair again and the other in the sheets, her hips trembling. With a groan, he stuttered in his rhythm.

"Don't stop, please—" She thrust helplessly against his fingers, her folds slick.

He rubbed her clit fast and hard, exactly the way she needed. "Yes, *cariño*, come for me," he whispered, his voice rough with need. "Just for me."

"Oh—oh, *Santi*!" At his words, she shattered, a million tiny pieces of fantastic pleasure spinning out into the universe. She soared, and when she finally came back down to earth, her entire body was buzzing and limp.

It took several minutes for her to recover, but when she finally reached for him, he inched down the bed.

"I told you my plans," he said with a grin, "and I'd hate to give them up." He kissed his way down her stomach, along her inner thighs, and then...

If she'd thought his fingers were magical, they had nothing on his tongue.

He lapped her up like she was his favorite dessert, his mouth attentive and all-consuming. The tip of his tongue swirled at her clit, then at her entrance, tracing an infinite figure eight between the two that made her arch and moan. He licked her with a mix of love and lust that had her shuddering with unspent pleasure faster than she'd thought possible. Her fingers searched out his hair, and a moan vibrated against her.

Unable to keep still, she moved against his ministrations. She thrust her hips up against his mouth, and his palms slid over her thighs, holding her in place while he ate her out. Fire crawled over her skin, burning her up. She arched off the bed. "Yes, like that, keep going, *keep going…*" Her grip tightened in his hair. She cried out as another orgasm washed over her, drowning her in pleasure. He lightened his touch, but she had to nudge him away completely, her throbbing clit too sensitive for contact.

Sated and loose-limbed, Mariana sank into the bed in utter bliss; Santiago crawled up to lie beside her, tracing his fingertips over her curves.

"How are you feeling?" he whispered.

"Amazing." She smiled lazily and ran her fingers through his mussed hair. "Mmmm. That was…some next-level shit."

He kissed her lightly. "Good. I want you to feel good."

"Oh, you definitely accomplished that. Whew." She blew out a long breath. "But what about you?"

"I'm happy making you happy."

His erection begged for attention, though, and she wanted to explore with him. Explore *everything*. She trailed a finger along its length.

His eyes closed, and the tip of his tongue darted out to wet his lips. "You don't have to do anything you don't want to do."

"Who said I didn't want to try?" She swept her thumb over the tip. Her other hand went to the waistline of his boxers. "Let's take these off."

"Anything you want." He slipped his boxers off and dropped them onto the floor, baring himself completely.

Her gaze fell to the dark hair trailing from his navel to the base of his cock. She curled her finger in a silent come-hither gesture. He knelt in front of her on the bed, and she grazed her fingertips over the trimmed curls, then up his erection.

He lurched at the contact. "*Tesoro...*"

She dragged her gaze up to his face. "Come closer. I want to feel you."

Santiago leaned in and kissed her, and she tugged him into herself until they fell backward onto the pillows. Her legs parted around him, and her ankles crossed at the small of his back. He caressed one hand down her body until he found her core. She expected him to do the same thing as before, but instead he massaged her there, a gentle, sensual rubbing. She hummed in interest, her legs falling farther apart to grant him better access.

"You like that?" He pressed his lips to the underside of her jaw.

"Mm-hmm."

"Good." He kissed his way down her neck, then took her nipple in his mouth, sucking gently.

Sensation thrilling through her, she clasped his head to her breast. "Mmmm."

He groaned and circled the tip of his tongue around the bud. She trembled. His fingertips slid between her lower lips, slick and easy. With a low *ohhhh* she parted her legs further, wider. Unexpectedly, she liked the openness, the vulnerability of being spread open for him. He had the reins in this moment, and his priority was her pleasure.

Then, one finger slipped inside her and curled at an angle that made her breath catch in her throat. "How does that feel?" he whispered.

"Good. Really good." She lifted her hips, searching for more. "Will you...?"

He withdrew, entered again, over and over, curving his finger into her most sensitive spot.

She sighed, pleasure tingling at her entrance as he moved in and out. "Yes. More." He slid in a second finger, and she closed her eyes as she thrust against his movements.

He lowered his mouth to her ear. "You feel amazing. I've imagined being inside you, and it has nothing on the real thing."

Her cheeks heated, and she met his gaze. "Really? You imagined being with me like this?"

He flashed his dimples. "With such a beautiful woman next to me every night, it was hard not to." His free hand caressed her curves, stoking the fire inside her. He kneaded her breasts, played with her nipples, trailed his fingertips down her abdomen and around her hip to grip her ass. All the time, his fingers pumped in and out, and her breaths shortened with desire. "You're so sexy. Every inch of you makes me ache."

"You *ache*, huh?" She traced her palm down his chest, down his stomach, to his erection and palmed the silky hardness. His hips pumped into the contact; his eyes went half-lidded, and his rhythm inside her stuttered. She caressed him up and down, up and down, until he tugged her in for a deep kiss, his tongue lashing into her mouth as he trembled, trying not to thrust into her touch.

She pulled back for a breath. "I think I'm ready to move forward," she said archly.

"Whatever you want." He pulled his fingers out of her and licked the wetness from them.

She swallowed hard. That tongue had done some wondrous things. Maybe she could get him to taste her again after this...but first, she wanted him inside her.

Foil crinkled, and then he settled between her thighs, his cock brushing the lips of her sex. Unable to resist harder contact, she ground down on him. Groaning, he thrust up so that her lips parted around him, her wetness soaking his length. Not inside, but all up against her. She rode him like that, instinct taking over where experience lacked; she rode his erection and, with a moan, tucked her face into the arch where his neck met his broad shoulder. Pleasure pooled in her belly, but it wasn't enough. She felt empty, wanting. "Santi, I need more. I need you."

With a rough noise, he kissed her again, and this time, his tip settled at her entrance. "I'll take it slow."

"No. Now." She trembled with want. If he made her wait any longer, she might die. "*Please.*"

He looked deep into her eyes. And then he slid inside her, filling her up, stretching her without hurting. Absolute perfection. When she adjusted her angle beneath him, he partially withdrew and thrust back in, finding a part of her that lit up like fireworks. She dug her nails into his back. "Holy shit, *cariño*, that—do that again."

He pulled out, pushed back in, hitting that spot again, and she arched in pleasure. "Santi, yes. Oh my God, yes. More."

Then he was in and out, in and out, lighting up her core, grunting with the effort. She reached up with one hand and fisted it in his hair the way he liked, and pulled hard. He groaned, gripped her hip, and thrust harder. She pushed back against him, taking all of him, feeling him everywhere.

"Mari, I—nngh—" His thrusts stuttered, and she found herself taking over the rhythm as his hands fisted in the bedsheets. "I'm going to—"

The pleasure radiating from him, how close he was, all his smooth words stumbling, thrilled her. More desire coiled in her. "Do it, Santi," she whispered, echoing his own words to her earlier. "Come for me."

One last thrust, and he came with a raw sound in the back of his throat. He collapsed on top of her. She wasn't done, though, so she snuggled him while he recovered, but once he sat up... "Will you go down on me again?"

His grin shouted yes.

Chapter Twenty-Four

In Which They Finally Get a Dog

DECEMBER

> CUTEST WIFE IN HISTORY: *leaving work now*

> CUTEST WIFE IN HISTORY: *dog* 🖐 *time* 🖐 *dog* 🖐 *time* 🖐 *dog* 🖐 *time* 🖐

> BEST HUSBAND EVER: *dog tiiiiiime!!* 🖐🐾

> CUTEST WIFE IN HISTORY: *do you have everything ready to go?*

> BEST HUSBAND EVER: *it's all by the door, ready for you to get here*

> CUTEST WIFE IN HISTORY: *can't wait!!! I'm gonna drive FAST*

> BEST HUSBAND EVER: *NO BE SAFE*

CUTEST WIFE IN HISTORY: 👀

Despite the chilly winter wind, blue skies stretched overhead as Mariana pulled into the driveway of their house and parked beside Santiago's car. Christmas lights lined the rooftop and front porch, and a blowup Santa sat in the middle of the lawn. She raced inside to drop off her lunch box and work things. Santiago was fussing with a dog crate, a basket of dog toys, a dog bed, grooming supplies, and more, which were set up by the door as promised. He caught her with a kiss as she passed, and she stopped to run her fingers through his thick waves before continuing on her way to the kitchen.

"Are you reeeady?" she sang as she slipped a Pop-Tart packet into her purse in case they got hungry before they returned.

"So ready!" He bounced onto the tile floor in his socks and almost slipped. "Well, technically I still have to put on my shoes. But other than that, yes."

While he searched for his sneakers, she changed out of her work clothes into a T-shirt and jeans. The carpet was freshly clean, and the dryer rumbled. Her chest warming, she poked her head out from the bedroom. "Thanks for vacuuming and doing the laundry, *cariño*."

He winked at her. "Anytime."

They picked up the leash, an adjustable collar, a squeaky squirrel toy, and an old blanket from the dog supplies on their way out the door and dropped them into the back seat of Mariana's car. She slid into the driver's seat; he took the passenger's seat. Once she'd backed out onto the road, he took her right hand in his left, tracing circles on the back of her hand with his thumb.

"You'll be a great dog mom. Especially with the million dog training videos you watched," he teased.

She glanced his way and stuck out her tongue. "So I like to be prepared. Sue me. But I guess you're gonna be a great dog dad too."

"You *guess*?"

She shrugged, then grinned. "Yeah, you are."

After ten minutes on the highway, they parked outside the Humane Society of Northern Virginia and strolled toward the front door. In the cool air, his hand was warm in hers.

"Pup-py time. Pup-py time," she chanted under her breath, and he laughed.

He opened the glass door for her, and they walked into the lobby. A few people sat on the scattered benches. Quiet classical music played from the overhead speakers. In one corner, a calico cat in a tall multilevel cage groomed herself. At the front desk, an older white woman with short gray hair greeted them. "How can we help you today?"

Mariana gestured with her thumb between herself and Santi. "We're the de los Reyeses. We have an appointment to look at dogs."

"Oh, right! We spoke on the phone. I'm Ellen." Ellen extended her hand, and Mariana shook it, then Santiago. "Let me take you back." She rose from her chair and shuffled out from behind the desk. Another employee took her place there.

"So what are y'all looking for?" Ellen asked.

"Definitely an adult, not a puppy. Two years old and up only. We don't feel up to an actual baby yet."

Taking Santi's hand again, Mariana scrunched up her nose.

"And one that's lower-energy." Santiago put his free hand in his pocket as they walked. "We're not super active people."

Ellen nodded. "I get you completely. Luckily, we have a few that could fit the bill for you." She opened a back door for them that led into a big room with ten dogs in spacious cages. She bypassed the first few—Mariana whispered hi to each pup—and stopped at the fourth. Ellen stepped aside so Mariana and Santiago could get a good look at the white pit mix inside. "This is Ziggy. Someone found him alongside the highway. Our vet thinks he's about four years old. We don't know much about his background since he's a stray, but he's played well with the other dogs while he's been here, and he's good with kids. He's a pretty laid-back boy."

"Awww, cute!" Mariana waved at the dog. "Can we pet him?"

"Sure. Let's take him out to the play area." Ellen unlocked the cage door, put a leash on Ziggy, and picked a couple toys from a bin. She led the three of them out back to a big fenced-in yard with agility equipment and a few benches. There, she handed Santiago a tennis ball and Mariana a tug toy and the leash. Ziggy leaned against Mariana's legs for pets.

She lit up. "He likes me!"

"Of course he likes you. You're the best." Santiago squatted to rub behind the dog's ears and in a higher-pitched voice, said, "You're pretty great, too, huh, buddy?"

Ziggy pushed his head into Santi's hand, tail thumping on the ground.

"Does he know fetch?" Mariana stole the ball from Santi with a grin and held it up.

Ziggy brightened, his gaze zeroing in on the toy.

"Oooh." Santiago straightened. "Looks like he might."

"All right, let's see." Mariana dropped the leash and pitched the ball across the yard.

Ziggy bounded after it with glee, picked it up in his mouth, and bolted back to them to drop it proudly at her feet.

"Good boy! Good fetch!" Mariana threw the ball again and surreptitiously wiped the dirt and dog drool off her hand.

They played with Ziggy until Ellen suggested, "We have a few more options you might like to meet. Are y'all ready to go back in?"

They put Ziggy back and moved a few doors down to a brown-and-white mutt with long ears and a speckled nose. "This is Spot. He was an owner-surrender last month. She was moving and couldn't take him. He's five years old and walks great on a leash. Heart of gold, and he'll do anything for a treat. Good with cats, good with other dogs, good with kids."

"Look at his little freckles!" *We could do better than "Spot" as a name, but it's accurate.* Mariana crouched to wiggle her fingers at Spot, who came up to the door and licked her hand. She giggled and stood. "Can we take him for a walk?"

"Absolutely." Ellen hooked him up with the leash and took them all back outside. They made a couple rounds around the play area, Mariana holding the leash and Spot trotting along between her and Santiago happily.

"What a good boy you are," Mariana praised the dog at her side. "You walk so nice!"

He smiled up at her, tongue lolling, and her insides seized with the cuteness. Unable to resist him, she bent to give him scratchies behind his long fuzzy ears.

"Do you know what breed he is?" Santiago too knelt to pet Spot, who soaked up the attention.

Ellen nodded. "He's a spaniel mix. Cocker spaniel mom and Cavalier King Charles spaniel dad. Quite a looker, huh?"

"He's the cutest baby in the world," Mariana cooed in a high-pitched voice. He might not be a puppy, but all dogs were babies to her.

Spot jumped up to lick her on the cheek.

Laughing, she gently pushed him back down to all fours. "Down, boy."

"He's a lover, not a fighter, that's for sure." Ellen shook her head. "I can't believe he's been with us for as long as he has. I thought he'd be snatched up in a minute."

"I can see why." Santiago snuggled the dog.

Mariana clasped a hand to her chest. *So cute. I die.* "Can we take him into the play area too?"

"Of course." Ellen opened the gate for them and ushered them in, where an employee was playing fetch with a Lab mix. Spot's little butt wiggled with interest, but he didn't pull at the leash.

Santiago picked up a squeaky toy someone had dropped in the yard and threw it long. "Go, Spot, go!"

Mariana dropped the leash, and Spot bolted after the toy with surprising speed. His little tail wagging, he brought it back to them and dropped it right into Santi's hand with a "drop it" command.

"What a good boy. Go get it!" Santi pitched the toy like he taught baseball instead of soccer, and Spot ran after it again. "He's great. I really like him." Santiago glanced Mariana's way. "What do you think, *tesoro*?"

"I love him. His little nose, and his ears, oh my gosh." She touched her heart. "And he's so well behaved. I wanna take him home and snuggle him."

"Me too. You think...?"

She nodded.

He looked to Ellen. "This might be the one."

"That's fantastic!" Ellen beamed. "Do you want to meet the last dog on our list, or is Spot your decision?"

Mariana looked at Santiago, and he looked at her, and Spot leaned happily against her leg.

Mariana smiled down at the spaniel. "He's the one for us."

*

CUTEST WIFE IN HISTORY: *don't forget I'm going to the gym with Yelena after work today*

BEST HUSBAND EVER: *awww will I see you?*

CUTEST WIFE IN HISTORY: *yeah, I'll stop by home first*

BEST HUSBAND EVER: *okay good*

BEST HUSBAND EVER: *I know I saw you this morning but I miss you*

CUTEST WIFE IN HISTORY: *you're a dork* ❤

BEST HUSBAND EVER: *are you saying you don't miss me??? I'm wounded*

CUTEST WIFE IN HISTORY: *I'm changing your contact name to "giant dork"*

GIANT DORK: *DON'T YOU DARE*

CUTEST WIFE IN HISTORY: *TOO LATE*

The afternoon sun shone through the house windows, glinting off the Christmas decorations and warming the rooms with an orange glow. Mariana picked through her dresser drawers, looking for workout clothes. So far, little success. Anything made for exercising was long buried from disuse. "I need something to wear while I work out. Are yoga pants allowed at Yelena's gym?"

Standing in the doorway, Santiago shrugged. "They have yoga classes, so I would think so."

"'I think so' isn't good enough for my anxiety." She brought up the gym's website on her phone and looked up the dress code policy. "Okay, cool. It doesn't say anything about yoga pants, so I think I'm fine." Giving up on finding any athletic shorts, she pulled out a pair of black yoga pants she'd unearthed. The calves were zig-zagged in a neat pattern. "If I wear a yellow top with this, will I look like a bee?"

He considered it. "If the shirt is striped, yes. Otherwise, no."

"No stripes, so I'm good." Mariana stuffed the yoga pants, a yellow T-shirt, her tennis shoes, and an empty reusable water bottle into a drawstring bag and tossed it over her shoulder. "I still find it hard to believe she invited me to go with her. I thought y'all were friends, not me."

"She invited both of us," he admitted, "but someone has to make dinner. Besides, this will give you two the chance to get to know each other better."

"I'm not opposed, just surprised." She perched on the bed. "I'm meeting her there in fifteen minutes, so I'll have to leave soon. But..."

He came over and sat beside her. "But what?"

"I'm a little nervous. It's my first time going to the gym in...I don't even know how long." She fiddled with the drawstring on her bag. "What if people laugh at me?"

"If anyone laughs at you, I will personally fight them." He kissed her on the forehead. "Everyone goes to the gym to get better. And besides, everyone's thinking about themselves, not about you. Except for me. I'll definitely be thinking about you. And how good you look in yoga pants."

She pushed him with a laugh. "You're a rascal."

He grinned. "Yeah, but I'm *your* rascal."

"That you are." Leaning over, she rested her head on his shoulder. "Don't miss me too much while I'm gone."

"Oh, I'll miss you so much, I won't know what to do with myself." He shot her a suspicious look. "Speaking of missing you, did you really change my name in your phone to Giant Dork?"

Mariana arched a brow. "Ask yourself this. Are you really a giant dork? If so, then yes."

He snatched up her phone and checked their text messages. "You did! I'm changing it back."

She grabbed for the cell, but he moved it out of reach and pushed her away. "It's a term of endearment!"

"Then pick another term of endearment, like My Dearest Love!"

"Don't tell me what to name you!" She swiped at it again.

He only held it farther away from her as he deleted *Giant Dork* and typed in the new name *Mi Media Naranja* with several heart emojis. They fought over the phone for a minute before she managed to wrangle it back from him. She stuck out her tongue, and he poked her in the side, but she didn't change it back.

She bundled up in a coat, scarf, and mittens and bounded out into the cold (well, the South's version of cold, which was still ungodly chilly in her book) to get to her car. She drove to the local gym and parked in the long lot beside the building. Windows lined the wall, providing a clear view of all the fit people working out. Insecurity twinged inside her. What if people whispered about the new girl trying to keep up?

Well, they could go screw themselves.

Her head high, she turned toward the front door.

She'd half expected Yelena to drive a vibrant Mustang at excessive speeds, but an ultra-safe Subaru hatchback pulled into the lot beside her. Yelena eased to a stop and waved at her through the window with a broad smile.

Yelena got out of her car and walked around to meet Mariana at her car door. "You ready?"

Mariana offered a piece of herself: "It's my first time at the gym in who knows how long, so go easy on me, okay?"

"Of course. We can go at whatever speed you're comfortable with. Was there something in particular you wanted to do? Treadmills, bikes, the track, strength equipment, free weights...?"

It all sounded out of her realm, so Mariana picked one at random. "Let's do strength."

They hustled inside to get out of the cold. Yelena scanned her membership tag on her keychain, let the staff at the front desk know that Mariana was there as her guest, and led her into the women's locker room.

Yelena put her coat and purse in a locker, then held it open. "Here, you wanna put yours in with mine? I have a lock."

"Oh, sure, thanks." Mariana reached inside and hung her things from the peg at the top. "Perfect. I was nervous about leaving it here free for the taking."

"No worries. I've got you covered." Yelena closed the locker and slid her lock into place. "So you don't go to the gym a lot. Do you work out at home, then?"

Mariana ducked her head. "Nope. I don't prioritize exercise like I should. But with Santi coming to the gym with you so much lately—"

"You don't mind, do you?" Yelena touched Mariana's forearm, concern clouding her expression. "If it makes you uncomfortable, I won't—"

"No, it's fine. Don't worry about it." Not so long ago, Mariana would've angsted. *Had* angsted, that first time. But Santi had made his affections clear, and jealousy was no longer an issue. "All I was saying was, his going to the gym with you is inspiring me to get into better shape. So here I am, trying something new."

Across from the lockers, a line of stalls had a tall mirror and a stool inside each one. Mariana took her gym bag into the exact-middle changing stall and stripped off her regular clothes. "What do you usually do at the gym?" she called over the stall walls.

Yelena padded into the stall on her left. The lock latched, and clothing rustled. "I like to run, and the exercise classes are fun."

Worry clenched in Mariana's chest as she pulled on her workout clothes. "Are you missing that because I'm here?"

"Don't worry about it. I'm glad to have you with me."

"Okay, if you don't mind." Mariana bent and laced up her tennis shoes.

"Definitely. I feel like you and I haven't gotten a chance to get to know each other, and this is a good chance to rectify that." Yelena's door creaked open, signaling she was done changing. "So tell me about yourself!"

"I never know what to say when people say that," Mariana said with a laugh. "Um, I like history. Obviously, since that's my job. I was obsessed with mythology when I was younger too."

"Nice. Greek, Roman, Norse...?"

"Egyptian. I had a little Bastet pendant I wore all the time in high school, actually." She emerged from her changing stall.

"Ooh, I love those pants." Now in a black tank top and green athletic shorts, Yelena pulled her hair up into a high ponytail.

Mariana smiled. "Thanks. I had no good gym attire, so I hope this works."

"Looks great, works great. Good choice." Yelena high-fived her. They left the locker room and went over to the strength equipment. "Want to start with the seated press?"

Mariana looked toward a machine halfway down the aisle of machines. *That's the seated press, right? Weird choice, but okay.* She took one step toward it.

She was wrong.

Yelena gestured toward the first machine in the row. "Do you want to go first, or do you mind if I do?"

"Nah, go for it." *Probably best if I have an example of someone who uses it on the reg, anyway.*

Yelena picked her weights and started the chest presses. She was slim, but damn was she strong. The heavy stack of weights moved up and down with each laborious push, ending with a final *clank* as she sank back in the seat for a short rest. She shook out her arms, then did two more sets.

Yelena pulled a tiny green notebook and a pen out of her shorts pocket and marked the weight and reps before sliding out of the seat and gesturing for Mariana to take her place. "You can do it!"

Mariana slid into the seat and evaluated the weights. No way could she press that much. She pulled the little stick out and moved it halfway up the stack. Her arms shook as she gripped the handles and pressed outward.

The weights landed with a hard *clank* after the tenth press. "I'm gonna be a One-Set Susie today," she muttered, her arms aching. *Whatever, it's my first time.*

"You did great!" Yelena held up a hand.

Mariana lifted one sore arm and high-fived her. "I'm gonna die."

"No, you're not. Shake it out." Yelena shook out her own arms as an example.

Mariana copied her, feeling silly, but it did help. "So tell me about you," she suggested as they moved on to the next machine, another one that Mariana didn't know the name of. Yelena slipped into the seat first and started using it with the confidence of someone who'd done this regularly.

"I live with my friend Alex in my cousin Dmitri's apartment complex. He's cool, my cousin. More chill than I am, that's for sure. Well, I don't know what to say. You're right—it's weird to have to describe yourself in a few words."

"Do you make your students do it on the first day of class?" Mariana's teachers over the years had all loved to use that icebreaker.

"Oh, absolutely. It's like a rite of passage." Yelena laughed. "What else about me? I like running, against all logic. I watch football but not basketball. I eat Lucky Charms for breakfast every morning, like a champ."

"Mariana?" A familiar voice came from the bike area. Embry slowed her cycling to a stop and dismounted. Leaving her water bottle in the bike, she edged along the aisle and came over to hug Mariana. "I didn't know you came here."

Mariana hugged her back. "I don't usually. I'm here with one of Santi's work friends." She turned to introduce Yelena. "This is—what?"

Yelena stood staring, blinking at Embry, a delicate flush crawling up her cheeks.

Embry propped one hand on her hip. Something sparkled in her eyes. "Oh, hey, it's you. I'm Embry." She stuck out her other hand.

Yelena shook her hand, biting her lower lip. "I'm Yelena. I'm the work friend."

"Nice to actually meet you." Embry turned back to Mariana. "Yelena and I are in all the same exercise classes, but our paths have never crossed."

A guy cleared his throat beside the seated press, signaling that they needed to move on or move away from the machines.

Embry pulled a face. "Guess we're blocking traffic. I'll let you get back to your workout. Mariana; it was good seeing you. Yelena..." Her gaze flicked down Yelena's body and up again in a quick motion, almost imperceptible, and her lips curved. "It was nice to meet you."

Yelena swallowed. "You too."

Embry edged back to her bike, and Yelena let out a long breath. "She's so...pretty."

Mariana cocked her head. "She likes girls. Do you want me to ask if—?"

"No!" Yelena blurted. "Oh my God. It's nothing. Please don't say anything."

"Okay." Mariana shrugged. "Whatever you want."

They finished up their rounds on the exercise equipment, changed back into their outside clothes, and hugged goodbye at the door. Mariana drove back home, her stomach grumbling and her muscles aching as she sang along with the radio.

Sore but satisfied that she'd done a good job at the gym, Mariana fumbled at the doorknob with one mittened hand. "I hate winter." Finally, she got the door open, and the icy wind blew inside with her, shivering the tinsel and greenery. She hung up her coat, dropped her gym bag in the bedroom, and recognized the sound of conversation and kitchenware. "I'm home!"

"I'm in here!"

The boiling macaroni had steamed up the kitchen window and bumped the ambient temperature by a few degrees as well. Santiago stood by the stove, stirring the pot occasionally, Spot lying at his feet. His phone sat propped up on the counter. On-screen, Lola and Maca lit up. "Mariana!"

With a mock scowl, Santiago returned to Spanish. "You're more excited to see her than you were when I called."

Maca shrugged. "She's nicer than you are."

"Oh, hi!" Mariana waved at the Skype window as she switched languages. "How are you?"

Lola smiled, tired but with more vibrancy in her expression than they'd seen all year. The edge of her chest bandages poked out above her neckline. "Thank you for sharing your inheritance money with us. I'm feeling so much better since I had my surgery."

"I'm glad." Mariana beamed. "Everything went okay?"

"No complications. I'm home now. My caretaker is doing a great job, but Maca still hovers over me like she's my mother instead of the other way around."

"Good." Santiago checked in on the details of her recovery, and after the call ended, Mariana rested her head on his shoulder and sighed happily. He kissed her on the temple. "I'm almost done with dinner. Why don't you go pick out something for us to watch?"

After changing into clean clothes, she flopped onto the sofa and stole the remote from the coffee table. "This is a whole lotta power you're putting in my hands. Hope you know what you're doing." The dog plopped down at her feet and let out a big sigh.

"After many moons of honing my craft," Santiago announced from the kitchen, "I have made the perfect box mac and cheese."

She kept her gaze trained on the slowly scrolling Netflix options. "So you honed your...*Kraft*?" She held up her index finger and thumb and twisted her wrist.

He groaned. "No."

She cackled.

Bent over as if the joke had broken his back, he carried two heaping polka-dotted bowls of pasta into the living room. "That was bad, and you know it."

She accepted her bowl from him with a cheeky grin. "There are no bad puns."

"Yes, there are, and that one was at the top of the list."

This, of course, did nothing to squelch her satisfaction, but she graciously let it go and gestured at the

TV screen. "What're we watching, pun-hater?" Well, sort of let it go.

They narrowed it down to a crime-show episode or a movie, and realized they had no popcorn. Planting one hand on his shoulder for balance, Mariana stood up and teetered behind him on the couch to hop off over the armrest. In the kitchen, she microwaved two packets of popcorn and dumped the sizzling buttery contents into a giant bowl before trotting back to the couch to nestle in beside the man she loved.

The man was currently shoveling macaroni into his mouth. "Shhnn-gsshh." Based on the inflection, she guessed he was thanking her.

"No problem." She pulled her own bowl of mac and cheese into her lap for demolition. "Thanks for making dinner, *tesoro*."

He swallowed his mouthful of food before replying, "No problem." Without thinking about it, he draped his free left arm around her. She leaned back and extended her legs over his lap. He jazz-tapped his fingertips familiarly on the crest of her calf before returning to his food.

She settled in with a warmth in her chest that had nothing to do with the hot dinner. Giving in to her overwhelming smile, she reached down and patted the spaniel napping at their feet. The opening credits rolled, and she nudged Santi. "We need a new name for the dog. Spot is too mainstream."

He considered this. "Cheese."

She stared at him. His love for mac and cheese had impaired his judgment. "You can't be serious."

"Cheese," he insisted stubbornly.

"We are not naming our dog *Cheese*."

"It's the dog or our eventual baby."

Mariana's mouth dropped open. "You wouldn't dare name our firstborn Cheese."

Unsmiling, he held her gaze. Dared her to take that chance.

A minute passed, and finally, she threw up her hands. "Fine! The dog's name can be Cheese. But you have lost your baby-naming privileges."

Awakened by the decision of his name, Cheese caught the scent of fresh popcorn, and his unbearably happy face poked over the edge of the couch with intense Puppy Eyes.

"Noooo," Mariana moaned, putting up her hands to fend against her Achilles' heel. "You're such a poooo. Nooo."

Santiago looked down, and his eyes widened behind his glasses. "What is this magic?" he whispered helplessly. "I can't even..." His hand drifted to the popcorn bowl. "One. We can give him one."

She squeezed her eyes shut and fisted her hands. "No," she forced out. "No—we have to be strong."

A telling silence.

"Don't do it, San—"

The quick crunch of a hand digging into the popcorn, and then puppy jaws snapped to catch the tossed treats.

"Santi!" She opened her eyes to mock-glare at him...before taking some popcorn herself to throw for the dog. "He's such a poo. We're just enabling him."

They enabled Cheese through most of the movie, despite multiple promises to each other to stop, until the whine of a passing motorcycle drove Cheese to the window and out of the Danger Zone. At the loss of the Puppy Eyes, both Mariana and Santiago collapsed back with sighs of relief. And stuffed their faces with popcorn before the adorably manipulative dog could return to finish it off.

Once Cheese figured out that the motorcycle wasn't coming back to play with him, he scampered back to them for comfort. He rested his head on Mariana's stomach at an angle that had to be uncomfortable, yet he held the position, unbothered. Now free of food, Santi absently petted her legs, stopping every so often to squeeze or tickle a sensitive area. Each time, she jerked and laughingly complained at the familiar, friendly play. Each time, he dropped a playful kiss on a different part of her face and continued as she wanted him to.

When his kisses found her lips, she caught him to keep him there longer. As the kiss deepened, they forgot about the movie.

After they came up for air, Mariana picked up both her and Santiago's phones—the light on his was blinking purple. The notification blurb read, "USCIS Case Status Online: Case Update."

She hopped in place before thrusting the phone toward him. "Santi! There's an update about your green card!"

He snatched the phone from her. "Please, God, let Harrison have not screwed us over," he muttered.

She wrapped her arms around him and watched over his shoulder as he swiped to open the notification. He entered his receipt number into the Case Status Online website and clicked Check Status.

Congratulations, Santiago. Your Green Card has been approved.

Mariana squeezed him. "Holy shit!"

"I can't believe it!" He hugged her back. "After all that..."

"You've got it!" This green card would last two years, and then they'd have to reapply to have the conditions removed from his residence. Now that their relationship was legitimate, though, there was no reason they'd fail.

Santiago was here to stay.

She kissed him. "Congratulations, *tesoro*."

Once they made themselves go to bed (a little late), Mariana slipped into his arms and wrapped herself around him, easy as breathing. With a hum of pleasure, Santi nuzzled at the crook of her neck. He didn't need to tell her he loved her—she knew it already—but he murmured it against her skin anyway. She whispered it back, relaxing against him.

Two best friends fell asleep entwined, their dog at the foot of the bed, and they couldn't have asked for anything better.

Acknowledgements

First, a huge thank you to my partner, Liz, who put up with long hours and many mood swings over the years as I worked on Mariana and Santiago's story. You've been so supportive, and I can't imagine this journey without you.

Many thanks to Allie for all her love and support throughout the creation of this book. You're the best friend I could ever ask for.

Thank you to my beta readers: Nora Watkins Bray, Sarah Skrlec, Erin Kinsella, and Anna Hurtubise. Thank you also to Jessica Snyder for that first developmental edit on the roughest draft. You all saw this story in its earliest stages and helped it become its best self.

Shoutout to the real-life Maca for answering my seemingly random questions about Spain and the Spanish language, and for letting me use your name.

Thank you to my family for supporting my writing and teaching me to love books. We're kinda weird, but in a good way.

A big thanks to my editor, Elizabetta, for all your encouragement and hard work making this story shine. I so appreciate having you on Mariana and Santiago's team from commas to character arcs.

Thank you to Neimy Kao for the gorgeous cover art! I still stare at it in awe every day.

Finally, thank you to the team at NineStar Press for bringing me into the family and for everything you've done to bring my stories to life!

About Ivy L. James

Ivy L. James wrote her first story on Post-it notes as a child. Since then, she has graduated to regular paper and enjoys writing inclusive, heartwarming romance as a way to counterbalance the negativity in the world. She lives in Maryland with her partner and their corgi, cat, and two snakes.

Email
authorivyljames@gmail.com

Facebook
www.facebook.com/authorivyljames

Twitter
@AuthorIvyLJames

Website
www.authorivyljames.com

Instagram
www.instagram.com/authorivyljames

Pinterest
www.pinterest.com/authorivyljames

Other NineStar books by this author

Make the Yuletide Gay

Coming Soon from Ivy L. James

Love, Lorena

Lorena García Fernández has built her matchmaking company, "Love, Lorena," from the ground up, but her parents refuse to acknowledge the business as legitimate. Hoping to impress them, she travels to Ìovoria to find the crown prince a match. However, when he unexpectedly abdicates, his wild sister, Rosamund, becomes the crown princess and Lorena's new client.

Lorena knows "Rowdy Rosamund" from the news headlines, but as she helps the princess, she learns there's more to Rose than her public persona. The two women grow closer with each date, and Lorena finds herself falling for Rose.

With only a month to find the perfect match, each failure increases the pressure to succeed. How will Lorena choose between her duty and her heart?

Also from NineStar Press

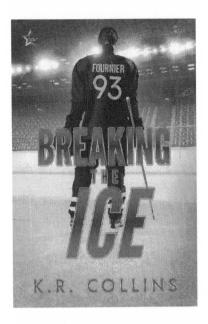

Breaking the Ice by K.R. Collins

Sophie Fournier is the first woman drafted into the North American Hockey League. Playing hockey is something she's done all her life, but she faces new challenges as she finds her place on the struggling Concord Condors. She has to prove herself better than her rival-turned-teammate, Michael Hayes, and her rival-turned-friend, Dmitri Ivanov, and she has to do it all with a smile.

If she's successful then she opens the door to other women being drafted. She can't afford to think about what happens if she fails. All she knows is this: if she's not the best then she doesn't get to play.

No pressure, though.

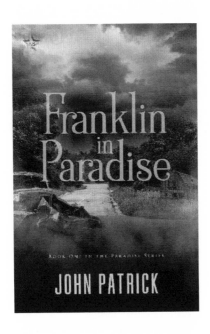

Franklin in Paradise by John Patrick

Life is good for eighteen-year-old Franklin. He lives on the spectrum, structuring and organizing his days, avoiding messy situations and ambiguity. But what he really wants is a boyfriend.

Twenty-one-year-old Patrick has a past he can't seem to shake, and a sexual identity that's hard to describe—or maybe it's just evolving.

When a manmade virus sweeps the globe, killing nearly everyone, the two young men find themselves thrust together, dependent on each other for survival. As they begin to rebuild their world, their feelings for each other deepen. But Franklin needs definition and clarity, and Patrick's identity as asexual—or demisexual, or grey ace?—isn't helping.

These two men will need to look beyond their labels if they are going to find love at the end of the world.

Connect with NineStar Press

www.ninestarpress.com

www.facebook.com/ninestarpress

www.facebook.com/groups/NineStarNiche

www.twitter.com/ninestarpress

www.instagram.com/ninestarpress

Made in the USA
Middletown, DE
27 April 2023

29501954R00187